BLOOD DIAMOND IN MY MOTHER'S HOUSE

A Shadow Files Thriller

ROSE SANDY

ROSE SANDY

BLOOD DIAMOND IN MY MOTHER'S HOUSE

A SHADOW FILES THRILLER

PROLOGUE

1854
The White Room
Buckingham Palace, London

The last maharajah of the Sikh Empire thought hard about the curse of the Koh-i-Noor blood diamond. Those who owned the diamond would rule the world but have nothing but sorrow. Only a god or a woman could wear it without fear. Yet, should the stone be returned to its homeland, no foreign invader could ever conquer its people.

The maharajah had worn the diamond.

He had made the wrong decision; the jewel had made life so much easier for his people in India. Somewhere behind the shimmer of the Koh-i-Noor diamond, there was an even deeper secret. The truth had long held the maharajah, Duleep Singh, in awe—even more so now that the gem was so close to him and yet so distant.

His robe crossed the entrance of the magnificent room in unison with his steps, silk raffling against taffeta as he stepped into the grand White Room, the Queen's private state apartment. His turban impeccable, a magnificent outfit, had been prepared for the portrait painting that Her Majesty had commissioned. The long-tailored shirt reached to his knees, with a flowing scarf draped over the left shoulder.

A sound behind him called his name. It was her—Queen Victoria, the Empress of India—followed by the royal portrait artist, Winterhalter, his hands full of paints, brushes and canvases. Duleep saw no fear on her face; all was calm.

In a flash, he turned to confront her and spoke. 'You honour me with your presence, Your Majesty.'

Her face softened, and she seemed content watching him as she entered the room. He did not know what to make of it.

'I thought you may like to look at this,' she said.

His eyes widened as his gaze followed the velvet pillow she carried. Duleep peered down at the gem, his fingers curling. 'I presented my royal jewel to you several years ago under the treaty of the Lahore Agreement, and now I am reunited with it. Just like that, handed from one kingdom to another, when I came as a defeated prince boy to your shores. For a blood diamond that had started and created wars, it was an amicable exchange.'

'The diamond was fresh from uniting the enemies that surrounded you. You presented the jewel without a hint of apprehension,' she said.

'They say it was a gift to you, in gratitude for—

Queen Victoria watched him, studying his expression. 'Are you not grateful?'

'Your Majesty, I'm honoured to serve you and to be called on to do such an important act on my queen's behalf as posing for this portrait, but I'll take it one step at a time.'

The Queen blinked, then advanced towards a family portrait on the wall, a shadow on her heels. She paused for a moment and glanced back. Eyes pensive, she progressed towards the stone nestled on the velvet cushion, ready to be part of the adornment for his portrait.

She picked it up and held it out in front of him. 'Is there any reason I shouldn't keep this diamond?'

Duleep's loyalty was now in question. She was testing him. He took the stone from her hands, admiring its glint as the sun hit it. 'There's no gain in reminding me of my past life. It's behind me. Just, you came to our nation in a moment of need.'

'Do you like the Koh-i-Noor?'

'There's nothing like this Mountain of Light. Do you know the curse that follows the Koh-i-Noor?'

'The Mountain of Light. Such a befitting name. So that's what they called it?'

'Yes. Have you worn it?

'Should I? It's beautiful and nothing like anything in my collection.'

He studied her pensive face. She loved England. Fond of her subjects and her Great Empire, there was nothing they would not do for her.

'Can anyone give a queen who has the world in her hands anything to match her influence and sovereignty? Tell me this. What about my land in India?'

'What of it? You are but a boy, my prince, who has everything they could ever want.'

'But my line of succession and honour.' He wanted to hear her say it. He repeated his question. 'Do you know of the curse?'

'I've heard many stories, countless rumours.'

'Then your Lord Dalhousie didn't tell you?'

That was enough to put her on high alert. 'Tell me what?'

He took a deep breath and watched her closely. In her fear, Duleep couldn't detect any danger. 'All you can do is wait. You see this jewel was once worth half the daily expense of the world and was mined in the Golconda region of my country in Andhra Pradesh. It was once the shape and size of a small hen's egg. History in my land documents its path well—including a curse, lethal to male rulers who wear it. The curse read; "Only God or a woman can put on it with impunity". You see many emperors, and sultans dared to own it, only to suffer misfortune including invasion and their lands facing conquest. The diamond has hypnotised many with its value and status.'

A smile crept its way onto her countenance as she approached him as the artist prepared his materials. 'Did you wear it?'

'I did. I can only spare you my misfortune by taking back what brought a curse to my kingdom. You should return it to me.'

He raised the stone. It glowed under his gaze. The Koh-i-Noor found on the sacred Yamuna River had caused men to raise their swords and lose battles. It was as if the stone could see into the minds of its masters; as if it could read his thoughts.

'We both know the value of the jewel. If you don't surrender it, the power of the diamond will remain.'

Winterhalter moved to where they stood. 'We're ready to begin.'

There was a silent pause before she spoke. 'Albert can have it now. He says that it needs to be re-cut to display its true beauty. I'm not bothered either way, but he wants the world to admire the Mountain of Light for what it's worth. Like all jewels, it might never go back to where it came from. They tell me we must cut every diamond down from its original size. This will be the final cut. You are free from its curse. Let go of it so it can't recede into your past.'

Her laugh this time more resembled regret. 'Albert wants to spend £8000 to slim it down to about 105 carats. They say the people at the Great Exhibition will admire its brilliance. A new form will give it lustre.'

'The stone has more glory than it needs.'

Her smile faded. 'That is what we will do. I'm grateful for your friendship, Duleep. It means more than you know to my subjects and to the future of our two nations.'

'What will happen to my country's diamond once they have exhibited it for the world to see?'

The Queen smiled and circled his robes. 'I'll set it in my imperial crown, and now that you say the curse follows the male line of monarchs, perhaps my decree should be that it be worn only by female consorts to the monarch and a reigning queen.'

Duleep studied her confidence. Her voice was deep and harsh, like that of something dark and inhuman. However, she seemed to comfort him, to tell him she, too, would not carry the burden of the diamond.

He glared out the tall windows for a moment. 'I'm still a young man and was a boy when I came here all alone. I lost my family, familiarity, but I was too young to even know what that meant. Even if a palace were built by magic, could it withstand the force of the Koh-i-Noor?'

The Queen withdrew the stone from his hand and slid it back onto the cushion. His eyes, ready to scream, stared at the rock. If he didn't act now, the diamond was lost to him forever. His voiceless scream burned within his throat as if it could echo off the hills of the Himalayas and resound in the room.

How could the curse be lifted now?

The curse of the Koh-i-Noor diamond that could make and break empires.

Duleep's soul burned with defeat. The freedom of his empire and legacy, gone, withdrawn from his sight on the cushion of a Queen as Winterhalter gave it back to the palace jeweller.

Duleep knew.

Had he been able to reach for it, reclaim it, he would have fulfilled a well-known prophecy.

For though the Koh-i-Noor carried a curse, it also carried a prophecy he had memorised the day they took it from him.

To break the curse the stone had brought him, he had to return it to his homeland.

He had to break the curse, or someone else had to.

I

Present Day
Hanimaadhoo
The Maldives, Indian Ocean

Aria was known not for stealing from the rich but rather from dead pirates. At least that's what the media said. Dead pirates and ancient hoarders. The map in her hands dating to the eighteenth century was just the fun she needed right now. It wasn't hers but belonged to the Middle Eastern billionaire standing in front of her, eyes hooded like a pelican beak.

She glanced at his expensive-looking groomed face with his silver beard and eyes that peered through her soul. 'I take fifty per cent commission on everything I find.'

'Thirty per cent,' he replied.

'The fee isn't up for discussion. It's my boat, my men, and my strategy.'

The billionaire made a move towards the bar of his yacht. 'And when will you deliver the finds?'

'The day after I lay my hands on them,' she said, grabbing a beer from the bar. 'I'll expect the bank transfer after delivery, right here in Hanimaadhoo. I will let you know when to dock your magnificent yacht.'

'It will cost me a small fortune,' he said.

'I'll deserve it and earn it.'

He said nothing as the sun's rays hit his eyes.

A few minutes later, a man strode into the vast space, then leaned against the wall next to the bar. His hair was a matted mess, and a pair of black jeans hugged his tall frame. His skin appeared smooth over, and the skin on his arms and underarms showed a deep tan.

'He'll be your contact,' the billionaire said, nodding to the man.

'As you wish. You ask no questions, and I give no answers. Those are the rules I work by.'

'It's my map. My information.'

Aria narrowed her eyes. 'Then, why do you need me? Grab the next tough guy to get it for you.'

'None are as resourceful and successful as you at retrieving lost stones and identifying historical jewellery.'

'Is that what they told you?' She neared him, her face an inch from his. 'They told you well.'

'My man goes with you.'

'No. Besides,' she said, giving his man a quick look and stepping back, 'he can't keep up with my team. I do this my way or no deal.'

'I know you work hard at the game. That's why you are here,' the billionaire said, studying Aria, looking back and forth between her and his aid. 'I respect your work.'

He thought for a moment, then looked away before turning back to her, shaking his head. 'A few years ago, I would have done this myself. I'm the luckiest of the lucky few.' He stared at her, his fingers pressing against the edge of his whisky glass, and then he turned and leaned forward. 'I'll get everything I want out of this relationship.'

'I'm sure you will. I'll get to work,' she said. 'And remember, no tagalongs or the deal is over.'

That night, Aria awoke in a cold sweat. The night before she'd dreamed she was speaking to her sister again. Then she heard water coming out of the bathtub from her bathroom. 'Huh?'

She thought hard, but no words came to her lips. Aria stirred and realised that she was naked from the waist up, her hair a mat around her bare shoulders.

She peeked at the clock with a sleepy eye.

2:03 a.m.

It was the fourth time.

Aria launched a pillow to the other end of the room and lumbered to where the sound of vibrating came from. She grasped the phone.

Hand over her forehead, she mopped the sweat beads away. The same unidentified caller. She wiped her brow. How long had she slept?

Aria tossed the phone to the floor, then pulled the warm pillow over her head.

A downpour beat at the palm trees outside her home, slashing one down until it smashed into her outdoor patio. A rare storm at this time of the year, it had moved into the North and gotten worse.

Her small bungalow with a secluded beach and a terrace gave her views of the turquoise lagoon on moonlit nights, but not tonight. White drapes flew in the wind, and gales tore at the curtains and whined. She stomped to the floor-length windows and shut them.

The mobile phone's loud shrill continued to vibrate, even

through the dampening of her pillow. For the last twenty-four hours, every three hours, a text flashed across her screen.

She hesitated and rose to retrieve the phone. She glared at the screen.

What if it disappeared again? She'd thought all day about going to the tech expert she knew on the main island. Could they interpret the scrambled code?

Her high-tech office equipment, even though efficient at underwater signal detection, wasn't sophisticated enough for this. This person knew what they were doing.

The secret intelligence services in London would have much to debate on how such a signal worked. She should know —for years her father had talked about GCHQ's sophisticated signals intelligence development—but who was this, and why her?

She unlocked the phone with her index fingerprint then slid it over the smooth surface. Her patience with this individual was approaching its dire end.

Night shadows of palm trees danced on her bedroom floor, and she sank back on the bed. Aria raised an eyebrow as a last surge of defiance swelled inside her. How could she deny a simple request? She set her hand on her sweat-beaded brow and sighed with exaggerated patience, trying not to let panic overwhelm her. Then it appeared again.

A sharp breath left her lips, and she rubbed a palm across her neck. Her eyes skimmed the words.

Gibberish.

She went to the desk and connected the phone to her laptop. Huffing, she then launched a programme pirated from her father's government server access. It had only taken a few minutes to hack the automated data discovery software. There was one way for governments to know if agents were creating unauthorised data files to try and sell or compromise government data.

The software could check data in real-time and unscramble sensitive information if necessary. Could it work?

If only she had a programme to spy on her father and the secrets he kept from her. He'd done it for years.

She started the programme, and the phone, like a magic wand, decrypted the information. It read:

It's Emily.
I only have fourteen days.
Burn the will.
Burn the diary pages.
Please!

Aria dropped the phone, and it landed on her big toe. She yelped in pain and reached down to grab her foot. It was the first time she'd read or even digested the message. Her heart raced, and a tight knot formed in her tummy. Unsure what to feel, Aria's hands fumbled for the cool glass of water by the bedside. Unsteady fingers collided with the glass rim and sent it crashing to the floor.

Her mouth parched as reality blurred with what she'd known for thirteen years.

Emily.

It couldn't be.

But she's dead! Emily had died thirteen years ago. It was the explosion at Altaneus Corporation. That's what the police and the papers had said.

The Louvre Museum
Paris, France
06:55 hrs

The museum had been without water since Thursday. It was the last thing Ramond wanted, another scandal. A weakness formed in his legs, and he needed a few seconds to rest. He drew in a sharp breath as he scuttled through the lower level halls of the Louvre Palace. First, he passed the entrance on the ground level, then he raced past Roman, Greek, and Egyptian sculptures. When he reached the Apollo Gallery, he stopped.

He swivelled and faced a tall shadow with a smirk. Ramond's eyes bulged. 'Who are you?' he asked.

With a lean build and protruding eyes, Ramond watched as the man stretched out a hand. 'Amos Hudson.'

'The name means nothing to me.'

'We have a way of knowing things, including your little mess. You've lost the Koh-i-Noor diamond, haven't you?'

'Who is we?'

'Never mind. You've lost England's treasure—and only days before it's due to appear in The International Court of Justice.'

'We've lost nothing.' He raised an eyebrow. 'How did you get in here?'

'I would worry less about how I got in here and more about how the Koh-i-Noor diamond got out.'

'Alain Ramond!'

Ramond turned his head at the sound of the approaching footsteps. 'There's a man here to see you,' a low-ranking security official said as he shuffled into the room.

Tension tightened Ramond's neck tendons as his employee

stepped into the small space. His tongue felt too thick to form words. 'Leave us. He's already here.'

The junior officer shuffled from the gallery.

Ramond's attention shifted back to the man. 'I'm going to ask you to leave.'

'Not a chance. But I do have a proposal for you. We can make all this headache go away for you; give me your CCTV footage files from last night. I need everything from before and after the break-in.'

Ramond studied Hudson. 'Who sent you?'

'It doesn't matter. We have eyes and ears everywhere.' The man handed him a business card. 'If you want none of this to get out to the press, I suggest you cooperate, as in two seconds this will be all over the world's media.'

Hudson was not giving away much, not even a hint of what he was thinking. He flashed a business card with just a number on it. Ramond would have raised a gun to his intruder's face. He resisted and reposed a finger on his trouser pocket. The man left twelve minutes later with full access to his CCTV footage on an expensive phone.

When the man had gone, Ramond glanced at the business card and scratched his chin. One blasted number.

No address.

No details.

Who were these people?

'Flandres!'

The junior officer returned, shaking his head. 'The diamond was here last night,' he said, his eyes reflecting the overhead fluorescent lights. 'I don't know. I turned for just a second. We followed all the procedures for the exhibition. The security system and cameras respond by following the area of activity.'

'What else?'

'It should all be on CCTV camera. The system also sends an alert message. There's no way—'

'Well, somebody got to it. Maybe someone who knew we would use the system.'

'Only the government has access to these servers.'

Ramond moved his hand from his chin and leaned forward. 'We must alert Madame Konstantina. The head of the museum won't want to wake to this media attention. She would have to produce a statement. It'll be chaos. I don't need this now!'

He strode to the window where his eyes fell on the posters the teams had erected outside the Louvre's inverted glass pyramid. The architectural draw constructed of glass never ceased to amaze him. Right now, its triangular segments reflected a prism of colours in the early dawn light.

The transparent architecture of the pyramid in the courtyard reflected the views from the interior of the lower floor of the museum reminding Ramond of a deep well.

The grand entrance would accommodate the growing number of visitors the Louvre continued to receive, and the figures would only increase with this diamond on loan.

With all the controversy over who owned the blasted thing, this disappearance would make his life more than a little untidy.

This exhibition was of international importance. It would also mark his career.

The marketing department's commotion about how the display, mostly around how the two-month loan of the Koh-i-Noor diamond should be presented to the public, was still fresh in his mind. Ramond fought back a sick feeling in his stomach. The gem was to go amongst France's own Crown Jewels—including the Crown of Louis XV.

How could they have been so careless? This was an exceptional and conditional loan.

The Koh-i-Noor had never left the United Kingdom since the young maharajah from India presented to it to Queen Victoria. Forced to become a subject of the British Crown, Raymond's thoughts on the matter were irrelevant.

They had timed every part of the exhibition launch to the last minute, from an early press conference to the speech by the royal representative from the Tower of London.

How could he lose this diamond?

What had happened?

He wiped his brow. Fourteen days to go before the inquiry at The International Court of Justice, and media hype was only about to begin.

'We can't afford such publicity when the Indian government has made a serious claim.'

'When did they do it?' Ramond said.

'Do what?'

'Start the investigation?'

The officer scratched his head. 'The press started reporting on The Court's intentions about seven months ago.'

This was the type of case the DEI sniffed around. How had they gotten to the theft this quickly? It didn't matter.

In less than two hours, he'd have no job.

10:29 hrs

These days, Aria's routine involved more than sitting at the beach. Horde hunting in the ocean was tough work, but it was one way to forget Emily.

If she could kill one thing, it would be her mobile phone. It had never been the bearer of good news, and now, it was the home of a ghost.

Someone was playing a cruel joke, or there was more to it.

Aria never felt brave when she'd come to the Maldives.

The diary.

She drew a flash drive from her office drawer in the main room in the bungalow. It would be a difficult decision, but she could not keep the diary here any longer.

Aria rotated the flash drive in her hand, then slotted it into the laptop on the desk. She turned on the machine, then took photos of the last seven pages of the diary with her phone. It had text on each page. Personal stories, time in India, and her great-great-great-grandfather's thoughts about his experiences drew her back to the 1800s.

It had been page seven that had made her stop and document the material. Something was wrong in those pages. After saving the picture on the flash drive, she slotted the diary in a box.

Had Emily known?

Aria scanned the room for her backpack, and then she placed the flash drive in the centre sleeves of the worn luggage.

Glowing with red intensity, with streaks of dark scarlet and black, she examined the red beryl gem. She had always wanted to find one, as red beryls were rare.

The sudden ringing of the phone beside her bed pierced through the silence.

Her hand reached for the phone. 'Yes?'

It was Maxwell.

'You better come here and look,' he said. 'Do you know the full extent of what you have found? Do we really get to keep fifty per cent?'

'Yes, we do.'

'We need to authenticate all of it. Come check it out. It's indeed payday. The guys are also following another lead out at sea. We should get going.'

'Be there in a few minutes,' Aria said.

'Still can't believe you did it—and in less than twenty-four hours. I'm still amazed at how you know to search farther than most and longer than all..'

'Now we keep it until he pays in full. I will build that museum. Come on, Maxwell, for every 150,000 gem-quality diamonds we find, only one red beryl crystal appears. For decades, countless expeditions have been searching for the shipwreck we found that took place in the late 1800s. I always knew it was a few miles from Kudahuvadhoo Island, but it was our client's map that filled in the missing pieces.'

'Well, you didn't come to honeymoon in the Maldives. You revel in the treasures that lie on the ocean bed.'

'It has been worth it now. I needed this.'

Aria had spent six hundred thousand pounds on the small oceanographic centre she'd set up with Maxwell—an equally qualified geological oceanographer she'd met at Wellington Square at the University of Oxford.

They were doing anything but examining the seabed, for rocks and minerals out in the Maldives, or anything that their degree afforded them, like a career at NASA, the European Space Agency, Airbus Space or the Ministry of Defence.

'Your business is a disguise for what you care about, isn't it?' Maxwell said.

'What do you mean?'

'Hiding from your father while finding lost valuable treasures on the seabed and making media headlines. It's one way to get his attention.'

'I still don't understand what you mean.'

'If a degree in Oceanography and qualifications as a

gemmologist is the way to your father's heart, then count me in. Not to mention countless hours of diving instruction.'

'I've been here for three months because I like it here. Nothing else. What we found last night has been lying on the ocean bed for two centuries. That's what gives me a buzz,' she said.

'All right. Get back out here then.'

She set the phone down and then slotted it into her jeans.

Payday it most certainly was. The things the ocean hid for her to find had drawn her here. Most people wanted treasures; old, or shipwrecked, or forgotten, it didn't matter.

She'd bought her own little expedition fleet and hired a crew of five led by Maxwell, and she could go anywhere in the world looking for these finds. The next part was easy. Find the highest bidder for them so she could fund her museum.

Aria made a mental note to call her father as soon as possible, then she turned the phone off.

Outside, the crash of waves and the fizz of foam made her stop and peer towards the beach. An ocean breeze crept through the open window and slapped her face as she handled the rare gem.

Aria strode to the back of the bungalow where she'd parked her motorbike. Her eyes caught sight of the white sand and the lagoon. She took the little stairs down to the beach. The late morning sun scorched down on her skin. She'd barely had time to put on any sun cream or even grab a swimming costume.

Would her father be proud of her now? A knot settled in her belly, and she scrubbed a hand over her forehead. Was it Emily who'd sent the text last night? Surely not...

Tightness formed in her chest.

She glanced at Emily's photo on her phone. 'You'd be proud of me.'

Amsterdam
06:17 hrs

Jave Lincoln hated packing.

He crossed the length of the hotel room towards the window and peered behind the curtain. Three men leaned their backs against the wall of the shop downstairs on the street corner, clad in black attire. He'd seen them before. Just the other night, in fact. They had followed him from the restaurant past several streets in Rembrandtplein until he made it to his hotel. He narrowed his eyes, stiffness growing in his jaw. They'd blown his cover.

With one toss, he threw all his belongings into his overnight bag. Careful to find his passport and mobile phone, he stuffed the last items into the carry-on. That's all he needed.

He slung the backpack over his shoulder and crossed to the window one more time to peer outside. The three men had disappeared.

Soon he heard thundering footsteps on the south side of his hotel room.

So, they weren't giving him any time at all.

Damn it.

He secured his backpack and threw it through the open window. A bang sounded outside his door, and it pushed open. A bullet whispered past his ear in a high-pitched whine as the men from outside thrust themselves into the room, one after the other. The first guy advanced, a handgun at the ready.

He stepped out in front of him with a finger growing tight on the Sig-Sauer, then aimed it at Jave's chest. Another man shouted, 'There's no way out, Lincoln!'

Jave stopped in his tracks. His thoughts ran over the next steps he needed to take. The others remained motionless.

The larger one spoke first. 'Our reason is simple," he stated. 'It's about the price you paid.'

Jave had only seconds to think. In a swift movement, he backed to the open window and threw himself outside onto the balcony ledge, his back straight as he stepped against the wall. The air temperature was inching above boiling. His heart pounded in his ears; his fist shook from his adrenaline.

He reached for the fire escape and pulled himself towards the top of the building. He had no choice and crossed the length to the helicopter pad.

Where was the chopper?

His pursuers flashed towards him. Out of the corner of his eye, he saw the bird.

Late.

Shoulders adroit, he found his gun and fired a shot past the three men behind him.

He only needed one minute.

'Aria!'

She turned to see Maxwell, a little envious of the way he tanned as he approached, showing off his well-built shoulders and torso. He was her favourite Scandinavian with that deep voice.

Maxwell was irresistible to women, and if today was anything to go by, she knew why.

'Incredible,' he said, holding two red beryls from the deep dive hoard they'd found late last night.

The team was camped at the beach by the pier, inventorying the gems. In the secluded part of the island where they'd made a home, Aria didn't expect much trouble from bystanders.

She'd given up at midnight, leaving Maxwell in charge.

His deep green eyes shone at her. 'This alone will pay for all our annual expenses on the pier, the diving equipment, the boats, and our security,' he said.

Aria smiled.

'After several weeks, our investment has paid off. It's been worth it. I didn't believe all the historical stuff you were talking about. Was it really pirates?'

Aria smirked. 'Do you believe me now? Pirates off the coast of Africa stole the Indian Ocean red beryl hoard.'

'Yeah, but come on.'

'Still a nonbeliever?' She fingered a stone. 'They sailed towards India and were shipwrecked, survived, but their loot ended up at the bottom of the ocean.'

She reached for a red stone from his hand. 'AHe nd now it's ours at least fifty per cent.'

'I don't get you, Aria,' Maxwell said, lifting his head. 'You knew the missing piece of the puzzle was that dusty map the sheikh bought at an auction in London. Several years ago, you told me you'd been looking for that. You don't need any of this. The money. Your family owns half of England, right?'

'My family has never been good news.'

Maxwell raised an eyebrow. 'Come on, your family isn't that bad. You should try my dysfunctional lot. Your parents loved each other.'

'Compliment noted. Maxwell, you're such a romantic. I'm afraid I'm not. Ever since I lost Emily, my relationship with my father has been one of walking on coals. The old man doesn't seem to get me. I love him, but I just can't understand his silences or his long-term absences.'

'He can't be all that bad. You know men are not that dreadful.'

'I'll believe you when my father explains the countless evenings he spent when I was growing up making secret calls on high-tech mobile phones I'd never seen in any shop—and also the way he carried them with him constantly. Over the years, the phones have changed—as has the technology—but he always had that encrypted phone,' Aria said.

'Don't take it out on the phone.'

'When my mother lost her battle with cancer, it broke his heart, and going on diplomatic posts has filled his time, but it has also taken him away from the guilt he feels over the loss of Emily and my mother. It's just the two of us now.'

'I'm so sorry, Aria,' Maxwell said.

'I know. Besides, it's not the money I'm after,' she said with a wink.

'Then what?'

'I don't know. I need more.'

He raised an eyebrow. 'Like what? Diamonds?'

She curled a lip. 'We overrate diamonds. Too easy. Next to diamonds, red beryls are an excellent find.' She glanced at the security boxes containing the jewels the team was selling. 'Now, we need to find the right home for them.'

He raised an eyebrow, and the sun hit his face where a streak of sand had found its home from his morning dive. 'Our underwater museum project. I don't think we can ever raise that much money unless... A museum people dive to. Do you think it will work?'

'We continue taking clients unless I cash out all my inheritance from my mother.'

'I won't let you do that. Listen, we've been searching for treasure in the Indian Ocean for three months. Nothing will top this find. It's top-notch. Just because of some greedy moron centuries ago. Including deserters from your very own British East India Company,' he said.

She searched his eyes. 'There's more to find, Maxwell. The bottom of the seas and oceans have been a dumping ground grave for many centuries, and they have hidden some of the best finds in history. Everything from Indian temple gold, jewels, coins, lost ancient continents, armoury, history and more. I want to find it all, and then I want to finish our underwater museum.'

'It would take years; don't you ever want to settle down?' Maxwell asked.

'That's overrated too. I like the beauty of the Indian Ocean. We have Asia to the Northwest and Africa too. We just live here or sail as far as Australia or Antarctica. It's no surprise that they named it in India as *Ratnākara* in Sanskrit, "the mine of gems". And that's what this life allows me to do—mine for gems.'

'I only ever want one gem, and that's the one that will be fit for the heiress with perfect sapphire-coloured eyes, long chocolate hair, and lips that belong to a goddess.'

An uncontrollable flush of heat crept up her cheeks, and she cleared her throat. Was he saying what she thought he was? She liked Maxwell and trusted him with her life, but not once had she imagined he may want to take things further. 'Maxwell—

He flashed her a cocky smirk and produced a jewel box he opened, revealing a solitaire diamond. 'I can change this to another stone,' he said, placing the diamond on her finger. 'I guess we've got the rest of our lives to sail the Indian Ocean.'

A lump settled in her throat as she studied the diamond ring. He was serious and would not take no for an answer. She would have to tell him the truth, eventually. 'I'll call my family lawyer. He's worked with my family for years. I'm sure he will have a few ideas about how we can cash in on this hoard,' she said.

They moved in silence to the edge of the water and dipped their feet in the tide as the team they'd hired hauled the finds onto the secluded beach. 'Maxwell, I—

'No, let's enjoy this day and discuss that another day.'

She had enough to deal with and couldn't be distracted by her lack of feelings for Maxwell. He was possibly the sweetest man she'd ever met, but men, however sweet, always broke her trust—starting with the only man in her life she'd never been able to forgive.

She didn't like how she'd left things with him. High Commissioner Raith had a lot of answering to do.

Her heart sank when a text surfaced on her phone—the same encrypted message.

Fourteen days.

Fourteen days till what?

2

Andhra Pradesh
India
13:27 hrs

James Parkinson read the sign above the restaurant and bar facing the Golconda Fort.

On the western edge of Golconda, the sixteenth-century fortified city stood on the summit above him with its crumbling walls only above shantytowns. The evening was a fresh 20°C.

Dead clumps of grass half surrounded weather-worn stone pillars and crumbled buildings.

Crimson sunset fog hung between the city's landscape like blown flour. Having rained earlier that day, and with no sign of any moisture still in the air, Parkinson fought a parch in his throat. The travel website had mentioned that this was a suitable place to pass the time, but his mission here was anything but to look for air-conditioning and cheap drinks.

He moved towards a scanty building. Loose wires hung from the entrance, and a Coca-Cola sign swung from the entrance door. The menu on the board by the door offered local specialities—mostly meat items and vegetarian dishes. It tempted his eyes to involuntarily shut. Jet lag was setting in.

He pushed the door open and stepped into the cramped space beyond. It was nothing to write home about, but it was clean and dark. A stench of beer filled the air, as a commotion from the bar area made him turn his head. He made his way slowly to the counter. 'One Kingfisher beer.' He studied the bartender who looked like he would know the locale well. 'I'm looking for someone,' he added. 'They told me there's an old man here who knows Golconda's mining and diamond history.'

The bartender gave him one glance and nodded, drying out several water glasses.

Parkinson's beer arrived warmer than he would have liked. 'I serve beer, and that's it. If you're looking for the lunatic who speaks nonsense, then there,' the bartender said lifting his chin towards the corner of the bar. He snickered. 'That's the only man I know who claims to know Golconda better than most. Between you and me, you will have to decide what you believe from him. I don't know why anyone bothers with those ancient ruins.'

Parkinson slowly turned his head to the small crowd gathered around the voice coming from a cross-legged man seated in the room's corner. Nothing about the man gave away his real motives for entertaining the small crowd. He kept shaking his head slowly.

Parkinson grimaced and listened.

'Until Alexander the Great came to India, no one outside the subcontinent had heard of diamonds. This was the place. He knew it.'

'What's his fee?' Parkinson asked the bartender.

Wiping out several whisky glasses, the bartender shot one

look at the man covered with a blanket around his small shoulders.

'For what? Talking? Don't waste your money.'

The old man's beard almost touched the table.

'Rumour has it he's a cobbler from northern India. He says he's 179 years old, so lots of the locals give him food and drink. We see him as good luck. He is a heck of a storyteller.'

What the bartender said was correct. Many had gathered around him with their whiskeys and plates of curries.

Unable to see, the old man's eyes stared blankly into space. Parkinson took one look at the dog by his feet and gathered he was blind.

'Do you believe his stories?' Parkinson asked.

'He certainly tells some remarkable ones. The tourists love it, so we let them come in here. He can tell as many stories as he wants as long as people keep eating and drinking.'

'What does he talk about?'

'It all depends. My personal favourite is how he was born in the 1840s. Also, nobody can exactly verify this, so we all believe he's 179 years old. He's even been in the newspapers.'

'I'm glad to see people believe in longevity,' Parkinson said.

'People are trying to live longer, so they will believe anything. In India, anything is possible.'

Parkinson grabbed his drink and moved towards the small crowd around the old man. He listened to the man's story as he spoke in heavily accented British English.

'*The legend of Golconda says that the meteorite came down at a ferocious speed as it approached the Earth and hit Golconda. There was a little boy who lived in that village. He was out in the fields tending to goats and saw the whole thing. You see, this part of India had been cursed for centuries but also filled with blessing when the diamonds appeared.*

When the meteorite hit, the young boy looked up. It hit on the outskirts of this town. Several of the meteorite rocks scattered. One was so dense it hit and created several caves and split rocks that came down the river. The meteorite then smashed into the village, and the porous stones glowed. Several moments later, no one saw as a large rock dropped on the shores of the riverbeds. It smashed into two diamonds. Later the villagers saw several miracles. Babies born that year all were rumoured to live beyond a hundred and twenty years or more. Like myself.'

The old man stared at the tourists. Parkinson observed him imagining the man had told the story many times before. Myths around gemstones and diamonds sometimes intrigued anybody who'd worked in geology.

Golconda was where the experiment had taken place. The forbidden warehouse that later closed, which had claimed the life of Emily Raith's young life. It had all happened here. The experiment centres had burned down. It was classified, and no one knew about it.

He damn well did, because he'd barely escaped with his life and hadn't been back since. He just needed one sample. One sample from the caves.

'Is this all of it?' Aria said as the man hauled the last box with the ocean finds and placed it in the security trunk.

'Yes,' said one of the crew and left the room.

Aria had only ever met one person besides Emily that was capable. Maxwell.

The man could get anything done. She faced him across the table on the terrace of her bungalow. 'My attorney will be here to take the jewels to inventory until we decide what to do with them.'

Maxwell stared at the seven boxes containing the beryl

gems. They were rare. She'd calculated their value at six million, and Maxwell's face said it all. She was glad he'd taken her offer to join her as a business partner.

Inspecting one gem, Aria studied the red glow off its surface. Its red colour came from the amount of manganese the gems held. Red beryl was a rare mineral because it formed in a unique geochemical environment. They'd told no one yet about the find. Most of the crew had signed nondisclosure agreements anyway, and they would keep their mouths shut if they wanted to get their fair cut and commission.

Aria had two choices. Find a buyer and use the money for the museum, or make it part of the museum collection. The likes of Christie's and Sotheby's would want to auction the find, but that wasn't the right decision. That's where they would make the most money. However, it wasn't money that had brought Aria out to the great seas. It had been Emily.

Emily once told her she could do anything, including one day, find the treasures she longed to hold. Aria had always wanted to see what history had hidden from the world, especially history lying on the ocean and sea beds. That's why she'd become an oceanographer, and she would stay out here until the museum became a reality. She would find even more treasures to put in the museum's public display.

'It's time,' she said, turning to Maxwell.

'I'll get this in that hundred-tonne safe you bought. You were right about getting a large safe. You have more faith in this museum.'

'More than you know. Listen, I need to make a quick call. I'll be right back,' Aria said, stepping into the kitchen that overlooked the ocean.

She fished in the pocket of her denim shorts for the cell phone and tapped a set of digits. 'Can I please speak to the British High Commissioner?'

She waited until a voice came on to the line.

'British High Commission, New Delhi. Can I help you?'

'Caroline?' Aria said.

'Yes.'

'It's Aria? Aria Raith?'

'How are you? It's been a long time.'

'Yes, it has. I'd like to come and see my father soon. Is there a good time in his diary?'

'He'll be pleased to see you. When would you like to come?'

'I was thinking as soon as possible.' Aria hesitated. 'I really need to see him.'

'Very well,' Caroline said. 'Your father has been busy recently. I'll see what I can do and get back to you as soon as possible. Maybe I can clear two days for him.'

'Too busy to see his only child. I understand,' Aria said.

'His schedule looks full, and he has several guests coming in tomorrow night for a High Commission reception, but I'm sure after that I can open up his diary.'

Her father would do anything rather than face alone time with her. Ever since her mother had died, he'd needed a hostess by his side. It came with the territory of his diplomatic duties. Aria couldn't step into the shoes of a diplomat's daughter. Besides, that wasn't her life, the proper lady. It had never been her. Her mother had been an aristocrat to the bone. She was anything but. Her idea of fun was escapades on a boat in shorts and a bikini.

She didn't know how her father coped with diplomatic missions by himself. The life of a diplomat demanded a commitment to packing up your life every few years and starting again. The physical and mental resets that came with moving and uprooting were more than she was prepared to take on.

She moved to the window. How did her father make essential decisions about their country? He was at the disposal of not only the British Prime Minister but also key members of the government. He also had to head up an entire High Commission and deal with staffing and security. No, not the life for her.

She bit her lip for a second. 'Caroline, could I speak to him?'

Caroline's voice dipped a fraction. 'He's just walking into the room now.'

Aria waited for the deep voice that she knew well. 'I didn't realise you were free. I'm told by those who know you you're normally somewhere in the ocean recovering gems and national treasures, or should I say international treasures?' her father said.

A weight settled in her stomach. 'Father, we need to speak. It's important. I really need to see you.'

'What's going on? Can it wait? I'm so sorry,' he said. 'I can't drop things now. It's just been busy. I could be available for us in a month.'

'Father! It's about Emily.'

'Emily? Aria, you need to stop doing this to yourself. You can't bring Emily back.'

A soundless breath passed through Aria's dry lips. 'You never tried, Father.'

Crawfordton, Dumfriesshire
Scotland
18:17 hrs

'Did the princess's estate ever go back to the Swiss bank?' Cicero asked.

Iver Fenderson couldn't keep his cool. His hand covered his face, but he didn't dare say anything. Then he spoke after several seconds of silence. 'They were not idiots. She was the daughter of a maharajah, intelligent, and a debutante at Buckingham Palace in 1895. They would have gone back if only to keep her memory and that of the boy prince alive. They kidnapped him, you know, from his native Punjab. I've heard stories, but I have no information to back it, but then again, the Swiss vault was empty. The maharajah's vault was wiped of any secrets—perhaps evidence of what he'd faced in England.'

'What about the bank? What information did it give regarding the estate's visit?'

'The bank?' he said, his voice hoarse. 'My father could have helped if he had known, but it was impossible to get back in there to look. He never had the heart to go back, but I did, a month ago,' he muttered. 'It only took a little bribing and coercing, but we found the vault. My father got involved in the estate.'

'How?'

'That's not important. What is important is that several years ago, it outraged the media—so-called Switzerland's 'Nazi gold'. The Swiss Bankers' Association then published a list of over 1,800 untouched accounts and other deposits unclaimed for the past half-century. Hers was one of them.'

'Are you related to the maharajah, Mr Fenderson? None of his offspring had children. It was the Koh-i-Noor curse, you know?' Cicero said.

Iver didn't answer but scrunched his forehead. 'One of the abandoned boxes in that Swiss bank vault belonged to that Indian princess, and my great-great-grandmother was her caretaker and tutor. No one had heard from the princess who had possibly lived, in 1942, in Penn, Bucks. She was the daughter of Maharajah Duleep Singh, last Emperor of the Sikhs.'

Cicero's brow arched. 'You never told me you were of Indian descent? For crying aloud, your skin is as pale as Scottish toast and doesn't have a hint of Indian ancestry.'

'Looks can be deceiving. It makes me troublesome to figure out and hard to see coming, but I've waited long enough for the Koh-i-Noor. It's rightfully mine.'

'You should get in line. The international court case for its return to India dominates the news every day. Now, even more. It's gone. Doesn't that bother you?'

'The estate discovered that the maharajah's box was empty, but it was not. What I found in those vaults after much investigation tells me there are larger forces at play, and they all connected to one family, one man—Garen Raith—and his daughters. I'll find that diamond and finally, give it the place it deserves in history.'

'You aren't yourself today, Lord Fenderson.'

'How long have you worked for my family, Cicero?'

'Well, for as long as I can remember. Being in the Scottish Highlands, I don't get to see much of the world, but I wouldn't change it for anything,' Cicero replied. 'I think that's why I have never left this draughty old place for seventeen years, but then you have done a beautiful renovation on it.'

Iver rose from his armchair and strode to the window. His eyes looked past the valley as light from the outside came in through the windows, casting sunlight on the crystal chandelier. It had rained that morning, and now the sun broke through the parting clouds.

Iver pushed the terrace windows open, then stepped out onto the porch of his Scottish baronial mansion as it stood above Dumfriesshire. The smell of fresh-cut grass wafted past him, and he took in the scents from the vast gardens and the several dark sycamore and beech trees dotted across the grounds on either side of a path that wound down to the valley below.

'Cicero, organise the car to go into town. Everything must be in order. Have they prepared the one room we talked about?' Iver said.

Cicero raised an eyebrow. 'You mean the one past the separate chapel.'

'Yes, that's the one. I want it to be ready.'

The home had been in Iver's family for years, but along the way, the deeds had passed hands, and his family had lost it during the war. Now, however, it was time to bring the Koh-i-Noor diamond home to its rightful place.

'You know that she has the documents,' Iver said.

Cicero's jaw clenched. 'You mean the missing Lahore Agreement?'

'Yes. I have now found the documents, and it's about bloody time. We should be able to begin. Did I ever tell you the diamond was in my family?'

Cicero raised an eyebrow. 'Because of the princess's caretaker? You're as Scottish as they come. How could the Koh-i-Noor have possibly been in your family?'

Iver moved back towards a cabinet in the den. 'The only way we'll get to the diamond is if we use the offspring.'

'What offspring?' Cicero asked.

'History has a funny way of repeating itself, and the apple doesn't fall far from the tree I hear. It's a fascinating thing, family, and blood even more so. Sometimes it takes generations before there is closure to a long-disputed issue, and it is time.'

Iver opened a drawer on a large desk. He fished deep within its contents and pulled out three documents. The bold letterhead read the British East India Company. 'This is a letter from Lord Asterley himself. He never got away from anything regarding the Koh-i-Noor diamond. He may have led people to believe that his interest in India was education and prospering the British Empire, but I think they were more details to it than that. One of which would be things buried inside the vaults of the East India Company.'

Cicero's eyebrows knotted. 'Like what?'

There was a knock at the door, and a tall man marched into the room. 'It's time. The ship can sail in three days.'

'Have you mapped out the coordinates I sent you, Seeds?'

Seeds shook his head. 'I want to warn you. This isn't the best time for the ship to be sailing out to the Indian Ocean.'

'Don't tell me you believe in old wives' tales, Seeds? If I didn't have a funny arm, I would go myself. You want to make sure that all the diving equipment is intact. This could take a while, so make certain we equip your crew appropriately.'

'What about the minor matter of admission into international waters from the Maldives government?'

'Let me worry about that,' Iver said.

Aria paced out to the back of the bungalow that led to the beach as Maxwell and the others cleaned grit off the diving equipment. Until then, the gigs in the ocean were it—unless she could swallow her pride and turn to her father.

Her gaze wandered back to her room and to a picture of her mother on her bedside table. If only Aria's mother's will hadn't stipulated, she couldn't touch the small fortune she left Aria until she turned thirty, she'd finish the museum within three months.

Still two years away.

Her mother had been a beautiful woman, a lady. Bright brown hair and light compassionate eyes that used to make Aria smile. She'd worn expensive clothing and had many jewellery pieces she'd left to Aria.

Aria turned towards the men as Maxwell waved from the beach. It was good to be with him and not have the pressure to give him the answer he had been waiting for. Or was it? It was only yesterday that he'd proposed to her.

She would respond when she was ready.

Maxwell shot her a boyish smile, one that women craved. 'Have you had time to think about my question?'

Eventually, she would have to give him an answer, but perhaps today was not the day. Aria pursed her lips. 'Maxwell, I value you as a friend and—'

'As a friend? It's okay. I know the ring I gave you can't compare to what's at the bottom of this ocean,' Maxwell said. 'I think we might have something extraordinary.'

Aria squirmed under his gaze. 'Listen, Maxwell, let's talk about it when I get back from India. I'm going to see my dad. There's a lot of stuff I need to sort out, and I think my head will be a little clearer once I've done that.'

'All right.' He took a long breath and stared out to the ocean. 'Now that's some museum we will build, but I want more. I want you,' Maxwell said. 'I know it's your dream. You found out exactly what you want—and now you have it with this latest find. I don't see what else you could be waiting for.'

'No, Maxwell. I haven't found what I'm looking for.'

Her most crucial question had yet to be answered. Somewhere out there, her sister was alive, or someone had started a sick joke.

Aria reached for her diving gear. She secured her scuba buoyancy compensator to the edge, sliding the straps over the chamber and tightening them. She lifted the tank by the shoulder straps to check it had fastened tightly enough, then removed the tank valve cover and screwed the knob on the regulator before removing the dust cover.

When she was satisfied with the equipment, she attached the tank and fastened the inflator hose to the valve of her equipment. She took a deep breath and turned on the air. With the gauges face down and away from her, she used her other hand to open the tank.

The air pressure was stable, and she tested the regulator by pressing both buttons and breathing through the mouthpiece.

Taking a quick breath, she reached for her wet suit. Aria glanced at the inviting water in front of her. She gave Maxwell a quick nod. He frowned; his expression stony. Maxwell had planned the proposal for several days, and if she took off and left him, he'd probably forgive her but never recover.

The Maldives had always had a special place in her heart. Here she had gotten to know Maxwell better than at university. He'd been kind to her. This place was now home, and she wanted it that way, but she needed to make amends with her father if she was to understand the texts someone was sending her.

Maxwell turned to her. 'You ready?'

She nodded.

'You're exquisite and know what you want. Anything related to the ocean and underground treasures is no mystery to you. You've dedicated your life to understanding what the ocean has to say to us, and I want to share that with you. There's so much we can learn from each other. Don't you see?'

'Maxwell, I—'

'Just a friend.'

She smiled. 'Give me time.'

'Okay.'

Maxwell was being sincere and meant every word. That's why she'd made him a friend. Lover, husband? She'd never looked at him that way. Eventually, she'd have to let him know.

She had met Maxwell because they'd shared the same interests. He'd had the same thoughts about the ocean at Oxford. He was patient with unwanted lab results and brilliant in his study of rocks.

She had once thought she could warm-up to his advances, but something was missing, and even as she watched him, his muscular body in a wetsuit glistening in the sun, she couldn't tell what it was.

When her equipment was secure, she waved to the men out on the boat, and they waded out to deeper waters. Several minutes later, Maxwell and Aria stood on the deck of the boat, ready to go in. 'We should be about an hour,' she called to the crew.

Sunshine hit her face, and she moved over to where the men were busy hauling equipment onto the boat. 'Hey, Maxwell, you think we could strike gold again?' she said, trying to lighten the mood.

He flashed her a smile. 'So, it's gold we are after now?' Maxwell said.

They slid on their masks, and as the team on the deck prepared them, he winked at her. It was their routine. Both she and Maxwell checked that the oxygen straps were lying flat and had no slack. They also checked that the releases were secured and that they could undo them in case of emergency rule.

With masks on, Aria raised a thumb to Maxwell, and they both plunged into the water. They swam down several feet. She had marked the museum's territory. Seven hundred feet away from the mainland, yet naked to the invisible eye. That would make it easier when they finally built the underground museum and opened it up to the public.

They returned to the ocean bed where they'd found the red beryl gems pouring out of a traveller's chest. The biggest challenge remained securing this area of the water and dealing with the Maldives' authorities.

They headed down farther towards their secluded hideaway. If the world knew it was here, that would be the end. The world wasn't ready for it yet.

For now, they had to keep this location secret. The sandy floor, shoal buttons, and seagrass waited for their arrival. Aria looked around herself and studied the half-buried shells. She ran her fingers past sponges and exoskeletons of crabs as she manoeuvred through the colourful sea glass. Spiky dark virtues swam past her mask as shafts of bold light filtered down.

They neared the spot as manta rays invisible against the ocean's colours drifted past.

She heard her breath, magnified, through the diving tube, and her pulse beat in her ears. The ocean floor was a museum. She took stock of the enveloping beauty. The Mediterranean and the Indian Ocean were both places of mystery.

Floor bed treasures deserved the best treatment, one that no government would ever fund. That's why she needed to raise as much money as possible.

They waded past coral reefs. The surrounding water was nutrient-rich, and feeding sponges clung to the wall sides. Coral reefs had made a spectacular comeback after El Niño was rumoured to have destroyed ninety-five per cent of the region's coral. Soft corals lined the ocean bed, and beautifully coloured fish swam past them. They made it to a lagoon. Colourful invertebrates filled the little cove.

Congested with shrimp, manta rays, and other large marine

species, this was her world to protect. The perfect place to have chosen for the underground museum. A large manta ray slid past her, and she smiled.

Aria let Maxwell lead the way. He was a skilled diver. As they got to the area where they had found the treasure, she thought back to how particular a voyage this ship must have taken. Taking its journey in the eighteenth century, the British Empire ship had left India full of rubies and gold and was making its way through the Indian Ocean towards the Maldives on its way to Kenya. Many were off to build the East Africa railway when it was shipwrecked.

Her eyes moved around the shipwreck from broken floorboards to shredded ship sails.

Maxwell took her hand and pulled her towards the most significant part of the cove. The underwater museum was a dream. This was where the treasure was found, and this is where some of it would stay.

She sensed movement.

A figure.

She turned as a school of fish bolted past her, but it was too late. An attacker swam in from the right, grabbed Maxwell and pinned him to the ocean bed.

Sand drifted around her scuba mask. She pushed towards him, her heavy equipment impeding her speed. It was then that a second assailant pulled her away from him.

Maxwell kneed the heavy man off him. He then hurried forward towards Aria and flung the attacker off her back.

Dizziness and nausea overwhelmed her. Aria had just enough time to gauge what was going on, and her eyes enlarged as two more sinister figures shot their way.

Maxwell gave her a nod.

She read his intent.

One quick look at her mask showed they had detached it

through the struggle. Fast-moving underwater currents pulled at her as the men charged towards her. If she didn't hurry, she'd run out of oxygen.

She had to go back above the surface.

Air was everywhere except in her lungs. With as much rapidity as water resistance would grant, she hurried upward until her head rose above the water.

Aria thrashed towards shore as hastily as the cumbersome equipment would allow, then a sudden tug pulled at her feet. Without a moment to think, the force of the pull ripped her backwards under the water's surface.

3

Parkinson eyed the man's hands as he fingered a glowing diamond. 'You may call it a myth,' the old man said, 'but it was the start the Koh-i-Noor's legacy. The stone that means *'mountain of light'*. Make sure you visit the site before you leave our town, and be sure to climb the fort.'

'What happened then?' a listener asked.

'The rocks disappeared from the village, and children were no longer born. Many foreigners came to our land and plundered it for the Koh-i-Noor. A curse follows it.'

Parkinson swallowed hard. It was a story manufactured for tourists, but maybe there was more to it. Could he get someone here to guide him to the Golconda caves? That's where he'd been. All he remembered were three caves. He had to make sure he got there before the Department of Economic Intelligence found Altaneus' last place of operation.

He had been a physicist most of his adult life, but this he had never expected. Had he come all this way to listen to nothing but an old wives' tale about mysterious diamonds? He chugged down his beer and set the empty bottle on the bar counter. He tossed the bartender three-hundred British pounds. 'Rumours in intelligence circles say you know the way to the Altaneus factory. How about we take a little a trip when you close the bar?' Parkinson said.

Aria could feel the air leave her lungs. Her equipment was getting heavier as force pulled her farther down. She did not understand what strength she could use to lift and kick her attacker farther beneath her. Aria removed her diving equipment and pulled herself upward as she made it back towards the surface. She swam, determined like a frantic squirrel, and hurried to the beach.

With a quick glance over her shoulder, she turned back where she'd been. There was no sign of Maxwell. She took several moments to catch her breath.

Should she get help to Maxwell? Was he okay? She then saw him heading towards her and to the beach. Three assailants flashed right behind him.

It was then that she saw the man who had tried to pull her down only metres from where she stood on the beach. He was only sixteen feet away. Dumping her equipment, she darted towards her cabin.

She had to get out.

With a fluttering feeling in her chest and only a brief moment to pick up her backpack, Aria charged into her bungalow. She dashed to her bedside and found her passport and threw it in with her wallet. Her mobile phone had remained by the bedside. That too went into her backpack. She slid the bag over her shoulders, grabbed her shoes, and advanced to the rear of the house.

Her trusty motorbike was parked in the outer courtyard. She leapt onto it and started the engine.

The motorbike sped up the dust path until it slid onto the paved carriageway. She had no desire to know who was after her. Her sole aim was to get to the airport and hope a flight off the island would give her escape.

Aria turned her head for a second. A thug was hot on her heels and had been joined by two others in a car at the end of the road that led to the bungalow. She swerved around the bend and put the motorbike in full gear.

Aria joined the motorway. At this speed, she would make it to the airport in twenty-five minutes.

Aria had lost her pursuers about twenty minutes earlier, but it would not be long before they caught up to her. She left her motorbike in the car park and bolted to the terminal building. At this time of day, the small airport only had two flights to the main island. She glanced back to see if they had followed her. So far, so good. No thug was in sight.

Taking a deep breath, she hurried to the ticket desk. 'One ticket to Male International Airport,' she said breathlessly as she nearly collided into the counter.

'Aria Raith?' the male attendant said. 'You normally like to book in advance. It's not like you to leave in such haste.'

'Thanks,' she said as she grabbed her ticket and shoved it in her wet suit. 'I'm late for a wedding,' she lied.

She must've been a sight, standing in the airport terminal, wearing a wetsuit. It was then that she saw the dark car that had chased her stop in the tiny parking lot outside. Aria scurried towards the departure door that led out to the airfield. She pushed past a handful of passengers she was to travel with. Aria threw down several dollars at the end of the counter then grabbed a large cotton scarf. She tossed it around her shoulders, then blended into the tiny line heading towards the aeroplane.

Her heart in her throat, she quickened her pace. Who the heck were these people? Was Maxwell, okay? He was a robust man and could handle himself, but what were his chances against three armed men?

Aria found a busy café in the departure terminal. She sat still for what seemed like an eternity, her scarf concealing her head and part of her face.

Close to thirty minutes later, she held her breath as she took her seat and stared out the window for a few moments. Slapping the seatbelt into place, she held her breath as the aeroplane engines started to roar.

Hands tight around the seat handle, she glanced behind her and forced down a sick feeling as the plane soared off the tiny island. Several minutes into the flight, Aria scanned the passengers. She suppressed a shudder as her eyes locked with a passenger in row seven.

He had the same dark eyes that had borne into her on the coral reef floor.

Department of Economic Intelligence
New York Headquarters
10:27 hrs

The office was quiet as Agent Hudson entered the room and placed his gun on the table. Feeling too old for games, he rammed his hand into the wall.

Damn it!

His body locked up with rage. Why couldn't he find anything on this guy?

Hudson took the stairs two at a time to the seventh-floor archives room. Parkinson's file was like a ghost, and the CCTV footage from Paris had yielded nothing to connect him to the Koh-i-Noor's disappearance.

How could it? No one had seen him in twenty-five years.

The agency database had little information on James Parkinson since he had disappeared so long ago. Hudson scratched his chin, then he turned away and stared out the window. He had made this trip and had been in and out of the Department of Economic Intelligence for the last few days. The bosses wouldn't like this. They would be after him.

He sank down in the seat. Muffled voices in the hallway alerted him. It was lunchtime, and he had to finish the report. Without Parkinson, he had nothing.

Eighteen months was a long time to spend on a case, and now with the disappearance of the Koh-i-Noor, it was even more imperative to find a lead. Anything.

James Parkinson. Why were no answers surfacing? Parkinson had vanished from every database known to him except for the files they had in these archives.

He turned on the computer as a tall brunette made her way towards his cubicle and dropped a box on the desk.

'What is this?' Hudson asked.

'That box hasn't been opened for a long time. Figured you might find something there. That was the last time the agency looked for Parkinson, just before closing his file and marking it with a large *S* for Shadow File.' The woman ran a hand over the dust that had accumulated around the edges of the rectangular box and pulled it open. 'As you can see, this file was closed exactly twenty years ago when the agency gave up and officially classed it as a Shadow File. Nobody bothered to digitise any of this material. As far as the Department of Economic Intelligence was concerned, it was a null case.'

Hudson slowly grazed his fingers over the dated papers in the box. His eyes caught sight of a photograph of the man he had yet to meet. 'This him?'

She raised an eyebrow. 'Yes, that would be him twenty-five years ago. I'll be in the other file room if you need anything,' she said and left him with his thoughts.

Hudson studied the shot taken outside in a car park with a long lens. Parkinson had a nonchalant face. In the photo, he was blond and had symmetrical brown eyes, with a young beard on his face. Over his right shoulder, he carried an overnight bag. It looked heavy. Important.

The photographer had used the zoom lens to take the picture of Parkinson commissioned by them. A smirk on his face made him appear younger than he probably was.

Hudson examined the date of the image. They took it a few days before they knew Parkinson to have disappeared. He scanned the notes on him. The man had a brilliant career.

He'd been born in England, then his family moved to New Mexico, and he had studied in San Francisco. He studied chemistry for a while, and his grades were curiously not good at first. His real interest was geology and physics. Chemistry was something he picked up much later in life.

Parkinson had a PhD in chemistry. His doctorate earned him a mention in the Nobel Prize magazine, but they left him out from the accolade because the study got dropped compared to the other sciences. Parkinson taught at Princeton University for several years, lecturing in geology and later gemmology. The man had been working on something for years. Hudson only wished he knew what it was. The government had recruited him to work on a few classified projects. There was no detail about the projects, but there were photographs of diamonds of varied sizes and several references to quantum computing that he did not understand.

His eyes read the notes closer. A memo attached to the files, over ten years after they closed the Shadow case, revealed that Parkinson had appeared but then gone missing together with Garen Raith's daughter, Emily Raith. Altaneus Corporation had recruited the two. There was no information on what they had recruited them to do.

Emily Raith was seventeen at the time.

Hudson's finger filed through the last page of the box. An old black-and-white picture of the mine stared at him with a note and the date.

Golconda Mine, India 1927.

As he scrolled through the files, his eyes narrowed onto the personal data section. Parkinson was approaching seventy-seven years of age.

Where would a seventy-seven-year-old researcher hide? His eyes caught a copy of Parkinson's last known location. Twenty-five years ago, he'd boarded a flight from JFK to London Heathrow Airport.

He'd gone to the United Kingdom.

Why?

4

They'd been inflight for thirty minutes, and it would be another hour before they would land.

Aria's pulse raced. How was she going to get off the plane? The man wouldn't be far behind.

She slouched in her seat and dragged the scarf around her head. Pulling out her phone, she went over the text. Emily had been very guarded in the days before she'd disappeared. She'd not responded to a request Aria made to visit her for her birthday. There was no way of knowing what had taken place. Aria had been too young to understand it all. All she knew was that her sister had joined Altaneus. They were teenagers. She was fifteen, and her sister was seventeen.

Her mother's death had hit Aria like a brick wall. Both she and Emily had left her. Too soon. The police reports had all been vague.

Incomplete.

Aria drew in a deep breath as her mind clouded with dark thoughts from the past. The last conversation she had with her father about Emily had ended in a dispute; it was distasteful.

. . .

'Why did you stop searching for Emily? I blame you, Father. I was only a child, but now I know more. You let her leave. You didn't stop her going to that research corporation. You had access to classified information from MI6 and other government agencies. Altaneus went into administration, and you didn't see it. All their records from the time vanished under your watch. Why didn't you go after her, stop her, damn it, and not let her go?'

Her father's face had been granite. 'Emily was seventeen years old. She knew what she was getting into.'

'You had a duty to stop her joining Altaneus Corporation.'

'What's done is done. It's in the past. She's gone and not coming back.'

'You let her go and hurt me deeply. Father, why won't you let me in?'

The conversation had lasted only two minutes, but it might as well have been an hour. Aria wrung her hands together, fed up with secrets.

She peered over her shoulder, and a lump crawled to her throat.

The man's seat was empty.

Hulhule Island, North Male Atoll
Capital of Maldives

She turned to a woman with a little baby next to her.

'Could I borrow some clothes?' Aria asked twenty minutes before landing in the capital of the Maldives.

She reached for her backpack. 'Here's seventy-five US dollars.'

The woman frowned, but then she nodded slowly as she studied Aria's wet suit. 'Here, you can have my long skirt and a T-shirt.'

With the scarf over her head, Aria hurried down the stairs as soon as the plane landed at the arrival station on the tarmac. She rushed into the terminal building, following the directions for her connecting flight to New Delhi. Glancing over her shoulder, confirmed her fears as she folded into the arrival crowd.

Fingers tight with her nails biting into her palms, she huffed as she hurried through arrivals with one eye hunting for the ladies' room. The man from the plane set off in a run behind her.

She dodged into the toilets and scanned the room for a free cubicle. Aria threw back a toilet door and turned the lock. She needed to think.

She plastered her ear to the door for sounds of footsteps. Maybe even screaming. There was no way she could slip out into Male unnoticed by those who were after her.

What chance would she have in one of the smallest capitals in the world? Aria needed to board that flight to New Delhi within ten minutes.

Aria crouched her hand firm on the handle of the cubicle. Certain no one had followed. She unlocked the door and glanced both ways. Two women she'd not seen on entry cast her stunned glances as they washed their hands.

After several calculated moments, Aria stomped out of the toilet cubicle and headed towards the bathroom door.

A hand grasped her throat.

She riveted backwards, her back slamming into the rear wall.

'Where is it?' her attacker growled.

Gurgling for breath, she opened her mouth. 'Where's what?'

Aria soaked up her strength and glared at the man. He was the thug from the plane. He reached around, gripped her backpack, and ripped it open. Its contents dropped to the tiles —her wallet, research papers, and her passport.

'The stone. Where is it? We know you took it. You make a living collecting expensive rocks!'

What the heck was this all about? Had she left a debt unpaid? She felt his breathing on her shoulder. This time her voice was calm. 'What are you looking for?'

'Don't play ignorant with me.'

It took every ounce of courage. Head high, fists tight, and with one steady kick, she booted him in the groin. Hands on his crotch, he crashed to the floor, his face twisted with agony.

The women shrieked; their voices hoarse with dread.

Aria sped to the door, then spun around to retrieve her discarded belongings. She whisked to the window. Rattling on the doorknob made her stop in her tracks.

She heaved. 'How many of you are there?'

Her shaky hand reached for the latch and yanked it open. With one haul, she thrust her weight through the open window.

The landing was brutal and left her with a grazed knee as she rose from the dirt and scrambled back towards the terminal building.

Once inside, she scoured the departure terminal for her connecting flight.

Three minutes to departure. She took to her heels, scanning faces for the woman who'd given her the clothes. Aria knew they were headed the same way.

Seated near the departure gate, the mother raised her head and smiled.

Aria flashed through the halls to departures, arriving breathless before making her way to the woman in line for the India flight, balancing her infant and a changing bag. The baby's discomfort made the woman step out of line for a nappy change.

Aria gestured to the woman. 'Allow me to watch your bags if you wish to change your baby.'

'Really?'

'Sure. You look like you could use a break. You've been travelling a long way by yourself.'

Aria took the baby's changing bag in one hand as the woman changed her baby.

'There, all clean now,' the woman said, rocking the child before retrieving her bag. 'You going to New Delhi as well?' the woman asked.

'Yes. I think we are on the same flight,' Aria said studying the woman's information on her hand luggage.

The woman headed to the departure gate with less than a minute left for boarding.

Aria smiled to herself, rotating a flash drive in her fingers.

The flash drive she'd placed in the baby's changing bag on the flight over. It had taken a few seconds to pull it out from underneath the nappies where she'd laid it.

The man had said something about a diamond. Aria had no idea what diamond they were talking about. For now, at least, she had the diary photos.

Either way, the diary was far away from her and on its way to her bank vault in Switzerland—together with her fifty per cent from the sheikh's job she'd just completed.

5

British High Commission
New Delhi, India
15:20 hrs

They had had little time to discuss anything.

The look her father had given her when Aria arrived at the British High Commissioner's residence in New Delhi with no luggage but a plastic bag carrying her passport, wallet, and mobile phone was something she still had to explain.

She'd gone straight to bed. Once she'd settled into the second-floor guest room, Aria had collapsed into an exhausted sleep.

The following day, late into the morning, Aria made her way out in the sunshine of the palatial gardens. A Portuguese-Colonial style villa, the ambassador's residence spread across several acres of land. Traces of the British Raj still hung from its interiors and adorned the stunning mansion.

With the sun warm on her skin, she toured the property.

Her eyes drifted to the three-storey walls of Indo-Saracen architecture with its latticework fit for an Indian prince.

Though her father had invited her countless times to India, she'd only broken her silence with him over twenty-four hours ago.

Well-manicured gardens dotted with palm trees and sculptured shrubs surrounded the villa and begged her to continue her tour. She stepped on the terrace bordering a lawn of endless well-tended vegetation that stretched for what seemed like miles.

A noise behind her startled her. An Asian gentleman dressed in a crisp suit and tie pushed through the porch doors pulling a tray of afternoon tea with him. He glimpsed at her, his stare lasting longer than it should. She returned the smile; she needed a friendly face.

'I'm your father's butler,' he said. 'Could I offer you some Indian *chai?*'

As the British High Commissioner representing Her Majesty's government in India, her father, husband to the late Duchess of Asterley, had certain privileges afforded to him.

Aria hadn't seen him in three years, and her last words to him were, 'I never want to see you again unless you tell me why you let Emily down.'

Would he listen to her now that she was here? Uninvited. Her father was what one would call a career diplomat, having made his way through the ranks. Aria thought about her dual heritage. He'd been born American and met her mother, an aristocrat before she was born. He'd become a British citizen when he was about twenty-five—after his family had sent him to England to boarding school.

The butler smiled. 'Your father will be down soon, *memsahib*.'

She glanced out to the home office door where her father

was finishing a meeting dropped in that morning. She bit her lip and could still sense the cold silence that stretched between them like a tight rubber band. Emily's disappearance created a vacuum that had endured far too long. Aria stood up and wandered to the far edge of the garden.

Standing at six feet tall, her father was a fair-skinned man, with his round face, slight cleft chin, full lips, and dark-blue eyes that communicated confidence every time she saw him. His light brown hair was greying at the sides, and Aria remembered the smell from his tobacco pipe that he loved to smoke after dinner.

At her mother's will reading, her mother had left the majority of the wealth to her father and also left each girl a hefty sum to enjoy at thirty years of age. It was then that she'd decided to build the underwater museum. She hadn't told her father as much, and when she couldn't touch her money, she'd turned to lost treasure hauls and deep-sea diving.

She wouldn't bring it up. Today was about Emily and the diary that none had ever explained to her—the one she had inherited.

The sun kissed her bare arms. Why hadn't her father used his diplomatic connections in the government to help Emily if she'd been in danger? Emily had been overseas, but once the police and Interpol had closed the case, the reports had concluded with 'an unexplained lab accident'. Someone knew something.

Aria found a bench in the grounds of the High Commission and took a seat. A gentle breeze caressed her skin against the scorching sunshine on the Indian March day.

Her father wouldn't approve, anyway. She could never ask him for capital—because he'd want to know what she'd spend it on. The money had allowed her to start her own business down in the Maldives, including funding the ocean museum, the boats, and everything she required. She'd made the best of jewel and treasure hunting, but the museum fund needed so much more investment.

She twitched in her seat. As an heiress who would receive a significant sum from her family on both sides of the Atlantic, she was a target by many standards and travelling the seas was exposing her to greater danger. Her inheritance,—an American one from the steel business, and one from the Duchess's Asterley fortune—were possibly what those men had targeted and any jewellery the family had. What diamond did they mean, though?

Aria turned her head, then moved to the veranda for shade.

She stopped.

A man advanced to the far ends of the grounds. Instinct drove her behind a palm plant.

She recognised that voice.

Jeff Avent?

What was her father's American attorney doing here? A lawyer who could get anything done in intelligence circles. He was a long way from home.

She heard another set of footsteps come down towards him. Her father neared him. She watched the two men. Aria knew better. These two were up to something. Jeff Avent was the man her father called on to fix problems and make others disappear.

Jeff spoke first as Aria listened from her hiding spot.

'You need to be careful, Garen. You can't have this coming back to haunt you. My private investigators have only managed to come up with this information.'

Garen reached for the piece of paper that Jeff held out. He scanned it. 'You saying Emily got involved with this Iver Fenderson's criminal organisation? She was just a child.'

'I know. Read on. There's more.'

Garen's eyes widened. 'An explosion? How?'

'Says here an explosion led to several gas leaks, and all suspects had alibis. Iver's been cleared.'

'So, we've nothing that leads to him in all of this? Jeff, it's been thirteen years! How can nothing come up?'

Her father had lost his American accent years ago. His voice now had many traces of the Queen's English, with only a slight twang that hinted at his Pennsylvanian roots.

'We have a damaged flash drive that was discovered later at the explosion site. Here.'

Jeff handed something to Garen.

'So, this proves everything.'

'If we can read it. We haven't been able to, and now the Koh-i-Noor has been taken. You and I know it's not for its value alone.'

Aria squinted as her father placed whatever Jeff had given him into his shirt pocket.

With a knowing nod from Jeff, both men moved inside the building.

15:27 hrs

'We didn't get much time to talk last night, did we?' a voice said from behind.

Aria rose, then hesitated as her father reached in to peck her on the cheek. He drew her into a hug as she studied his face. Tired lines streaked his brow, and his tone was hoarse. He ran a hand over his forehead.

'No, we didn't.'

They took seats next to each other on the veranda, an awkward air between them. The butler came and poured him a fresh juice.

'Father...'

He held up a finger as if to tell her to wait until the butler had gone. As the man made his way back into the house, her father's eyes bore into her.

'Father,' she said. 'Why didn't you call Jeff back then? Why didn't you file a missing person's report until thirty-six hours had passed? I know I was only fifteen, but we accepted the statement from the accident. What happened to Emily thirteen years ago? We haven't talked about it?'

Garen's shoulders slumped. 'Why do you bring it up now?'

She leaned in and mumbled, 'Something's happened.'

'What?'

'I...'

Aria couldn't make herself tell him about the text, the diary, the ambush, her run here, the flash drive information she'd saved, and everything that had happened in the last couple of days.

'Father, Emily sent me a message. Well, at least that's what the encryption said. Someone's trying to reach me. Maybe even kill me. I barely made it here alive.'

Garen rubbed his chin and broke eye contact with her. 'Are you okay?'

She nodded. 'What's happening? There are some things I've wanted to know.'

'Do you?' Garen said.

A thickness grew in her throat. 'Father, please.'

'When your sister left, it was by her own choice. We argued, and I didn't want to fight her. I respected her, and I needed her to walk away with dignity. She was seventeen. I never considered she would go through with it.'

'Go through with what? Why didn't you stop her, Father? I never even said goodbye.'

'She was determined, just like her mother. She wanted to

take her money, and I let her. Little did I know what she would do with it.'

Aria fought the uncontrollable flushes of heat in her body. She ignored the thudding in her chest. How would she word it? If her father had let her sister get away and take her inheritance, had he suffered? What had Emily wanted with the money? The fluttering of a butterfly nearby made her stop when it landed on her. She flapped it away.

Granted, Emily had achieved more with geology and physics than most. A child prodigy, the papers called her, and then she was gone.

'Father, when Emily died, our gardener, Parkinson, disappeared around the same time. Where did he go? He was the one who introduced her to Altaneus Corporation. He used to teach us science and physics, you know. He was obsessed with geology too and the way nature behaved.'

'That's what made him a good gardener,' Garen said.

'But he went away the day after Emily's memorial service.'

Garen kissed her on the forehead and stood up to leave. 'Tonight, I want to show you something. Now, though, I must go back to the office. Come to my High Commission reception tonight. I have made arrangements for your wardrobe as it's an important affair. We can talk more about this. There's something your sister left, and I'd like you to have it.'

Once he'd gone, Aria rose. She had three hours to kill.

6

British High Commission
New Delhi
20:03 hrs

Aria's gaze caught the eyes of a man at the end of the large reception hall; his stare was fixed on her. Tall with an athletic build, his body fit nicely in an expensive tuxedo. His broad shoulders narrowed to lean hips. He gave her a nod of approval as one arrogant brow shot upward. This display of masculine charm wasn't wasted on her.

Clearing his throat, he arched a quizzical brow and then turned to a chatty brunette.

Aria tapped her chin with her fingers. Men shouldn't be built like him. A fiercely handsome face with the heightened presence of a Roman centurion. His stony expression revealed nothing of his thoughts as he towered above other men.

Her mouth went dry, and her hands moistened. Aria didn't need distractions right now. She'd never once taken such notice of any man, but his face was more attractive than was permissible. She had to turn away.

Aria's stare was cut short as Avent reached for a glass of champagne from a floating waitress several feet from her. She drew one sip of her drink and set the glass on the passing tray as the tingling bubbles loosened her throat.

'You look like a fish out of water,' a large man said approaching.

A search of defiance swelled within her as she locked eyes with his brooding face. 'That's because I *am* a fish out of water. I don't like dinner parties where I have to wear dresses I can hardly move in.'

'That dress looks magnificent on you,' the man said.

His accent was thick with Russian tones. Aria studied the middle-aged man in front of her. He was jovial enough, but in the glamorous environment she'd been in all evening, he was the first person who had bothered to chat to her.

'You're the diplomat's daughter. High Commissioner Raith's charming girl,' he said, his arm around a tall blonde woman.

'Seems you've guessed who I am, but charming isn't the word I would use. More like calculating, Mr Russian Ambassador. Are you enjoying your evening?'

'That obvious, am I?' he said.

'I believe you are. You wear the pin of Saint Peter's which is one of the lesser-known, most remarkable gems found in Russia. Correct me if I'm wrong, Your Excellency, but I believe your wife is also wearing stones that come from within the state of Romanov. Russia has gained many of these diamonds over 235 years. The jewels and diamonds collected by the Romanov dynasty began with the reign of Peter, known as Peter the Great, correct?'

'Tell me, do you like diamonds?' the Ambassador said.

'I hate them.'

'But your jewel knowledge is impressive.'

'I get by.'

Lips pressed together, Aria felt a tightness in her chest. This would be a long night. She had to wait until the High Commission reception was over before she could even get a word to her hosting father. She felt herself disengaging from the conversation and wished the ambassador would stop talking.

'Excuse me, Mr Ambassador,' she said, preparing to leave.

'You're a jewel expert, I see,' he said.

'I only follow the best, but not diamonds. Diamonds killed my sister. You see, Mr Ambassador, she went looking for the largest ones. That's why I hate them. Enjoy your evening,' Aria said, nodding to the ambassador and his companion.

Shock grew in his eyes as Aria left him and crossed to the front entrance. Eyes from the man across the room were still on her, intense, too curious.

She retreated for a second when she saw Jeff in the main reception room a few feet from the exit. Arms to her side, Aria turned back in search of her father who remained in deep conversation as the host of the evening. The clink of a glass brought on a sudden silence, as her father began a very casual speech to his guests.

When it was over, she turned to the door.

'Tell us, High Commissioner Raith. Where does your government stand on the missing Koh-i-Noor diamond? Surely Britain would want it back in the royal crown?'

The voice came from the Russian ambassador.

Her father cleared his throat. 'Tonight's Commonwealth celebration isn't about the debate of the Koh-i-Noor diamond. Like you, I'm shocked at its disappearance.'

So that was the diamond? The Koh-i-Noor?

She backed away, dodging towards the stairs. Out of the

corner of her eye, she studied Avent on the floor above her, oblivious to her scrutiny.

What did the royal diamond have to do with her? If her father wouldn't talk to her, then maybe Avent would.

With firm steps, Aria crossed the length of the hallway, passing doors on the residential wing of the High Commission. She stepped out onto the second level of the grand residence.

What was Avent doing in this part of the High Commission?

The building's top floors boasted mid-century design and radiated magnificence. Though a Colonial home, it housed contemporary levels of artisan imagination. What she liked about it was the solace the top floors offered and the privacy they so needed.

She crossed the hallway to the private library at the end of the wing. Sturdy books lined the walls. Multitudes of hardback volumes stacked on shelves reminded Aria of the library they had at Asterley Castle. The tick of the grandfather clock at the end of the room was the only perceptible sound. The dry smell of crispy paper and that of the musty carpets under her stilettos made her think of England—a home that she'd left many months ago.

She raised her eyebrows when she heard a clamour behind her, then pivoted.

Nothing.

Avent had vanished in the maze of rooms.

Music from the reception ball below filtered through the open windows. A warm breeze blew in her face, and she suddenly felt her body temperature rise. She returned her focus towards the far side of the library and hitched up her gown for easier movement. After peeking out to the grounds, Aria shut the window, convinced Avent wasn't on this floor.

Where the heck had he gone?

Satisfied there was nobody to find, she paced back the way she'd come. The hallway was now lit. Crossing a series of canvases on either side, many were evocative of the British Empire's history in India. The British Raj art it portrayed in streams of paintings glamorised the crop fields and diverse details that had made the East India Company what it was in Colonial India.

Once her father had spelt out at a diplomatic convention that several monarchs of Great Britain protected the trade of the East, but to what outcome?

She tiptoed to a new wing on her right. Court and community rooms boasted of the great Empire's history and made Aria's stomach churn.

Her brows lowered in concentration. The door at the end of the hall stood ajar. That was her father's private office.

A shadow fell on the floor ahead of her. It had to be Avent.

She stole a quick glance behind and advanced towards the room, sweat dripping from her brow. Aria took each step with caution.

Was it the plant in the corner? Was it the watercolours on the wall that had changed? She strode past her father's desk and advance into his office. A beautiful mahogany desk strewn with papers piled high, and a row of family pictures greeted her. Aria's eyes fell on her mother and sister's last photographs.

Her belly knotted, and she let out a deep breath.

The shadow moved again—this time by the window.

She crossed the room. Fear had held her hostage for two days.

Not tonight.

Not anymore.

She drew the adjacent floor-length windows open and stepped onto the marble terrace that overlooked the grounds of the High Commission. Guests had left, and a line of limousines ambled along the path stretching to the far end of the gate and beyond the compound walls. She checked her watch.

10:45 p.m.

Chin up, Aria filled her lungs and moved back inside the room. Had she imagined the shadow and Avent?

Her fingers slid over the old books on the shelf to the left, then she reached for an early paperback edition of a *Catcher in the Rye*. Her father enjoyed fiction. It was his way of contextualising what he had to deal with every day and all the events that affected his country.

A sinister shadow detached itself from the darkness, and fear knotted inside her. One wrong move would cost her her life.

Then, a bullet whistled past her ear.

The all-knowing eye of the gun peered into her soul, but her opponent was unidentifiable, his face concealed with a mask. His weapon never wavered as he cursed and clawed for a full clip.

In an instant, he darted back the way he'd come.

Aria raced to the window as a drone crashed through the window and exploded. What the heck was happening? Shuffling and screaming followed the eruption of gunfire on the floors beneath her feet. A crowd filed on to the lawn, and others scrambled for cover in now stationary limousines.

Shoulders curling forward, Aria found it challenging to breathe. Her brow furrowed, and her body hyperventilated as screams and shrieks sounded below. She thrust her back against the wall, realising it exposed her. Fear knotted her stomach as her head snapped around, and she tried to figure out how to get out. Her stomach clenched as High Commission security returned fire, but to whom?

Closer.

Behind her ear.

The shadow again.

Her heart rose to her throat, and the pounding in her ears nearly made her faint.

As gunfire was exchanged on the grounds, the sound was deafening. This time the earlier shadow took a new form. The assassin saw her coming and readied a blast.

Tightness formed in her chest. He had been watching her. In this very room.

Silence.

Gunfire pierced through the night air like the popping of a firework. When it sounded, a hail of exploding gunshots followed. She dived for the floor.

Sound-suppressed weapons whispered through the room.

Aria held her breath.

She kept her head down, the mahogany desk her only shield against ruthless shots.

How had anyone gotten past the military guards at the High Commission? *Damn it!*

She waited for several moments before tiptoeing towards the door. Her eyes fell on the staircase. Maybe she could make it down to safety. Whoever was here was scouring the floors.

Her heart pounding within her chest, frantic interchanges on the lower floors made her dart back into the room.

Aria held her breath, wanting to scream, but apprehension held her back as her hands clasped at her ears. Another shot. Despite the darkness, she saw just enough to know she was in trouble again.

Aria had been nowhere near a gunfight or even open fire, not until now. Was this her father's life? Was he now an international target?

She turned her head enough to glimpse outside where shifting bodies over the grounds in military uniform swarmed in to protect the High Commission.

Where was her father?

If anyone wanted to make an international statement, this was it with every government represented amongst the guests.

She waited.

Footsteps stomped to the door.

Aria remained still.

Her eyes fell on the doorknob as it twisted.

With insistence, and in one swift movement, a hand fell across her mouth.

7

The hand moved to her shoulder. Was this to be her last breath? The man twisted her around to face him.

Aria glared deep into the eyes of the tuxedoed man she'd seen earlier that evening. He'd since discarded his tuxedo for black tactical gear, and his presence numbed her as he held her tight, his grip commanding her to stay quiet. His eyes communicated to her she should remain still.

He wasn't here to kill her. His gaze fell back on her, and she held her breath. Shoulders straight, he placed a forefinger to his lips.

The door burst open, and the horror was too much and made Aria turn away. A pall of dread hung over her, numbing her to inaction.

Then a shotgun roared.

Her protector lunged sideways, then clawed for his shoulder holster. He smashed the intruder across the face with his pistol. In one insistent movement, a hand on her back threw her to the floor, out of harm's way.

As the man turned, his bullet caught one attacker in the leg, and they shuffled to the door.

With the thug now standing facing her protector, outside gunfire raged. Her protector took careful aim, and he popped off a quick shot before ducking.

She covered her ears, then lifted her head briefly. Her defender was to her side. He charged to the other man and smashed a fist in his jaw. Her eyes followed the drop of the large-framed man, a thud sounding loud in her ears. Hand to her heart, she stared straight, her mind registering the now unconscious face of the assassin.

Her protector turned towards her and pulled her to her feet. Her heart still hammering in her chest, Aria's eyes moved to the men who had marked her—now both on the ground unconscious.

'You okay?' the man asked his accent American.

'I think so,' she replied.

He darted into the hallway. She fought the urge to follow him but remained still. She heard him talk to the High Commission team. 'We have accounted for everyone. I've found the High Commissioner's daughter. She's okay.'

Aria couldn't believe that this man had crashed the thug into the wall unconscious.

He returned to the room with her father at his heels.

'Aria, are you okay?' Turning to the man who had helped her stay alive, he nodded. 'Thank you, Jave.'

'The High Commission is secure. They came with blanks to scare you, but I don't think they'll carry blanks next time.' Jave turned to her. 'Sorry. We haven't been introduced. I had my hands full.'

Aria studied his cocky grin.

'Jave,' her father said. 'You saved my daughter's life. Thank you.'

Her father scanned the room, first past the overturned chairs, then to the torn curtain. 'Must've been quite a fight,' he said.

'Nothing I can't handle, Garen,' Jave said.

'Whatever they were looking for, they got away with it.'

'I wouldn't be so sure about that,' Aria said, still shaking.

'What do you mean?' her father said.

'Never mind.'

'Don't worry about it, Aria. They didn't get you.' He turned to Jave. 'We need to get Aria out of here.'

'You sure that's the right move?' Jave said.

The High Commissioner paused as a flash drive fell from Aria's dress to the floor. He moved towards it and picked it up. 'This is way more dangerous and more valuable than the Koh-i-Noor.' His eyes narrowed into Aria. 'You always were one with a knack for having an insurance plan. What did you do with the diary?'

Aria cleared her throat. 'Kept it far from you and from me.'

Aria glared at the men. Her lips twitched at the corner as her father laid his hand on Jave's shoulder.

'What's going on here?' she said.

'This flash drive has the contents of the diary, right?' her father asked.

She flinched under her own surly thoughts. Was that all they wanted? The flash drive with the diary pages?

Hands on her hips, she huffed. She'd only taken the pictures so she wouldn't have to carry the blasted diary around. Shipping it to her Swiss private bank vault had been the best idea. It would be safe by now.

She shot Jave a glance. His frown gave her little

encouragement to continue her train of thought. He'd been watching her with those beautiful eyes, below a raised self-confident eyebrow—a lethal combination.

Whoever this man was, her father knew and trusted him. The concentration in Jave's eyes shook her willpower as he circled his finger around his gun. What was his relationship with her father?

The British High Commission
New Delhi, India
0:03 hrs

Aria pinched her lips together, drawing breath in her lungs as she ran her hands through her hair.

Her father stood watching her, then he moved confidently towards the window. He glared out at the terrace. His gaze met hers, saying nothing.

Blood whooshed through her veins with every beat of her pounding heart. 'Have they gone?' she asked.

'Yes. Security has contained the situation,' he said, 'but they haven't managed to identify a single person. We don't know who they were.'

'How's this possible? This is supposed to be the safest place in the country. This is the British High Commission. How can anyone just walk into a High Commission?'

'A security breach. Jave will work with our officers to find out,' her father said.

'First, in my bungalow in the Maldives and then here. They must have an international operation.'

Before he left the room, her father raised an eyebrow. 'What?'

'Nothing.'

'Why's this happening?' Aria said. 'I don't understand.'

Jave's face was severe, dedicated. It was his eyes, pale blue with a splash of green, that made him intoxicating. There was no other word for it; his was a life and a body built for action.

'Aria,' her father said. 'I think—'

'What he means to say,' Jave said, 'is that it's time you had a heart-to-heart after that episode in the Maldives.'

How did he know about the Maldives?

Jave moved to the door. 'I'll be outside if you need me,' he said before he left the room.

Her father turned, his face granite-like, yet focused. She knew with pulse-pounding certainty that whatever he was about to say wouldn't be what she wanted to hear.

'I'm so sorry this happened. I owe you an explanation of some sort, and I have a feeling it is overdue. Especially about your mother and sister, but this isn't the time to get into that. There's more at stake. Our family history isn't an easy one, and it is the reason they took away your sister from us in an explosion.'

She listened, but could she believe him?

Thirty-six hours ago, she would've laughed if someone had told her she would be in a crossfire fight. What was this to do with Emily, anyway? The texts? She had to sort out her thoughts, arrange them, and impose some semblance of order.

'Your great-great-great-grandfather, Lord Asterley, was involved in the British occupancy of India. Have you ever wondered why I wanted to be posted here as British High Commissioner? Lord Asterley once led the East India Company. Of all the choices for diplomatic posts they gave me, this is the place I chose, and the reason I did is that I needed answers. I needed to protect you. We have a complicated past that has come back to haunt us. The family.'

Aria stood in a hush. 'I'm tired of the secrets. What's going on? I nearly lost my life trying to get to you, and tonight—'

He tapped the top of the desk with a pen, thinking. 'You're right. You can't move on until we resolve this. Believe me, this is not the time. You need to be safe.'

She squished her eyebrows and studied her father's determined face. It was the only solid reality in her shifting world. A myriad of questions flooded her mind, then an idea slowly germinated within her. 'Who is Jave, really? He saved my life. What's he doing here? Is he protecting you? What's he doing at the British High Commission? He's a US Navy SEAL, isn't he? I saw how he handled himself, and his accent means he's not SAS. One thing about being a diplomat's daughter is you get wind of things that work in secret. What happened to your regular security team?'

'I asked Jave Lincoln to come here. For you,' he said.

'Why would you do that?' Aria said.

'Because you connect history and the future relationship of three great nations. India, the US, and the United Kingdom. Aria, your great-great-great-grandfather on my side was sent to the colonies to pay off a personal debt for the Civil War. That deal went messy with him and Lord Asterley.'

'Is that what this is all about? What debt? What's that got to do with the Koh-i-Noor? Father, there are people after me, and I don't know why. I've had to dodge bullets, moving vehicles, and God knows what else, and I am not even safe around you.'

'You're right, but my adopted country, Britain, has a debt to pay, and someone has declared it payday. We took something out of India, and until yesterday, it sat in one of the most guarded places in the world. The most highly secured establishment of national heritage—and possibly the most fortified museum in the world. The Tower of London. It was a debt.'

'Really?'

'Your great-great-great-grandfather paid off the debt using a jewel known as the Koh-i-Noor diamond. They used the diamond as a truce between two superpowers at the time, but it never made it to the New World. Instead, it went to Queen Victoria. Both the new colonies and the British government during the Civil War had an interest in India.'

'That makes little sense.' She pinched her eyebrows.

'What's wrong,' he said.

'That jewel's not American. It doesn't belong there.'

'Some would also argue it's not British either. Well, the debt was never paid, and a debate has hung in the air as to its rightful owner for centuries. So, you see the feud over its ownership has been resurrected, but more disturbing is the fact that it has gone missing for the first time in known history—two nights ago in Paris. You are the best jewel hunter in the world, according to Interpol. You'll be on everyone's watch list, including those who have taken the jewel. When that diamond came to Queen Victoria during the British occupation of India, it was somebody else's bounty, promised by your great-great-great-grandfather to someone else. That someone must blame our family.'

'The Koh-i-Noor diamond has always attracted controversy,' she said. 'So, what now?'

Her father's expression was pained, as though he had been wounded. 'We have a problem beyond its disappearance. Dangerous people want the diamond, and they know you are an expert at finding lost gems. My guess is that's why they're after you.'

'Shouldn't we involve the police? Interpol? Anyone who has the power to stop this?'

'London doesn't know about you being here. It's my job to make sure that London doesn't know where you are.'

'I really don't understand how I fit into all of this. There are better and far more experienced gemmologists than I,' Aria said.

'Not all have a family whose history is linked to the jewel's messy past. Someone wants the diamond badly, and they've pegged your name to it. With the jewel now missing, these facts have resurfaced. Your sister, Emily, died in an accident while investigating the future impact that diamond could have.'

Aria held back a gulp. She'd almost forgotten her sister's urgent ask in the text. Could it be why the texts had involved the diary?

'Father, I read the journal. It can't be right.'

'There's an organisation called the Department of Economic Intelligence, or the DEI, and it blames the British government for this mess we are in—and the court case that opens in eleven days to decide the controversy around the diamond. They work in secret and have marked you and me to produce this diamond and defend it.'

A wave of panic washed over her. 'I don't hunt diamonds, nor do I even like them. You can't be serious. I can also never be forced to look for something I don't want to find.'

His eyes shimmered with the intensity. 'Jave is here to help.'

Aria would ask the obvious. It was clear to them, but not to her. She sucked her bottom lip between her teeth. 'And if it's missing, do we know who could have taken the diamond?'

'No, I can't get into that now,' her father said, his lips compressing into a thin line. 'You and Jave have to get out of here before they return.'

'Is Jave with the US authorities? He seems to be in charge tonight, Father,' Aria said.

'He's someone I trust.'

Didn't mean *she* trusted him. Aria's throat parched, dry as dust. 'Father, I came here so I could avoid secrets. So, I could trust you again, but now I don't know. I've got so many things going on. I don't need this now. Can't you make it go away? I have to decide —' She stopped. 'There's this man, Maxwell.' She sank into a seat by the door. 'He wants to marry me. I just don't feel I can move on without knowing certain things about us in our family, and now I have the world after me—and Emily. I can't take any more of this.'

'I know, my darling. I just can't give you more information without further endangering you.'

'I'm already in danger.'

He stood straight and set a hand on her shoulder. 'The less you know, the better for you. Just know that it's the truth for now. I wish I had stopped you from coming here. They know you're at the High Commission. Let's get you safely out of here. Somebody has marked you to retrieve that stolen blood diamond.'

Would the diary really stop anything? What was in her journal that linked the Koh-i-Noor to her family? Her dad would be mad to think she could just disappear. The people after her were skilled marksmen. It would only be a matter of time.

The diary wasn't with her. She forcibly quelled the urge to scream. 'Why was the Koh-i-Noor allowed to go to Paris?'

'It was on loan from the palace. A diplomatic gesture between two nations.'

'From HRM?'

'You being a jewel expert, an oceanographer and treasure expert, and my daughter, has made all this worse. You know that the Koh-i-Noor was once the largest diamond ever mined. With each change of hands, bloodshed has followed, and we need this to stop before it comes to the forefront of the media.'

'Why now?'

'Like I said, in eleven days, the fate of the Koh-i-Noor diamond will be decided. With new evidence, there are many contenders on the table.'

'What new evidence?'

'Your diary. And now your flash drive.'

Garen set his hand on the small of her back and pushed her towards the door. 'Everything has been arranged. You're leaving tonight, and no one must know where you are going. I've asked Jave to take you.'

'Take me where?'

'I can't tell you much more. For your own safety.'

02:17 hrs

When Jave returned to his temporary accommodation in the High Commission, the bruise on his head started to throb. The ice in his whisky glass rattled, and he set it on an antique table. He stretched his neck and rolled his shoulders. It had been that kind of day since he had landed from Amsterdam at the small airport just outside New Delhi. It was no way to start this investigation.

Now, he had to ferry the ambassador's daughter to safety. The DEI would be after his neck if he didn't get this right.

How long had it been? Six weeks of threats?

This time they had been sending these thugs after him for the significant part of five weeks, and now he was so close to finding the answers.

He thought back to the evening's events. Before tonight. Jave had never met the High Commissioner's daughter. His mission was more robust than he had signed on for. Who had the whole picture here? Was Garen lying, or was it his beautiful daughter?

Jave liked the way she'd looked at him. With midnight black hair that flowed over her shoulders and strawberry-coloured lips, she had to be the most beautiful woman he'd ever laid eyes on. Her Amazonian figure fit well with her athletic body. Eden green eyes had glowed at him with a charming sparkle.

She didn't trust him, though. Should she? Heck, he hadn't been precisely charming tonight. The woman was beautiful with her waist-length hair that she kept flicking over her shoulder. He didn't need a distraction like her. Nothing would dissuade him from his mission.

Another swig of the hard liquor went down quickly, like water down a pipe. He set his gun on the table and reread the brief on his phone. Like Aria, Jave needed answers from Garen. This whole thing with his daughter should have been finished by now. Yes, they would deal with all of that shortly.

He made his way over to the bed. He'd barely slept the previous night.

The attackers, more like assassins, had left Aria rattled but with a stern warning. They'd slipped out of his grasp.

He peeked outside as stars returned in the sky like glass crystals. Like this annoying diamond. He linked his hands together and stretched them over his head to relieve the kinks. A knock on the door made him turn his head.

Garen strode into the room and stretched for a glass of whisky from the minibar by the door.

'Not the best person to tell you this, Garen, but you know you will have to tell your daughter the truth. She's hard to fool.'

Garen jerked his head around to stare at him. Grim determination etched his hard features. 'I lost both my daughters a long time ago. I can't have this happen again. Aria has broken her silence after three years.'

'From what I know, she's all you've got left. So, you've got to make the most of your family,' Jave said.

'How about your family? Where are they?' Garen said.

'I'm not here to talk about my family but yours, Garen. You sure you want to take this plunge? We leave in two hours.'

'Yes, you guys need to go.'

'There's something I need to know. We only have eleven days to find anything about Emily and the diary. I want to help you with this dilemma of yours, Garen.'

Garen's stubborn jaw clenched. 'She's got a diary she inherited from her mother's side. The diary has something that could bring this international argument to a close.'

'Where is the diary?' Jave said.

'Not sure. My guess is that's why they were here tonight.'

'Then she must have it.'

'How much do you know about Iver Fenderson, Jave?'

Jave feigned an indifference he didn't feel. Aria was in trouble, and he seemed to care more than Garen at this point.

'With the diamond gone, Fenderson or someone close to him was keen to win the Koh-i-Noor diamond case, but he needs anything he can find on it, and right now that is Aria's diary. My biggest fear is he wants Aria to find the stone for him. That's what she does best. Either way, he wants any evidence that will support his and India's case with the diamond.'

Jave watched as Garen shoved his hand into his pocket and pulled out a document. 'What will you tell Aria?'

Garen's downcast expression pleaded for understanding. 'The less she knows, the better.'

'If Fenderson doesn't get the diamond or the diary, what will happen?' Jave asked.

'We mustn't find out. I'm in a bind with the Department of Economic Intelligence,' Garen replied. 'They know nothing about when the Lahore Agreement was first drafted. There are three parts to it. One is in the diary, one section was bought by a noble family—now headed by Count Valex in Austria, a man that I know well, and you need to find—and no one knows what happened to the third section. You need all three to piece together the evidence as to the true owner of the Koh-i-Noor. There's no straightforward way out for me, and I'm afraid. I don't know why I was the one to have two daughters connected to this diamond. I tried to protect them and keep them as far away from it as I could, but go figure, one daughter, Aria, learnt all about jewels and their history and my other daughter about the science that surrounds the future use of gems, and it killed her. I won't have that happen to Aria.'

Jave would stand firm in his assessment of the facts once he had them. 'We won't let that happen.'

'Aria's the best oceanographer and historical jewel expert this century has ever seen. She knows more about gem history, and their position and worth, than any other person. From an early age, she studied them, and she has given her whole life to understanding rocks. There's the funny thing. She hates diamonds and has even the ones she inherited from her mother, Clarisse. It took her away from me. I'll not let this take her away anymore. I need you to keep her safe. I trust only you. I've planned everything. When you get to Vienna, go to this address.' Garen sent an address to Jave's secure phone. 'Tell the Count everything. You can trust him.'

Jave rotated his head to release the tight tendons. 'How long has your family had the diary?'

'Decades. Aria inherited it, and it is one of the only heirlooms she has from her mother's family. I hid it from both the British and the US government. That's why it was important for me to have dual citizenship. I needed to be on both sides of the gambling table. What I can't figure out is how they knew she had it. Aria and I have barely been in communication since Emily died. I had this High Commission ball tonight. There's no way they could have known she would be there. The farther away Aria is from me, the better.' Garen's pent-up tension whooshed out of him. 'You need to get her out of here.'

'One last thing,' Jave said. 'What does Fenderson have on you?'

'Everything. He runs a huge organisation that made it onto the DEI's *Shadow Files*. They have several bases around the globe, including India and London.'

Jave remained cool. 'I'll do this, Garen, but only because I owe you. You saved my life once, and that's something I'll never forget.'

It wasn't a lie, but he also wanted to find out more about Aria, the daughter Garen had failed to mention when they'd met.

Garen wasn't done. 'Fenderson is a shadow himself. There's no time to give you more answers.'

'Why?' Jave asked.

'Three reasons. Three pages were ripped out of the Lahore Agreement, and one sits in Aria's diary. I let Emily work for Altaneus. Now I know that was a huge mistake, but I knew she could help stop something that had been brewing for years in the solar power industry. She learnt to be an exceptional engineer.'

Jave's stare drilled into Garen. 'What? What was brewing?'

'Emily could prevent the blasted scientific diamond experiments that required the Koh-i-Noor diamond's formulaic makeup. Crushed to pieces.'

'Really?' Jave said.

'Yeah.'

'Is that why the diamond's been taken, and why the MI6 intelligence that you showed me last night reveals no sign of a break-in at the Louvre museum?' Jave asked.

'Correct.'

'I just need to understand a few more things before you hand me your daughter,' Jave said.

'Perhaps another time,' Garen said.

Jave flinched. 'I can only help you if you give me more information. The more you give me, the more I have to go on.'

'Jave, I trust you. We can stay in touch via secure phone communication. You're the only person I know with the ability and means to get the DEI off both our backs and help Aria. The DEI's been searching and digging for dirt on my family for years. They confiscated a lot of my assets. This stops now.'

Garen's frown gave Jave little encouragement to continue, but he had to know. 'Do you want me to do this? You may never see Aria again. My job is to make people disappear. Do you really want me to do this, Garen?'

'It's the risk I must take. I have to save the only daughter I have left.'

Jave stiffened. 'Looks like you've made up your mind. I wash my hands clean of what may come next.'

8

Yamuna Riverbank
New Delhi, India
06:23 hrs

Aria turned her back towards Jave. The nearness of his body flustered her. At this moment, she had little control over where she was going. 'You put him up to this, didn't you? My father. Whatever you and he are plotting, I'm not interested.'

Jave offered no apology for dragging her to the boat dock. They had left just before dawn, and it had taken two hours to reach the pier. The sun crept over the horizon at a snail pace, then hit her face. She took in its warmth and puffed hard as she watched Jave, a stranger. Yet her father had decided she should trust him.

Jave walked in a slow circle around her. 'You don't have time to get upset with me.'

He set a hand on her shoulder, and she shrugged it away.

Jave's beautiful eyes squinted. 'If you want your father to stay out of the media, and out of trouble with London, I suggest you listen to what I have to tell you. Plus, if you want your fiancée to carry on with your wedding, then listen up.'

How had he known? *Damn it!* Maxwell's ring was still on her finger. She searched the unblinking depths of his eyes. 'Are you going to drag me?'

'If I have to.'

He scuttled along the pier towards the edge of the river where a small boat waited.

'This will take us to the airstrip. It's the most discreet way to get you out of here.'

'To where?'

He didn't respond.

Too weak to argue, her eyes left his face for a moment. He clenched his fist tightly around the rope of the boat. Without warning, a hand closed over her right shoulder. 'Ready?'

This had started as a desire to get answers about Emily and to settle in her mind what she would tell Maxwell. He'd called her earlier to say he was okay. When he'd insisted on knowing where she was, she'd not given him any information except to say she wasn't hurt.

Relaxing for a second beneath Jave's grip, she felt at once a corresponding lessening pressure from his hand. Aria nodded. 'Yes.'

She was beyond pain and hanging on to survival as she had been in the last thirty-six hours. The light wind on her skin was sweet, the air pungent. A dazzling white blur of sun now stood fixed above them.

She checked her watch.

6:27 a.m.

Where was Jave taking her?

They came to the edge of the pier and stopped, and Jave stretched out a hand. 'Here, let me help you into the boat.'

His tone held a note of impatience.

Aria's stare drilled into him. 'I've spent much of my time on boats. I think I know how to get into one,' she said.

He squinted at her and tilted his head to one side. 'Noted.'

She placed a clumsy step onto the wooden stairs of the boat and settled on a hard bench at the back, its size no bigger than the lifeboats on her large yacht in the Maldives. She fiddled with the overnight bag Caroline had arranged for her travel and turned her head away from him. Fumes of diesel fuel from the boat's engine tingled her nose as Jave roared the engine into gear. Murky water tossed into the boat floor as it picked up speed. This was one heck of a nightmare.

Aria had never feared for her safety, even now as she bit down bitter emotions from her father's vague story about her history. She raised her hand to shelter her eyes from the sun. In her youth, she'd done some dangerous dives in the ocean, but going off to God knew where, with a man an absent father trusted, was new territory.

She tried not to stare at Jave. Aria turned her gaze to where they'd come from, avoiding eye contact. His bare arms under a military shirt made her understand how he could take on an attacker with unleashed hell in one strike. He had a masculine force about him, a high presence of certainty. His clean-shaven face was etched with lines of concern. Why?

Jave pulled in his mouth at the corners as he started the engine. He stared ahead as the boat waded out to open water.

An idea germinated in her as her hand slid to her denims, and she pulled out her phone.

Timothy.

Timothy would get her out of this. Having spent close to six years in the Special Air Service, the SAS had toughened Timothy more than most. She'd known him since high school and hardly saw him because of his classified missions. Was he a match for Jave? Would her father object? Swift with a gun as she'd seen at the High Commission, Jave was no pushover. She swiped her fingers on the screen to start the text.

Timothy.

Am in India.

I don't know where we're headed.

Need to talk to you.

She took a deep breath, then hit the send button.

Jave's upper arm muscles flexed as he turned the driving wheel, heading north along the river. Where was this airstrip he'd mentioned?

Jave wasn't menacing, just sure of himself.

Ahead of them, a warm shoulder of sun reflected off the tides as morning broke, prompting Aria to remove the thin blazer from around her shoulders. An hour later, Jave killed the engine in the middle of the Yamuna River. He shuffled to the seat beside her and handed her an envelope. 'Here, your father asked me to get this to you. Something to use when we find Count Valex.'

Aria reached for the letter from his firm grip. 'Who?'

He clasped it for a moment. 'I know you don't trust me, and this is all strange, but I'll get you to safety—as I promised your father.'

She noted a hint of gentleness in his eyes, then nodded, biting her lip.

Jave watched her with searching eyes. 'I hope whatever it is, you can settle it with your father. I'm just the messenger.'

Aria pulled back her shoulders, taking in his musky scent. He moved his hand to rest on the deck. 'Garen mentioned I should give it to you once we were on our way. I think you should look to know what is ahead of us.'

Aria stared at the letter. 'You read it?'

'Your father asked me to.'

Her fingers were centimetres from his. She narrowed her

eyes and allowed a slight heaviness in her stomach. It could be anything. Would she open old wounds or find more questions? Was she ready to know the truth? Her family history had always been hidden in lies, behind closed doors. Even with the little information her father had shared the previous night, much still was a mystery around the diary.

'You should give Garen a chance,' Jave said. 'He cares more than you know.'

Aria took the letter from him and read its contents. 'Who's Iver Fenderson?'

'A billionaire looking to return Colonial goods stolen during the British Raj. Not too long ago, he found out that your father is one step ahead of him in finding and understanding his connection to the diamond's past. Turns out your family and Fenderson's had quite a connection. We don't know where Fenderson is or how he operates, but we need to be careful and keep you away from him. He could be tied to the diamond everyone is looking for.'

'Was that him or his people who ambushed the High Commission?'

'Possibly.'

'Why?'

'Probably looking for that letter you're holding now, and much more likely, your diary.'

'What's that got to do with it? This is just a letter referring to a treaty—'

'A treaty signed and executed in secret before The Last Treaty of Lahore agreed in 1849. It made the then maharajah relinquish control of India, including the diamond.'

'I know.'

'Of course!' Aria scratched her chin. 'The letter here relates to article three, which says, *'The gem called the Koh-i-Noor, which was taken from Shah Sooja-ool-moolk by Maharajah Runjeet Singh, shall be surrendered by the Maharajah of Lahore to the Queen of England."* Aria glanced up, trying to understand Jave's motivations. 'This letter can open up a can of worms. It points to another agreement no one knew of, one agreed before the treaty. This means the treaty may be invalid. Do you believe my father? The letter?'

'I don't know what to believe. I'm just doing a favour,' Jave said.

Aria's eyes softened. 'Why? You must have your reasons? It can't just be because my father's paying you.'

His fist grew tight, and he frowned. 'Listen.' He unwound his hands. 'Your father asked me to take you out of the country,' he said. 'And I'm taking you out of India. He's being watched. You're innocent, yet it's you they want. I'm sorry it doesn't help that you're so informed about diamonds and gems.'

'Do you know who took the diamond in Paris, and why?'

'No, but my guess is they think it's you.'

'Me? Why?'

Jave's eyebrow rose a fraction. 'The Department of Economic Intelligence. Iver Fenderson or anyone who wanted the diamond out of England.'

'All I know of the diamond is what any gemmologist would. What makes you think we can get this out of India safely? This letter and all this information are random and goes against what I know about the Koh-i-Noor diamond. It just put my life in even more danger.'

Her shoulders drooped.

Jave's hand on her knee was gentle. 'You're a jewel expert—

ironically with a connection to the history of the world's most sought-after jewel.'

She reread the letter. 'Who wrote this?'

'I don't know, but it looks like we will need every element relating to the letters your great-great-great-grandfather wrote regarding the pre-treaty agreement. There are three parts to that pre-agreement.'

'I read my diary excerpt. I must have one part of all three documents that hide the history of the Koh-i-Noor diamond that we do not know. Then just maybe everyone will stop going mad and realise I don't have the diamond.'

She glared at him. It was the first time she'd seen softness in his eyes. Aria exhaled a long breath, accepting his sympathy with silent inquiry. 'Before that happens, we need to find Emily. I think she's alive. She's the one who knew every intimate detail of the Koh-i-Noor.'

They arrived at a private airstrip bordering the river on the outskirts of New Delhi. Aria stepped into the small building as Jave spoke to a counter attendant. Her eyes moved to the runway where a Jet Gulfstream waited. She recognised it as her father's private plane. Jave completed the details with the counter attendant and led her towards the runway and through to the plane.

When Aria stepped into the plane, she tossed a few belongings in the first-row passenger seat.

She approached Jave. 'Where's the pilot?'

'We don't need one,' Jave said.

He stroked a hand over his jawline, and his long limbs swaggered to the pilot's seat. '22,000 hours of flight school training, military and commercial jet flying will just have to come in handy,' Jave said.

She held her next words. What other skills was Jave hiding? *Goodness!* Was he really flying this plane?

Aria sank into the seat next to him. Was he really the pilot?

Jave gave her a wink, then a smirk. 'You're sitting up front with me.'

'How upfront do you mean?' Aria said, raising an eyebrow.

'I'm flying us out of here, and I need a co-pilot.'

Her heart gave a little thump. The man was full of surprises. 'What are you? Military? Agent? A diplomatic attaché? A Navy SEAL? A spy? You're knee-deep in all this government stuff aren't you, Jave?'

She hesitated all of ten seconds, then made her way forward before sinking into the co-pilot's seat. How different could it be from navigating a boat? She'd done that several times.

The plethora of instruments was hard to grasp. There was no way she could help this man pilot the plane.

Jave oddly impressed her. She squinted. He would tell her where he wanted her, in his sights. The fact that he'd hired no crew to fly the plane meant that he was taking no passengers on this escapade. His was a life of secrecy, and worse, he'd drawn her into it.

Jave buckled up and started the engines. He communicated with the ground staff at the tiny airstrip through a headset. The modern plane stood out of place in the small Indian suburb as sunlight flooded the cockpit. She heard the doors close, and the aeroplane began a regular taxi on the runway.

After twelve hours around this man, Aria finally relaxed.

Jave was enigmatic, nothing like anyone she'd met. She armed herself with self-control and a calm, icy resolve. Soon they were airborne over New Delhi.

Aria turned to Jave as he piloted the plane north with the skill of an airline captain. 'Where are we going?'

'North towards Tibet, then out towards Afghanistan, then Europe.'

When they were cruising at 35,000 feet, Aria squinted at the shimmering lights hitting the cabin.

'Where are you from, Jave?' she said.

'Where do you think I'm from?'

'Hearing you speak, I take it you're from Washington or the East Coast of America. You don't wear your heart on your sleeve, and you possibly had a fallout with, I would say in this case, your parents or a very close relative. It drove you away from home.'

His grin was mocking and teasing. 'You certainly know how to make friends. What makes you say that?'

'That's why you joined the military. Way too pissed off at the family. Or was it some other armed forces? That you can pilot this plane makes me wonder if it was the Air Force you enlisted in.'

He let out a quick laugh, and his laughter grated on her nerves.

'You seem sure of yourself,' Jave said.

She smiled. 'Is any of what I've said correct?'

His smirk was amusing 'I'll let you speculate.'

Aria wasn't done with her questioning. 'How do you know my father? How did you two meet? Where did you meet?'

A look of distrust entered his eyes. 'You ask a lot of questions, Miss High Commissioner's daughter. You hungry?'

'You don't like talking about yourself, do you? How am I expected to trust you? How do I know you didn't grab the diamond for yourself? How do I know you will take me to where my father has asked you to? Even though neither one of you would tell me where that is.'

Jave gave her a cold shrug as Aria bit down on her bottom lip. 'You've adopted a life of secrecy. Just like my father. He never tells me anything. Never did.'

Jave was the silent type, but he had a calming soul about him. Something she found herself strangely attracted to. He differed from Maxwell, who was always open with his feelings. There was no way of cracking Jave. He audibly inhaled, and from his behind his pilot seat, he pulled out a packed lunch.

He gave her a smug grin. 'Aria, that's a risk you will have to take. You don't get a choice but to trust me.'

9

New Delhi
15:17 hrs

Garen's thoughts were blanking. Drained of energy, he could hardly walk and faltered in his decision. Jave would get the job done, but had he put them both in danger?

Someone they both knew had first introduced Jave to Garen.

He thought of the time he'd met Jave when he'd been in MI6. Garen nearly lost his life that day. The day the Russian informant had turned on the secret intelligence service. Jave had come in at the right time. He owed him much and was the only man he could trust with his family.

Sunlight glared through the open windows, and he choked back his anger as his muscles stiffened. 'Caroline?'

'Yes, High Commissioner Raith?'

Caroline poked her head around the door.

'Hold all my appointments for today. I need to make an important phone call.'

She nodded and stepped out of the office.

Jave and Aria would be on the plane and heading out of Indian airspace. If they timed it correctly, they would be onto the next destination within the hour.

He dialled a secure number.

No answer.

He dialled again.

After the third attempt, he finally got through. The silence was as if all sound had disappeared, and then he heard air cabin noises.

The noise rasped against his fragile nerves. 'Jave?'

'Garen?' Jave said.

'How are you keeping up? How's Aria?'

'Fine. We're at the Indian border.'

'How did she take the disclosure of the three letters? Her diary?' he asked.

'It's hard hearing news from a letter. You guys really need to sort your stuff out.'

'Can I speak to her?'

'Course,' Jave said.

Garen waited until Aria came on to the phone. Time had eroded away his confidence with his daughter. Could he blame Aria for not trusting him?

'Aria? How are you keeping?'

'For years, we haven't spoken, Father, and then I come to India to see you. The first thing you put in front of me is a letter that only opens up more secrets. You thrust me into the hands of someone I don't know, and you send me away, how do you think I feel?'

Garen sensed a hardness in his gut and found it difficult to swallow. 'You have every right to be angry, Aria,' Garen said.

'Where's Jave taking me? Emily might be alive, and if so, she is in a lot of danger by the sound of her messages.'

'You're going to Austria to speak to the Count. Aria, Jave will take you to him undetected. He's an old friend of mine and needs to give you information that can bring closure to the diamond's ownership with no one getting hurt. Your great-great-great-grandfather penned the agreement between two parties, the East India Company and the Boston Tea Party, only days before the Treaty of Lahore was agreed. Lord Asterley then sent that account to Queen Victoria ahead of the treaty being signed. He split the letters into three parts to secure their secrecy and sent the letters on three different voyages. Pirates intercepted all three letters before they arrived, and they were lost over the years. Now, someone knows those letters exist, and one is in your diary. Two more are out there, and I need you and Jave to secure them. You, because you know how to hunt lost treasure, and Jave, well, let's just say he is the best man to keep you safe. We need all three of them to understand what exactly happened before the Treaty of Lahore was signed by the then-boy Maharajah Duleep Singh's.'

'What about Emily?'

'Emily left us years ago. Why can't you accept that?'

'Why haven't you gone after the letters after all these years?'

'Because we never knew the third letter still existed until now. It has been missing for more than a century. It was only when I read your mother's will that I understood.'

'That's all I know,' Garen said. You're gifted, and your knowledge of jewels and gems and their history will come in handy.'

Troubled by horror, all Aria could do was listen. A wave of

apprehension washed over her. 'Why do I sense there's more to this?'

'Asterley wrote the letter to his US counterpart in the New World. The man you will meet will help you with the missing letters. Lord Asterley went to the colonies in the New World to pay off a debt to the Boston Tea Company. So, you see it negates ownership of the diamond.'

'What are we supposed to do with the letters when we get them?' she said.

'Jave will help you secure them by British diplomatic post to a safe place. Unlike normal diplomatic posts, this is electronic. The passwords, you know. The password is our first address scrambled with your first piece of poetry that I'll never forget. Nobody will interfere with opening that. I have given you both diplomatic immunity, so you can skip borders with no one asking questions, and no one should question your movements. Jave is working for the US authorities with me. Listen, Aria, don't trust anyone but Jave. Don't trust any government official. Don't trust anybody who comes and pretends to be the government. Even any person pretending to be sent by me. The sole person I'm sending is Jave. He alone is working with me on this.'

'I understand, Father. I assume that secrets will forever mask your life. It was always this way. Father, as I've repeatedly done ever since I was a little girl, I'll give you the benefit of the doubt this one time.'

'Thank you.'

'You've scared me so much in the last twenty-four hours. I didn't even have time to talk to you about why I came to India. You have let me down, and I needed you. I have to go now,' she said.

Garen heard her hand the phone to Jave.

Jave came on the line. 'We need to go. We've stayed too

long on this line; someone might pick up our trail. We have to go.'

'Please take care of her for me. It's hard for her.'

'I understand.'

When he set the phone down, Garen couldn't prevent the churning in his stomach.

Jave checked the controls in the cockpit. They'd been inflight for close to three hours. He'd asked Aria to take a nap, seeing that she had barely gotten any sleep the night before.

He stole a furtive glance at her. Eyes closed, chest softly heaving, she slept soundly in her seat. He hated to lie to Aria.

Damn it! She was right about many things. Yes, he'd been a Navy SEAL and had had a good education, and his life was one legacy of family issues. To be exact, his family was as she guessed. Unresponsive, mother left them. From the fighting, his father's shouting began at age twelve when his mother ran off for several months with the grocer in his hometown.

Headington, Illinois was a place not to create a life. It was a place to forget.

How could one woman have so much intuition into his past? He had experienced nothing like it. A life with the US Air Force later gave him the distance he needed, and the thrill of flying Air Force planes. *Heck! Why not?*

He checked his route on the dashboard. They would land on a small strip just on the outskirts of Central Vienna.

Eleven days until the hearing was placing a time constraint on them that made him shudder. Would they really find the documents Garen needed? The Koh-i-Noor? Maybe he should find it himself.

God forbid the DEI would not back down on their threats.

That's how Garen had come into his life. All thanks to the blasted DEI.

He hadn't met this Count Valex that Garen Raith had told him about, though.

Aria stirred slightly. So, she was engaged. He'd found that bit of detail interesting. It had slipped out of her unintentionally on the boat ride when she'd stared at the rock on her finger, contemplating whether to take it off. She must've also come to her father to get his advice, even though she'd not admit it. He'd been too caught up in his own mess to listen to her. She needed him despite how much she couldn't stand him.

Aria's eyes shot open. She raised her hands above her head in a catlike stretch. 'Am I allowed to roam around the cabin, Captain?' she said.

Jave smiled. 'Course you are. You didn't eat earlier. There's more food in the back in the small fridge on the right, and there are a couple of sandwiches here.'

Her eyes fell on the empty wrapper of his sandwich.

She nodded.

He enjoyed watching her. The left side of her lips twitched when she was unsure about something, and she moved with a strength that did not lessen her femininity. He'd seen her with her father. She was resolute by nature.

'Looks like you haven't eaten in a while too. Not since those canapes at the High Commission party,' she said smirking.

'Feel free to roam around the cabin. The captain has turned off the seatbelt sign. Also, feel free to grab the captain a drink from the back of the plane in the bar area.'

Aria's lips twisted into a vicious smile. 'I'm not that kind of crew member.'

She rose and crept to the back of the plane before returning with a packed salad and his drink.

He studied her quietly as she took her seat and buckled up.

She took a bite of her food. 'You don't enjoy flying with a crew member, do you?' she said. 'You've lived your life with no checked luggage or passengers.'

There, she'd done it again. No one had ever read through his thoughts like this. Jave watched her, her hair dishevelled, a black aura encircling her shoulder. He soaked in how she'd inherited a charm from her family genes. He raised his hands above his head and switched off the seatbelt sign then fought a chuckle. She hesitated before fumbling with her seat belt.

Aria wasn't one to be ordered around. It was easy to see why she didn't trust him. She didn't trust him because she didn't trust her father.

He'd been the man in her life, and he had let her down. Just who were these thugs the DEI had sent after her? Were they the same as those who were after him? God knew what was happening with this man that had asked to marry her. The poor guy was being taken around an unending mountain.

Hours on the flight while she slept had given him enough time to study her father's notes. An oceanographer. She spent a lot of time diving around boats and saltwater oceans. She was an Oxford grad, but one thing didn't add up. Why was she so hung up about finding lost gems for money?

Her family didn't need the money, and neither did she from what he could tell, but he could see from the smirk on her face; she wasn't about to make this conversation extremely easy.

His eyes narrowed as he studied his instruments, then he raised an eyebrow.

Two planes were on their tail. B-52 Stratofortresses by the looks of it and about thirty miles behind them. Both planes chased at close range. The grey bulk of the fighter jets cruised to either side. Who the heck would send jet fighters behind a private aircraft?

Jave checked their location. He might lose them. He shifted the plane's flight direction, sending a jolt through the aircraft. 'Buckle up, Aria.'

Her body stiffened. 'What is it?'

'We have company. Two fighter jets on our tail.'

'Fighter jets?'

She set down her food and checked her seat belt. Her fingers, white-knuckled, gripped the side of her seat.

A plane came into view, on her right.

Jave's gaze remained fixed ahead as mountain ranges appeared. 'We must lose them,' he said looking forward.

'The mountains?'

Jave descended to a lower altitude, and her stomach dropped with the plane's sudden descent into thicker clouds. She took a quick breath as Jave raced the flight down to several thousand feet. Aria could barely see through the mist of pure clouds. Engines roared in her ear, and she shut her eyes. Once at a low altitude, he cranked up the engine, and the plane gained speed, shooting forward through fog and hell. Jave would lose them if it were the last thing that he did.

New Delhi

Garen turned as Caroline announced a man by the name of Daniel Pepper as he stepped into his office.

'Don't believe we've met,' Garen said.

'That's because we've never met, High Commissioner Raith.'

One day, Iver Fenderson would catch up with him. Was it

today? Was this one of his men? It had been too good to be true to expect Fenderson himself to appear at the High Commission.

'Please take a seat,' Garen said.

Pepper sank low into the leather armchair. 'I'm under no illusions you know what this is all about.'

'Let me guess. Fenderson has sent you.'

'Who sent me is of no consequence to you.'

'You have some nerve attacking High Commission property,' Garen said.

'We grew impatient, and your resistance is not helping,' Pepper said.

Garen should have known better. Iver Fenderson had an army that could find him anywhere. It had always been so, but this time, it was personal.

Garen's lips pressed into a thin line.

Pepper, a tall man with long sideburns and silver hair, was built with broad shoulders. He was a man that had clearly seen the army. Yet his age contradicted his powerful appearance and upper-middle-class tones. Definitely from London, and an Oxford graduate like himself no doubt.

'You're to return something that belongs to us, or you stand to lose a second daughter,' Pepper said.

Garen held back a sneer. He chose his words carefully. 'Your kind has been here on two occasions, and I'll give you the same answer I gave them.'

Pepper huffed. 'The people who came to see you before only tested the waters. I want to make sure that, this time, you hear the message loud and clear. If I set foot on your High Commission anytime, you and your daughter are not safe—even in this establishment that you call the British High Commission.'

Garen's stomach clenched. The High Commission wasn't a

territory to play on. If Fenderson and his organisation had infiltrated the High Commission, then they were undoubtedly in more significant trouble than he thought. They'd already marked Aria. Perhaps as they'd marked Emily.

Pepper cut his thoughts and looked around him. 'That diamond was mined from this land. How you Americans and the British got involved is what this is all about. It's time that you restore it to its rightful owners. The Koh-i-Noor, like many Colonial goods, was stolen during the British Raj from this very country. You shouldn't be upset. We are only asking for something to be returned to us.'

'You're as British as I am. What do you care, Pepper? Fenderson is as British as they come, an Earl of Scotland, and in case you haven't heard, the diamond is gone.'

'All the more in its absence for the British government to act. I'm only the messenger. I'll be back, and I hope when I do it will be good news. That diary and the missing pages better be intact.'

He rose and headed to the door, then swivelled. A smirk grew on his face. 'Let's just say the clock is ticking for your daughter. If we don't have those letters before the international hearing in eleven days, or possession of the Koh-i-Noor, I don't think I need to spell it out for you.'

Garen took in a small intake of breath. 'Which country exactly are you representing?'

'Whichever side pays my fee.'

10

Jordan Border
10:56 hrs

Jave's focus remained ahead on his instruments. It was as if he didn't feel the bumps and the changes in gravitational pull.

The jet took sharp turns as Jave tried to lose his tail. Aria's limbs shook, her racing heartbeat causing pain in her chest. She held her breath, praying that Jave knew what he was doing on this plane. Aria swore her heart was hitting her throat. Soon Jave slowed the engines and then, silence. How Jave did it, she had no clue. She stared out into the clouds as the plane settled to quieter cruising.

Aria steadied her breathing, then felt a hand on her knee. Jave's face took on a grave look. 'That little number back there messed up my engine. We've dumped a lot of fuel, and we will have to land.'

'Where are we?' Aria said.

'On the border between Jordan and Iraq. I'm trying to make sure we enter into Jordan airspace.'

'Will we make it?'

'I always make it,' he said.

Jave turned on his communication, and someone at ground control fed a report of a flight position to him. Interference muted the line for several seconds before it went live again. He spoke on the radio to Jordan controllers. 'Roger that. Okay will touchdown in exactly twenty-five minutes,' Jave said.

She tossed him an uncertain look. 'Is this your idea of taking care of me?' Aria said.

'You're safe, aren't you? We just have to take a diversion.'

Her throat, scratchy and sore, ached from the ordeal, and she flinched. 'What's the plan once we are in Jordan?' Aria said.

Jave said nothing. He continued piloting the plane until they began their descent.

Her tongue felt too thick to form words. 'Okay, before that number you pulled, I sent a text to an SAS friend of mine, Timothy Seeds. He can help us.'

Jave raised an eyebrow and anger crossed his face briefly. 'What did you just do? Nobody's supposed to know where you are.'

'You're overreacting. Timothy knows how to deal with these situations.'

His mouth pressed into a thin line, and he turned from her.

She dug up the phone and dialled Timothy's number.

'Hey,' Jave said. 'I'm the captain. Turn off your mobile phone.'

'I'll turn my phone off when I'm done,' she said.

Timothy picked up.

Aria turned to her phone call. 'Timothy, listen, I'm in trouble, we're on a flight coming in from the East landing in Jordan, and I know they stationed you in Baghdad not too long ago. Can you help?'

She ignored the grave scorn on Jave's face but focused on Timothy's response.

'How did you get yourself in that kind of mess? I can spot your location using your cell phone. You are fifteen minutes out of the Muwaffaq Salti Airbase. I can get there within the hour or two after you land?'

'We just need a ride. A plane. We've had some damage and still need to finish our journey.'

'We?'

'Yes, we. I have this guy with me, and we need help.'

That remark caused Jave's jaw to clench. Aria finished her call and put her phone away. They were to land in fifteen minutes. 'Timothy can meet us at the airbase where we will land. I assume this plane can't take us all the way to Austria,' she said.

Twenty minutes later, they strode into the small building of Muwaffaq Salti Air Base owned by the Jordanian Air Force. Timothy, an army man himself had been in the Middle East for British Forces. From the fighter jets, Aria took note that they stationed squadrons here. Her eyes studied General Dynamites F-16 fighting Falcons she'd only heard of from Maxwell. Aria needed to freshen up to get away from Jave's anger at her.

The phone call to Timothy that she had made had upset Jave.

She dodged to the bathroom as Jave busied himself with some calls.

Two hours later, Timothy, with azure eyes and a muscular build, strolled into the base's main building with a makeshift turban around his head. He'd travelled by open Jeep from the dust on his clothes.

Aria rose from the small waiting area and ambled towards him. She threw her arms around him in a bear hug.

'Timothy! I'm so glad to see you.' Timothy gave her a peck on the cheek and a long hug. He lifted an eyebrow when his eyes fell on Jave at the end of the room with his back towards them. 'That your friend over there?' Timothy said.

Aria grabbed Timothy's hand and drew him towards Jave. Jave turned slowly, his eyes narrowing as he glared at Timothy. He pursed his lips in thought as he raised his chin.

'Timothy, I want to introduce you to a friend. This is Jave Lincoln,' Aria said.

Timothy shook Jave's hand an eyebrow rising. 'Hey.'

It was jovial enough, but Aria suspected this wasn't to be a comfortable ride with these two. The secrecy of this mission had been something both her father and Jave had warned her about. For crying out loud, she'd grown up with Timothy all her life. He'd bullied her in school until she'd drove a fist in his nose. They were friends ever since. He was like a brother to her.

'What brings you to this part of the world?' Timothy said, eyeing Jave with a curious grin.

'Ask Jave that,' Aria said. 'Listen, we need a plane, and I know you sometimes have access to, should I say... resources.'

Timothy smirked. 'A plane? So, this is your pilot? And that's your father's plane I take it?'

His eyes moved to the runway where Jave had taxied her father's jet. 'Your plane has suffered engine damage I hear.'

Aria rolled her eyes. 'Something like that.'

Timothy tightened his arm around her waist, in full view of Jave. 'The only way you get to fly my plane is if I'm on it with you.'

Taj Mahal Palace
New Delhi
18:21 hrs

Garen took note of each diplomat in the hotel bar. It was his business to know who came here and who didn't.

The Hungarian mingled with two women, and the Korean Embassy's First Secretary sat over a computer at the end of the bar. The place was squirming with European diplomats; he was done waiting. Garen moved to the end of the room.

It had been eight hours since he'd heard from his daughter. Time was running out. Every wasted minute was a step closer to losing the international case for Britain's cause. Something had to happen. If not, the DEI would get their noses into this one, but not until he was ready. This had to be on his terms.

His phone rang, and he shoved his hand in his pocket, then he waited three seconds for a secure connection. He'd always been comfortable around technology but even more today. He'd never feared for Aria's safety, even when she'd gone off to the Maldives and not spoken to him for years. He'd used his MI6 nose and placed a tracker on her boat for three months. He knew every sound the ship had made and every venue she'd been to. It was his way of keeping her safe.

'We have little time,' a calm voice on the other line said.

'Jave?'

'Yes.'

'Did you get to Vienna?'

'No, we had a diversion. Our plane had some damage, so we stopped in Jordan.'

'How's Aria?'

'She's fine, but we have company.'

'Company?'

'In fact, it's the reason I'm calling. Who the heck is Timothy Seeds?'

'Timothy?' Garen said.

'Yes, Timothy. He knows Aria very well.'

'He's ex-SAS and a man who knows how to disappear off the radar. He's very resourceful in our army. Why? How did he connect with Aria?'

'She called him. Must not trust me, and I don't blame her. She said she needed to call someone to help her out.'

Garen took in a deep breath. 'I see.'

'Listen, I need to know if there any other skeletons in her closet. Is this Timothy someone that we can trust? Should I worry? You know what's at stake,' Jave said.

Garen moved to a quieter corner in the bar. 'No, it's nothing for you to worry about. In fact, he might help you. He was someone she knew when growing up.'

'Then I guess we've nothing to worry about. However, the more people you include in the circle, the more we risk.'

Garen thought for a second. 'Timothy might come in handy. He's been severely loyal to Aria since they were in school.'

'Garen, we agreed to make sure she gets to Count Valex and then disappear off the map without a trace. Is that still your understanding?'

Garen swallowed hard. 'Let me talk to her.'

His child was in deep trouble. She had to see it his way. If she wanted to stay alive, Jave was her best bet. He heard Jave hand her the phone.

'Aria, listen, please be careful. I know you've asked Timothy to help you, but the fewer people who know about this, the better. I would do this myself, but I would raise all alarm bells if I leave the High Commission. I know you hate me right now. I may be a terrible father, but I care what happens to you. Listen to Jave before listening to anyone.'

'Father, Timothy has always been there for me. More than you have.'

'Just be careful, Aria. Now, let me speak to Jave again.'

Jave came back on the line. 'Please train her to stay alive. Teach her how to stay alive the same way I taught you.'

11

Banks of the Danube
08:27 hrs

Aria stole a quick glance at Jave as he fed gas to the engine and stared ahead. Timothy's chartered flight had dropped them off at Vienna International Airport an hour before.

His silence had to do with Timothy. Though it had not occurred to her earlier, the men were similar. Both men had had military backgrounds and almost identical training by what she could gather, although Jave had been on more overseas missions than Timothy. They'd eyed each other the same way two male lions do when claiming a pride of lionesses.

The drive up the winding road in the Austrian mountains continued in silence. The Range Rover cruised around the sharp turns on the Austrian cliffs.

Vienna was only a cross-border day trip from Prague and Budapest. Vienna was new to Aria. The mountains above Vienna showed their true majesty as the sunlight hit them, and the car navigated into a valley where the Danube continued to snake.

Aria had only grabbed new clothes and supplies once they arrived at the airport and later at the car rental place.

Jave peered at Aria. 'Do you know the count well?'

'No, I don't know him at all. I knew of him when I was a child. Interestingly, he isn't that much older than I am, but my father knows him well and has watched him grow up to be the count he is today.'

'He knows to expect us,' Jave said.

'He better, otherwise we will shock him out of his wits. The count has not seen me since I was five years old, nor I him.'

'Let's just see what happens.'

Aria watched Jave as his jaw tightened. He had not breathed a word the entire time Timothy had been around, although she was sure he could outmanoeuvre Timothy in a punch out. Jave was nervous about something. She only wished she knew what.

Count Valex's villa stood on the side of a cliff. Jave parked the car in front of the octagonal-domed entrance.

Exquisite in appearance, with its tall stone walls and arched windows, ivy ran down one side of the majestic building, and the gates opened to a resplendent garden and a driveway with a flowing fountain. Aria observed the Palladian portico heralding the entryway as they stepped out of the car.

'Something's not right,' Jave said as they hiked up the cobblestones to the tall oak door.

Aria took in a whiff of fresh moving air. A place like this should have been attended by a greeting staff of some sort. The entrance into the driveway had been a bit too easy.

'Let me lead,' Jave said.

Aria nodded, and they continued to the door. She stayed behind him and his careful approach.

He rang the doorbell. They waited for several seconds before the door pulled back and a head popped through its crack. A woman's gaze darted from areas to Jave's face. She was young, perhaps in her mid-thirties, with dark eyes and shoulder-length chestnut hair. One arrogant brow shot upward. 'Yes?'

Jave had taken the lead up till now, but it was Aria who spoke first. 'Hi, my name is Aria Raith. This is Jave Lincoln. Is Count Valex home?'

'He can be,' she said, her voice thick accented with Austrian twangs as she spoke English.

Aria studied her. 'The count knows my father very well.'

The woman didn't contest her answer and stepped back, allowing them to move into the entry hall.

A regency drawing-room came into view as they continued a steady march through the ground floor.

The woman turned and gave out a look that would quicken a pulse. 'The count will join you shortly. I suggest you make yourself at home,' she said. Turning, her stilettos clicked on the marble as she sauntered back out to the hallway.

Aria turned her attention to the art in the room. Her eyes sneaked to the walls where sixteenth-century art adorned the regal wallpaper. To one side of the den, Renaissance art had made its home above a Chinese chest bordering a Persian rug.

'It's really something here,' she said.

She then advanced towards several open cases storing Russian eggs, studying them carefully. These were not replicas. Her trained mind told her that the count had gained the originals. 'Count Valex's father spent time in the military and later was Austrian ambassador to Washington. I think that's how his father met my father,' Aria said.

It came in in a flash.

The sudden piercing shriek of tyres on pebbles reached their ears from the driveway.

They rushed to the window and scanned the grounds.

A metal can smashed through the window, causing an inventory gasp to escape Aria's lips as tear gas infested their nostrils. Her eyes rolled back as outside a Bugatti sped off through the gates, towards the valley.

Jave shot to the entrance after the Bugatti and watched it disappear behind the bend.

The woman was gone.

He turned around and surveyed the villa behind him. His instincts told him that something wasn't right. He'd never set eyes on the count, but either the DEI had gotten here before them, or that woman was no housekeeper.

'There's no one here,' Aria said, chasing after him. 'It makes little sense.'

'Stay close and do as I say,' Jave said. 'We need to find Count Valex.'

They swung back towards the villa and began an inspection of each room. The ground floor was intact. A tour of the upper floors confirmed Jave's suspicion. Whoever had come wanted something, and they had left their mark on each overturned cushion, chair, and drawer.

On the top floor, they entered the first room. Startled by a quiet man standing glaring out the window, Jave observed he was not much older than he was. However, his startling pale skin against the rays of sunshine that came in through the window made Jave stop and observe. The man stood with his back to them and remained still for several seconds.

'Count Valex?' Jave said, putting his gun away.

'Yes,' the count said and turned.

He placed an ash white hand in his pocket and a face, the colour of a ghost, stared back at them. Snowy albino eyebrows teased above, smiling bright eyes from an altogether young, attractive face. A sharp, yet confident look guided all this man's movements. His eyes were wonderfully calm as he stood there in silence watching them. His lips grew into a curious grin.

'Are you all right?' Jave said.

The count nodded.

'Who was that who just left your house? They robbed you blind, and you don't seem concerned,' Aria said.

'I couldn't be bothered. They've taken nothing I can't replace. I know who they are.' He sighed. 'It's all the handiwork of a feisty family feud. A feud that I can't seem to get behind me. And you are?'

'Count Valex, I'm Aria Raith, and this is Jave. Jave Lincoln. My father, Garen Raith, sent us.'

'Aria Raith? I have wanted to meet you for a long time.'

'Yes, here I am in the flesh.'

The Count stepped away from the window and made his way towards them. 'Your father called ahead, and I was able to get a car out to you in time.'

'Looks like someone came looking for something,' Jave said. 'You know what it is?'

The count didn't respond but turned and faced a row of family pictures on the wall.

Aria exhaled. 'You like family photos I see, yet you seem to have an issue with family. Count Valex, what happened here? Who was that woman? My father sent us to you in a hurry.'

'My sister-in-law. She's been sniffing for many months after something I frankly refuse to give her.'

'What is it you do?' Jave said as he stepped closer.

Whoever had come in and vandalised the place had brought a horde of companions with them. The room's broken furniture showed that there'd been a fight, but was this really a relative who had done this? Nothing was amiss according to the count, and he seemed bothered by something else.

Jave drew in a sharp breath. 'You let them walk all over you. Why?'

'She thinks I owe her something. It's one of those sibling rivalry things that you can't explain.'

'So, what is it you do?' Aria said.

'I'm a bit of the collector,' the count said.

'But you couldn't be a day older than thirty-two. What is it you collect?'

'Rare jewellery,' the count said in a rush of words.

Aria's eyes lit up. 'You collect rare jewellery?'

'Yes, I did, but in another life. I was with the Austrian intelligence, so that's how I met your father.'

'I thought my father knew your father,' Aria said.

'He did.'

'Just what did your sister-in-law come for?' Jave asked.

The Count's snowy eyebrows squished together. 'It's been going on for a while, but recently the invasions, the threats, and, frankly, the annoyance, have just heightened above my comfort level. My father had two sons—myself and my brother. When my brother died, his wife, the woman you just saw, took it personally upon herself to look after his estate. She's been trying to get his and mine ever since. For years she's been denied, and it looks now like she's hired some extraordinary help to look for something even more valuable than the estate.'

'Your sister-in-law hired thugs to come and ambush you, why?' Jave said.

'And she'll send many more until she gets what she wants, but they'll find nothing. They've been trying to threaten me for years.'

'I see,' Aria said.

'What is it you want from me?' the Count said.

'A letter of some sort. Something to do with an exceedingly rare diamond which has gone missing in Paris,' Jave said.

He rose an eyebrow. 'A diamond? Rare?'

'Yes, rare,' Aria said. 'And might I warn you to not leave Russian eggs that are valued at over $200,000 lying around?'

'So, you know about jewels,' the Count said.

'I make a living from it,' Aria responded as she forced remote dignity into her voice.

Count Valex circled the room. He gently traced his fingers across the expensive woodwork of a long table as Jave and Aria stood side-by-side. In one instance, the Count progressed towards the door and then stepped out of the room. Within a few minutes, he returned grasping something in his hands. 'You should be careful. Whatever you're looking for others have come for I'm sure—and many won't stop.'

Aria wasn't sure what to think as she observed Count Valex's face. 'We need your help to find a crucial document?'

'What could I possibly have that you need?' he said.

'Have you heard of the Koh-i-Noor diamond?'

'Like any other jewel collector, yes,' the Count said.

'What about the Lahore Agreement and documents that claimed its fate to make a remarkable journey to England several decades ago?'

'Okay, I'm intrigued,' the Count said.

Jave drew out Aria's letter and shoved it in front of the Count. The lines on Valex's face creased before he gave it a quick glance.

Jave pinned the Count with his gaze as he scanned the letter's contents, then handed it back to him. His instincts in the military had told him never to trust a man who lives a secluded life, and this count had secrecy written all over him. The icy-blue eyes against his albino skin communicated something different. His face revealed his desire for revenge.

He turned back his attention to the grounds and scanned them one time before turning to the Count. What was he up to? What was it that two siblings had done to each other to create such an enmity? He raised the letter in front of the Count's face. 'This holds sensitive data,' he said eyeing the Count carefully.

Count Valex shot one look at Aria. 'I've wanted to meet you for a long time.'

The Count wasn't much older than them, yet he spoke as if he had lived an entire lifetime. He took the letter and studied it. 'This holds sensitive information of an economic nature and forms part of the Lahore Agreement that started a struggle between two of the largest economies then.'

'We're running out of time, so anything you can do will be appreciated. In eleven days, a huge decision is to be made, and we need to make sure we have all our ducks in a row. We need to get a letter from you. Three documents can shed light on what really happened during the Koh-i-Noor exchange, and I think you can help us,' Aria said.

The Count moved to the desk and pulled out a laptop. He angled it their way. 'I'm afraid you have come too late. What you need is part of several family belongings we auctioned at Christie's last month. My sister-in-law and I fell out, so we sold several family assets. We had inherited a series of artefacts from India. My family is originally from The Netherlands. During Colonial times, the Dutch East India Company settled in Dutch Coromandel, notably Pulicat. My family comes from a very well-established Dutch merchant who lived then. The Company was looking for textiles to trade for spices they gained in the East Indies. My take is they got involved in something way over their heads. I wish you had come a month earlier.'

The corner of Aria's mouth lifted. 'Did you ever study the document?'

'No. I did no such thing. You see, until Garen called me, I didn't understand what I had.'

Jave took another glance out the window and caught a shadow in the bushes on the grounds. He set his hand against Aria's back. 'Come, let's talk away from the window.'

Were the DEI at it again? Or were these some of Valex's earlier visitors?

The damage here was the handiwork of a sniper. He did not understand how many were about, but by the look of the chips in the wall, there were a few. There was no time, and the grounds were exposed.

Jave turned to the Count. 'Is there anyone else here?'

Valex lifted his eyes. 'No. I sent them all away when my sister-in-law was due to come. She was here earlier to dispute the money we gained from the auction.'

'Do you know who your assets were sold to?' Aria asked.

'No, but I can make a few calls.'

'Wait here.' Jave stepped out of the room and set his back against the wall in the hallway. When he was sure he was out of earshot, he reached for his phone and his fingers tapped across the screen before he set the phone against his ear and spoke into a secure mailbox. 'If you don't hear from me within twenty-four hours, send someone to pick up Aria. She's the daughter of the UK High Commissioner to India. She might be in danger.'

He clipped the phone off as a thundering sound alerted him.

This time a new set of tyres screeched at full blast through the villa's front gates.

Three dark cars with tinted glass came into view.

Jave shot around as the cars raced up towards the villa. Sniper shots chased him, and he dodged behind the front door as bullets chipped the surrounding floor.

He fed his gun a fresh clip and hurtled back to the den where he'd left Aria. Jave shot back into the room and reached for Aria's hand. 'Let's go!'

Aria and Valex scrambled behind Jave, racing down to the front landing.

Jave winced. 'You've great taste in visitors, Valex.'

Valex pursed his lips. 'I also know how to get rid of unwanted guests. This way,' he said with a raised chin. 'Follow me to the cellar and watch your step. This villa is hundreds of years old.'

They flashed down several sets of dark stairs and emerged in a large room in the basement.

Jave's eyes widened at the collection of speedboats, jet skis, and other outdoor equipment. The Count was not as weak as he seemed. He was quite the albino playboy who'd had built a little getaway empire.

'My family set up this place,' Valex said. 'And they had many enemies,' he added as he led them towards a row of bagged-up equipment. 'There are many ways to get off this property.'

Fire thundered through the door above the basement, and the door flew off its hinges.

They crashed down a set of second stairs that took them into what looked like an underground mine.

Aria's thoughts raced. With the villa perched on the edge of a cliff, the only way off would be... She couldn't finish her thoughts.

'Tunnel carting is a favourite hobby of mine,' Valex said with a smirk growing on his lips. 'Follow me.'

Footsteps pounded down towards the last room of the basement. Valex made his way to a set of controls. He motioned to Jave. 'This way. Let's get both of you strapped into the carts. I can do my own.'

More gunshots sounded above them, and they jumped into the cart with a bolt of speed. Sleek metal seats were cold against their backs as the high-tech cart came to life.

High-tech engines roared as the Count pushed down a series of joysticks, then he joined them with a remote control in his hands. The cart sped along the rail track farther and farther into the mine in the Austrian hill. Soon the cart nosed out of a cliff to a waterfront edge underneath, a sheer drop into the River Graff.

'So much for your expert escape. How are we getting off this cliff?' Aria said. 'Any ideas about how one gets off your property that does not drop us into a waterfall?'

The Count smirked. He slowed the cart to the edge of the cliff where the tracks ended and jumped out. Aria and Jave followed him. Behind them, their pursuers hot on their tail had found a second cart, and as the tracks rattled, Aria drew in a sharp breath.

The Count made his way to the edge of the opening and pressed a button. A metallic wall began to rise.

Behind it, four wind gliders appeared. 'Well, are you coming? Did I tell you, Aria, that your father and I have glided off this cliff several times? We have a few amusements in common.'

Aria shook her head as Jave gave the sets of gliders a quick inspection. He hurried to one and began zipping up before helping Aria. 'You weren't joking, you know, about how to get off this cliff.'

The Count shot them a smirk. 'Like the back of my hand.'

They snapped on helmets and eye goggles in a flash before strapping themselves ready. The gliders' wingspans about filled the opening.

'You going to be okay?' Jave asked Aria.

'Watch me fly, pilot, and this time I'm at the reins.'

They edged to the opening, and Aria felt a breeze slap her face. She glanced down at the roaring waterfall.

Footsteps and bullets zipping past her ear were all it took to muster her strength. The Count turned to them, and as he hoisted each glider onto a ski lift with remote control, he completed the last preparations. 'The ski lift here will thrust you forward and drop your glider once it reaches the required cruising speed.'

Aria's eyes widened. 'You serious? I can't do this. I've never jumped off anything higher than—'

Before she could finish her sentence, the Count pressed the button down, and her glider propelled nose forward with the velocity of a jet.

Jave's body froze as he watched Aria's glider fly off the cliff.

'Ready?' the Count said.

Jave nodded as gunfire boomed and bullets shot past him. The Count held down the button and followed with his glider behind Jave. It was all of ten seconds.

Lift took over, and their bodies lost gravity and soared off the cliff in a steam of waterfall haze.

Several minutes later, Jave's feet touched the ground.

12

Janpath and Tibetan Market
New Delhi
13:27 hrs

The limousine pulled up on the kerb bordering the bustling New Delhi market. Sun-faded, striped fabric strung above rickety wooden stalls and shielded merchants and tourists from the sun's heat.

Garen pulled up the driver's divider, and his mouth went dry as he opened the window slightly. Scents of local spices, flatbreads, incense, and stale air blended with the heat infiltrating the air-conditioned limousine.

He reached for a cold bottle of water from the fridge and waited.

Goods from all over India and neighbouring Tibet hung from the stalls as merchants haggled tourists for their rupees. Piercing voices from vendors bargaining and calling out to passers-by filled the air as they aimed to offload crafts—hippy clothing, shoes, artwork, brassware, glassware, beadwork, leatherwork, hand-stitched bags, and cheap jewellery.

The passenger door to his left opened, and Agent Hudson sank onto a seat beside him.

'I do not know where she is. My High Commission was attacked, and they took off with her. Now it's just become a problem,' Garen said.

'Your not knowing where she is a huge problem for you,' Agent Hudson said. 'If you don't know where she is, then we don't know where the jewel is. How do you propose getting it back?' he added and smirked.

What would Agent Hudson do if he couldn't find Aria? Since she'd stepped off the radar with Jave, he knew that the agency would come after him. He was their next bet. He had factored this into it.

Hudson had now given the order to bring in Aria whatever the cost, and he couldn't let that happen. Had he put her in more danger by using her?

'We can go along with your plan,' Hudson said. 'She has either removed the trace that we told you to put on her or someone else has. That was your part of the deal, and you said the trail will lead us right to the jewel. If the Koh-i-Noor does not surface before the court hearing, you know what will happen. The deal was we would keep our distance from her, so she could lead us with that nose of hers to the diamond. That girl can sniff for a lost jewel anywhere.'

Agent Hudson had been a sniff since the day he'd come into his life. A DEI agent. They trained the best government agents on the globe, and their mission was one thing: get the job done.

Garen cursed under his breath, recalling his days as an MI6 agent sent to sniff them out. A particular trait that singled them out united them, and that was to reinstate the old British Empire. They wanted to protect the purpose of power and be ahead in science, technology, and new research. Their story spanned many decades of careful planning and the orchestration of major events in history.

Garen didn't know who headed the Department of Economic Intelligence. As soon as his mission had gotten close to finding out, the Foreign Service had summoned him. He knew one thing—DEI orders came from seven directions and avenues.

As the MI6 agent on the case several years ago, his intelligence on them was more in-depth than most, and they knew it. Now, Aria's safety stood between leaving or exposing them.

'I can't help you,' Garen said. 'You know as much as I do. You know I've never been able control my daughter or tell her how to live her life. Why do you think I can now? For crying out loud, we've barely spoken in the last three years.'

'We aim to secure your future from havoc.'

'No,' Garen said. 'You aim to create a new order, a mirror of the old Empire, rewriting history to secure your future.'

'Such nonsense does not exist—except in your own eyes.'

'If your man had put a tracker on her as I suggested, then you would have her now,' Garen said.

'I find it hard to believe that's what you want.'

'It doesn't matter what I want.'

Garen internalised a thought. Jave had done as instructed and destroyed that tracker the minute he'd stepped into the High Commission. That way Aria's reason to disappear off the radar would be justified.

A nerve in his forehead started to itch. He'd not expected the DEI to send their best agent, Hudson. This Koh-i-Noor outcome must mean more to them than he thought.

He had no clue where his daughter was. If the DEI was far from her, though, she was safe. They needed her to find the

Koh-i-Noor, and they couldn't eliminate her until they had what he thought she had.

Hudson breathed hard, then opened the door before stepping on the pavement. 'Keep me informed if you hear anything. Otherwise, you know what the consequences will be. I'll have to track her down myself.'

Hudson shut the door, then disappeared in the bazaar. Garen knew what the consequences would be, and they weren't noble. He called his secretary. 'Caroline, I need to get on a plane. Cancel all my appointments for the rest of the week and send all my excuses.'

'Yes, sir. What flight should I book?'

'Get me a diplomatic flight to London.'

Aria's feet touched the ground, and she steadied a quick run to halt the glider. Behind her, Jave did likewise followed by the count.

A dark limousine waited several hundred feet away in the isolated valley where they'd landed.

'This way,' Valex said.

Count Valex stepped up to the driver. 'Take us to Vienna and please have someone collect the gliders.'

They jumped into the back of the car.

'In Vienna, I may have someone help us locate the buyer of those documents.'

Aria gave him a sideways glance. 'Christie's won't give out information regarding their anonymous buyers.'

'I worked in Austrian intelligence. When we needed to find something or someone, there were always ways,' the count said.

Either way, Aria wasn't sure what to make of the situation.

Her sister was in danger, and her only means of finding her was finding these damn documents.

The count remained subdued, despite what he'd just experienced. Valex turned to Aria. 'When we get to Vienna, we will first pay my sister-in-law a visit.'

'Your sister-in-law? The woman who just tried to kill you for your documents?' Jave said.

'We're going to my sister-in-law's place because she won't be there. I banned her from that property when they divorced.'

Aria squished her eyebrows. 'Why does she feel she has any right to your estate?'

'Same reason we tried to stop the marriage," the count added. "'When my brother was diagnosed with bone cancer, we let him continue with his wedding—despite everything we knew about her. I've a feeling that whatever answers we are looking for; we might find something there. My brother knew more about our family history and who, if anyone, would want the items and documents I auctioned.'

The car nosed into the baroque streetscapes of Vienna. As the vehicle meandered up through Innere Stadt District 1 and past twelfth-century St Stephen's Cathedral, Aria relaxed.

The car stopped at the grounds of an apartment complex. They made their way to the main entrance. Count Valex took a key from his pocket and slid it into the front door.

Imperial in architecture, they followed him into the expensive lobby of the apartments.

Aria gazed above at the chandeliers and took in intricate details around them. She couldn't help but think of Mozart playing for royalty in similar surroundings.

The count pushed the door open, and their eyes moved to the destruction before them, with no item in its rightful place.

'Your sister-in-law had a head start here,' Jave said.

'You can say that again,' the count said, stepping over a broken vase.

He inspected the room before rubbing his forehead. Count Valex's lips twitched, then his eyes blazed with life. He led them to the den and pulled out his mobile phone. He then pressed in a code that removed the entire wall section from one side of the room. Behind the makeshift wall, rows of precious jewels, bonds, documents, and other expensive items stared at them.

'Being part of the intelligence services made me privy to acquire modern technologies ahead of their time. This is what we call an illusionist wall. I embedded it with sensors that move the room round to protect the contents of the safe,' Valex said.

Jave whistled and put his gun away. 'Smooth.'

Valex drew open a drawer and removed a stack of documents and a sleek tablet. He churned it to life. 'Here's a list of people who possibly could've footed the bill and the asking price I put on the auction. Your work is cut out for you as you try to find just who could've bought that letter. Also, the files have information on each candidate. These are the world's wealthiest people and estates, some of whom many have never heard of.'

The count wandered over to the smashed bar area and fished around for an unbroken glass. He mixed himself a dry martini. 'Drink anyone? I, for one, have had my share of battering for one day. You might require it for what I also need to tell you.'

'No, thanks,' Aria said. 'I'm just too nervous to eat. I'm worried that I might lose Emily's trail.'

Jave nodded. 'I'll have a cold beer if there's one going.'

'Your father may or may not have failed to tell you one thing. The Koh-i-Noor's exchange hid more things about his family than he wants to be revealed at the hearing. Bringing those letters together may be like opening Pandora's box.'

Aria's eyes widened as the count filed through more documents. 'Papers?'

'Not just any papers,' Valex said. 'More than you need on Asterley and his dealings with the East India Company.'

The count pulled out a small box that had held the top papers together. Aria's eyes stared down at the signatures on the stacks of papers. She would have recognised that signature anywhere. As a child, she'd tried to copy it.

Garen Raith's signature bordered several documents.

The count led them to an overturned round table and set it upright. He took a seat and offered Aria and Jave one. They spread the papers on the table. They were mainly old. Some were new, but they were all valuable.

Aria knew enough to determine the documents belonged to a jewel collector.

'The document you're looking for was filed with these ones years ago. My brother and I split the artefacts we inherited, and these are his—now mine after his death. We inherited these private letters from the times of the Dutch East India Company,' the count said, and he glanced up at Aria. 'Just like you inherited the documents your mother left with you.'

Aria drew in a deep breath. How did he know about her inheritance?

Valex took a sip of his drink. 'Your mother and my father had ancestry that brought them together. These are a series of secret documents from the East India Company. Have you heard of the East India Company?'

They nodded.

He pushed the papers towards them. 'I trust you'll return them after you find what you're looking for.'

Aria's eyes scanned the documents. Some of them detailed economic deals that had happened several decades years ago. What did this have to do with the missing Koh-i-Noor? What was it to do with the letter that she and Jave had?

It was clear that these papers had been collected over several years. Aria recognised contents she'd shared with a gardener that lived with them at Asterley Castle when she was a child. Most papers were old government documents. Even without knowing the full context, Aria believed shady business practices had gone on decades ago. Had her family ever been involved in embezzling goods during Colonial times?

Aria took on a feeling of heaviness. 'The Koh-i-Noor diamond, that has confounded many, has blood all over it and has mingled with royalty.'

'These papers tell of things history has hidden,' the count said. 'Years ago, two miners, one European and one American, went to India in search of their fortunes. They uncovered a precious diamond twice the size of the Koh-i-Noor mined with Victoria's diamond. The photo you see here is ancient, but look at that diamond. It was taken from a mining area where the Koh-i-Noor is believed to have come from.'

Aria's eyes widened at the size of the jewel in the picture. It was much bigger than the Koh-i-Noor by the scale of the hand that held it. In all her years of gem hunting, she'd never heard of the existence of a rock much bigger than the Koh-i-Noor mined at the same time.

Valex continued. 'A fight broke out between the two miners and the diamond disappeared. So, the precious jewel that made its residence in the Tower of London, also known as Queen Victoria's diamond, has a darker history that the East India Company concealed. The Crown Jewels are not complete. So, you see there is a missing part of history that surrounds Victoria's diamond, or should we say Duleep Singh's? What we don't know, though, is what happened to the other piece.'

Jave stretched his hands over the papers. 'How many people know about this?'

'No one. That's why the theft of the Koh-i-Noor has not only opened up the question of who owns the diamond but also just what mining history and conspiracy surrounds it—and why former members of the East India Company want to conceal that history?'

Aria readjusted in the chair as she tried to take in all the information. She'd been a gem hunter for a long time. She'd heard of all the details, and even been to the Tower of London herself to see the Crown Jewels, but she'd never imagined that there was a missing piece to the Koh-i-Noor diamond—however famous it was.

As a child, her father had always kept things from her. In fact, this had triggered her interests, but then when that silent gardener had come to live with them—a man who strangely knew much about the world's mining history and the geology of jewels—her love for these precious metals was born.

Come to think of it, he'd been as silent as the grave about his earlier life. Parkinson had been his name. She'd found in the gardener a mentor.

Then one day he left them for good.

Parkinson had created a lab at the far end of the grounds of her aristocratic home. Her mother had taken a liking to the man who somehow reminded her of her own father. This had allowed the girls, Emily and her, to take an interest in the man's work, and he'd sparked their interest in science.

Emily would go on to study physics and geology at such an early age. She'd graduated young and was one of the most intelligent people in her field before being hired by Altaneus Corporation at the age of seventeen as one of their researchers.

The count watched Aria. He seemed to communicate that he was following her thoughts. He reached for her hand. 'I know I can't do much, but I can offer some help. Though the Asterley letter you need is not here, these documents could change everything. Find the people who bought the letter at the auction and the people who know about the European miners. Everything from how the Koh-i-Noor diamond was split and why its history was hidden from the Crown. This will change everything in that court ruling, and it might help you find Emily. Your knowledge of hunting gems and understanding the minds of people who obsess with diamonds and jewellery will help you.'

'I'll help you,' Jave said.

Aria realised that her family was not blameless in much of the mystery, but she only had the diary's contents and Valex's documents to go on. It was all starting to make sense—right back to when Parkinson arrived at their home as the head gardener of Asterley Castle in West Sussex.

13

Twenty-Three Years Ago
Princeton University
Department of Geo-Sciences

Parkinson squinted an eye and lifted his chin. The laundrette faced a quiet square. He shot a glance at the student in the corner of the lit space. Head down, a young man bounced his head to the music in his headphones.

The boy rose and emptied a washing machine of its contents and put them in a basket. Three minutes later, he stepped out of the room.

Parkinson's eyes narrowed as a figure drew closer and moved into the open space. He was an agent, no doubt. The way he stepped into a room as if he owned it, revealed his purpose, his shoulders wide.

Parkinson's chin lifted. The agent moved to the window and looked both ways before turning around and hitting a switch by the door. The whir and slur of three washing machines stopped. That would make the laundry owners mad, but it was clear they wouldn't be back for several minutes. Longer. Parkinson had seen them step out for a smoke.

Only a few more weeks and the troubling experiment would be over. He traced his fingers across the top of the machine. The man was armed. He was that kind of agent. Probably hadn't missed a shot in his life.

'Parkinson, you've made me come after you,' the agent said. 'I told you what would happen if you led me to this.'

Parkinson didn't respond.

'We told you to close it down,' the agent added.

Parkinson continued about his business. The man set the gun to Parkinson's chin and looked at him square on.

Parkinson stopped what he was doing. His muscles froze. This man would pull the trigger if given half a chance. They were in a public place, though, and no Department of Economic Intelligence agent would take that stupid chance.

The man's eyes squinted. 'You realise that we can shut you down and not let you continue this line of research. *Damn it!* Ever since the NASA file report in India was finalised, we're sure there's meteorite activity in Golconda. The geological compositions need to start full steam on your desalination project. You could become a wealthy man, but not this way! Do it our way.'

Parkinson opened his mouth to speak. A vengeful response, though circling in his throat, didn't reach his lips. They had everything on him, his family, and his daughter he hadn't seen in five years. This was for her.

Completing this work meant that he could find her, and if he stopped now, then it would all be in vain.

The bleach he had used that morning still wreaked on his fingers. He opened his mouth to speak. 'I'll have it closed down by midnight.'

This agent was identical to the one they'd sent before.

Equal in manner and in demands, they were all aching to glimpse what he was working on, but not this time. He would find the Koh-i-Noor's origin, the missing piece to his research. He damn well knew it wasn't where everyone thought it should be.

The Department of Economic Intelligence agent removed his gun from James's temple. 'Good, and not a minute sooner,' the agent said, calling from behind his shoulders. He strode to the door. 'When I come back, I want to hear a different story. You get my drift? Otherwise, you'll regret it. Destroy all the evidence while you're at it.'

When the man had left, Parkinson made his way towards the door. He stared after the agent, then went back inside to gather his belongings.

A curse came to his lips. They wanted him to close the lab. What of it? He'd reached his breakthrough anyway. He hadn't expected to go this far. Earlier that morning, it had come to him. He didn't need several weeks before he completed the experiment. He'd done it. He would close the lab.

But nobody would ever know what he'd found. Not after what he'd seen in the formulas last night.

Two Days Later
Asterley Castle, Englan

Parkinson stared at the sixteenth-century country house. It was a palace by his standards, not a castle. He'd seen it many times on postcards his grandmother had sent him every Christmas urging him to visit, and he regretted never once making it here while she was still alive. She'd begged him to one day return home to his roots in England.

If this was the best place to stay off the DEI's radar, then so be it.

The black cab made its way towards the grand entrance. The car slowed on the pebbled stones, and he stepped out.

Parkinson took in the sight of the Elizabethan structure and its imposing grand facade, its stone masonry reflecting much of the splendour of the ancestry that had built it. He'd heard from his grandmother who'd worked here as a housekeeper for years that the house had thirty-five principal rooms, built in baroque style, and another eighty rooms of lesser elegance were also on the grounds.

Parkinson checked his phone and studied the name of his contact: Mrs Clarisse Raith. The family that built the house ran it. Possibly this Mrs Raith, who lived alongside the tourist business that kept up the gardens and the man-made lake in atmospheric shape.

This had been an easy escape. Moving with all his belongings had been a quick decision. He'd never had much anyway. Nothing connected him to this place. He had been adopted, and no one could link him to his grandmother. He didn't need the attention. Just a few weeks until he figured out his next move and finished the desalination numbers.

As a gardener, he'd work on the last required formulas. No one would ask why a fifty-something gardener was fiddling with unusual plants, rocks, and gems, while an ultra-modern computer could finish the calculations.

He'd find everything he needed here.

Parkinson patted his backpack and headed towards the entrance. What would the young family be like? The woman on the phone had said they had two young daughters.

Squinting upward, the sun signalled an early spring, Parkinson avoided the main entrance and slid to the inner courtyard where a young woman met him. She gave him one quick look over before turning towards the private porch off to the side.

Lush grass crushed under his foot. He took in the fresh air smelling the flowering plants that lined the bottom of the entrance. Staff flashed around the grounds as they busied themselves, trying to accommodate tourists and other happenings in the busy mansion.

'Mr James Parkinson?'

'Yes.'

'Welcome. They asked me to meet you here,' a woman said.

'Am I at the Raith residence?'

The woman stared at him and nodded. 'You'll find that this is the easiest way. You can avoid all the tourists that way, and I'm sure you'll soon have your own key to the residence. So, you're the new gardener?'

'Yes. I've looked after many gardens...and well,' Parkinson said.'

The grounds here are exquisite. There're plenty of avenues that will need a lot of attention, not to mention tourist fixtures. You must be something to look after twenty-six acres of land,' she said.

'I'm sure I'll have plenty of help. I believe the job comes with two junior gardeners,' he said.

'Well, Mr Parkinson, I sure hope you'll be happy here. Welcome.'

With that, the woman left him standing in front of a grand doorway. He searched for the doorbell and rang it twice.

The door cracked open, and a pair of large emerald eyes stared at him. 'Yes?'

She was a child of perhaps only five years of age, and her dark ringlets bounced off her little shoulders. 'Can you fix my doll?'

Parkinson couldn't help but smile. 'Well, I don't know whether your doll will allow me to fix it?'

The little girl giggled, then Parkinson heard footsteps behind her. A tall woman in Wellingtons and a burgundy sweater crossed the hallway, then came to the door. 'Aria, please find your sister, Emily. We need to leave in an hour for London. Can I help you, sir?'

'Hello. Yes, my name is James Parkinson. I believe you're expecting me. The agency sent me. I'll be looking after the gardens here.'

'Oh, yes. I am Clarisse Asterley Raith, but you can call me Mrs Raith. We have been expecting you. It's so good to meet you,' she said, shaking his hand. 'Come in.'

He followed her into the expansive room. 'Thank you. You're a countess?'

'Yes, my father and his father before him used to own this place, and somehow the work we do with charities and other endeavours has meant I can embody a title that adds years to my existence.'

Parkinson smiled. Mrs Raith radiated with life. She wasn't a day older than thirty-five and carried herself like royalty, even in her pair of faded jeans.

'Do you enjoy being a countess?'

'It is a title I believe I hijacked. I was sort of born into it.'

Mrs Raith was aristocratic and spoke with no words wasted. She indeed ran the house. This Mr Raith, whoever he was, wasn't around much, nor did he command anything by the looks of it.

They went to the kitchen, and his feet stepped onto the tiled linoleum flooring. The kitchen appeared used, its counter lined with dishes including a flowery ceramic jar with cooking items poking out. Though it was nearing 11:30 a.m., the smell of bacon and oil in a pan signalled that the family had had a late breakfast.

Clarisse led him to the wooden kitchen table. Low and Tudor-looking, it lined the entire room. A cocker spaniel scratched at the door wishing to be let out. The little girl who he believed to be Aria opened the door and sent the dog on its way.

'I'm glad you get to be part of our family. Mr Parkinson. The gardener's role here has always been a member of the family. We have your room and your place ready in our house. I understand that you like to work with flowers and plants, so there's a glasshouse for you.' Concern lined her face. 'I hope the glasshouse will meet your standards.'

'I'm sure it will,' he said.

'Your resume is outstanding. You've worked on some of the most prominent gardens in the country in the past I hear. Asterley Castle needs someone with imagination that keeps the tourists coming back, so, we need a functional garden.'

'I understand.'

'Once you have had tea, I'll show you to your accommodation and around the place.'

'It would delight me. Is it just you and the two girls that live on such a grand estate by yourselves?' Parkinson said.

'No. My husband, Garen Raith, lives here with us, but he is often away. He joined the Foreign Service. He often goes abroad.'

'You don't go with him?'

She pouted her lips. 'I can't keep up with him sometimes,' she said.

'Must be quite unsettling for the girls,' Parkinson said.

'Perhaps more for Aria. You see, Emily has always been an independent child. Aria is five, and she's a free spirit. My older daughter, Emily, is inquisitive. It won't surprise me if she finds lots of time to come and help you in the garden. She's an outdoors girl. She likes to understand how our world was created and everything that makes it work and tick.'

Aria strode up to Parkinson. 'Here's my doll.'

She handed it to him.

He took the plastic toy from her. 'I'll see what I can do.'

'Don't bother yourself, Mr Parkinson,' Clarisse said. 'I'm sure you have many other things to do besides take care of my younger daughter's musings.'

'I take it that with Mr Raith not being around much, someone can lend a hand. I'm happy to help, and I can begin by fixing your doll,' he said, staring Aria in her large eyes.

'I understand from your resume you have a particular interest in exotic plants and flowers,' Clarisse said.

'That's correct.'

'I hope you'll see this place as your playground. Experiment and show off Asterley Castle with as many exotic plants as you want. You can use the conservatory. I know little about gardening or how functional that glasshouse is, but we have equipped it as best as we can.'

Thirty minutes later, after tea and scones, and a tour of the central premises, Parkinson started up to the backhouse. Several flowerbeds lined the side of the outside walls, and the rear of the house bordered a man-made lake. With the gardener's house several hundred feet from the public places and commune areas, it was as private as he could expect.

Rough plywood walls lined the floors of the house, and one glance at the bedroom adjoined to a kitchen and living area put a smile on his face.

He moved to the adjoining glasshouse. The wind sneaked into the cracks of the glass edges as it whistled past the cramped space, full of numerous little flowerpots and a long counter with tools lined on one side. From the looks of it, the glasshouse hadn't been used in years. He would need to make sure the buds he'd brought with him would stay as warm as possible.

An overpowering stench of ammonia crept into the room. Parkinson would take care of that too. This was now home.

He placed his belongings on the bed. It was perfect. Here he would live undisturbed.

No one would find him. Not even the Department of Economic Intelligence. He pulled open his backpack, fished out a silver cylinder, and smiled.

14

Ten Years Later

Aria had two things on her mind. How was she going to explain the fight at school and the rip stretching around the tightness of what she believed was a Givenchy dress? She may be fifteen, but being a countess like her mum was not on the cards for her. She needed freedom, and this dress didn't have it.

'Aria, they delivered the dress,' she heard her mother call from downstairs. 'It's in your bedroom.'

And she'd found it to her dismay. Was she expected to walk around in this thing all night?

Her mother's voice was the voice of reason. Aria stared at her bleeding lip in the mirror. She could apply a little makeup to disguise it. Timothy *bloody* Seeds knew better and should've known what was coming to him. Aria recalled the events that had taken place three hours ago.

Timothy's voice still rang in her ears.

. . .

'Just because you get to live in a fancy home doesn't make you smart,' Timothy grunted.

'Timothy, you're my geology lab partner. We're here to finish this work. I refuse to come down to your level and discuss matters that have nothing to do with chemical ores and how they behave at depths of at least twelve metres,' Aria had said.

'You don't even need to bother with this. Just marry some rich aristocrat and let some poor person who actually needs an education take your place at this school. You're on your way to inherit your mother's millions aren't you,' Timothy said.

The pounding of Aria's heartbeat had grown loud in her ears. Her mouth felt dry, and her stomach tightened. She fisted a palm and aimed, then thrust it straight in Timothy's face.

She rubbed the blood on her jeans and huffed. Next time he would know better than to call her a spoilt, wealthy aristocrat. What started as a general discussion on heat and pressure within the Earth's mantle had turned into pure excitement in the top-floor classroom of Rochford Grant Secondary School.

The sound of the doorbell brought her back to the present. Aria had two things on her mind. What she would say to her mother and whether she should quit school altogether.

Suspended for a day, she wouldn't tell her mother. It would not turn out well the minute her parents found out. She couldn't worry about it now. Not now that she had to get ready for her fifteenth birthday celebrations.

It was July 22nd, and what a warm July day it was. In true Countess Clarisse style, the Givenchy dress stared back at her.

It was a crêpe midi dress with lace. Minimalist yet eye-catching—and perfect for an earl's daughter. An earl who was recently spending less time at home. A pair of new black pumps lay in an open box next to the wardrobe. Just what did her mother think a fifteen-year-old had business doing with a dress that cost several thousand pounds?

Something was wrong between her parents. She couldn't say what. She would ask Emily about their marriage.

Her mother's voice called from downstairs. Aria sank to the bed and put her head in her hands. She wasn't turning out to be the lady her mother wanted.

Her mother would surely punish her for the school suspension.

Aria had stopped wearing labels when she was seven years old, and she avoided dresses. Who needed them when all she ever wanted to do was study rocks and stones, and dive. She had better things to do—like practise for her swimming competition that weekend—rather than entertain half her mother's friends at a birthday party more suited for a duchess than a fifteen-year-old tomboy.

She'd always felt more comfortable in a nice pair of jeans or trousers and a good pair of hiking boots.

She stared at her faithful cocker spaniel, who was getting on in years now. 'Okay, Puddles,' she said. 'I'm in real trouble, but you better help me disappear after I've made an appearance downstairs for an hour.'

The little dog stared at her. Did he know that she'd secretly joined the international gem society and signed up for a course in deep ocean diving? Her mother wouldn't let her go, but she would try nonetheless.

Parkinson had given her some tips about dealing with her mother's expectations. Poor man, with no family but theirs, he was the closest thing in her life to a grandfather.

A noise behind her made her shift as her mother entered the room. 'Listen, Aria, the guests will be here soon. You're not even ready...'

Anger was evident in her mother's eyes. Aria didn't care. So what if it was her birthday.

'I've just walked in from school and should study...' she began.

'Aria, Emily's finishing sixth form soon. Then it will just be you and me. Emily has—'

'Turned out to be every inch the lady you wanted her to be!' Aria snapped.

Her mother set her fists on her hips. 'That isn't what I was going to say.'

'It's what you meant.'

'I know about your fight at school today. Aria, you need to shape up or—'

'I'll never amount to anything but a wife for an earl. You'd love that, but it's a little old-fashioned for me. I don't intend to, Mother, so don't make me. Times have changed.'

Her mother sighed and pouted her lips. 'Hurry and come downstairs when you're ready. The guests have arrived.'

Today, like all other days, she would disappoint her mother. Mother wanted a lady. She was no such thing. Growing up had been one heck of a struggle. Trying to fit into haute couture dresses did nothing for her. Laces and frills weren't comfortable. She preferred jeans and doing cartwheels on the lawn and just maybe jumping on a jet-ski. Everything a young lady shouldn't want to do.

She closed her eyes. Aria couldn't live up to her mother's ways for her.

She thought of Parkinson. He'd always kept to himself in that outhouse. Thanks to him, the gardens had turned into some magical adventure tourists flocked to, but not only had he kept their gardens, but he'd also introduced Aria to a world of exotic plants and botanical wonders. He also had an interest in intergalactic geology and possessed a small collection of rocks he claimed were from outer space. Parkinson believed in geology and especially geology concerning other galaxies. Sometimes people thought he was a mad scientist. He hadn't left Asterley Castle in years, and although he never entertained guests, nor left the house much, Aria knew he had someone special, perhaps a child.

She brushed her hair back into a ponytail. It would do. Her mother would feel content if she tried. Sure, she would wear the Givenchy and possibly attempt to look like Audrey Hepburn.

She checked the result in the full-length mirror by the door as Emily poked her head around the door. 'Aria?'

'Coming.'

Emily moved with the elegance of a gazelle in a remarkably similar outfit that complimented her auburn hair and cool good looks. 'Here, I have something for you.'

She placed a gold necklace around Aria's neck. Aria looked up from the gold chain with her name on it. 'It's beautiful, Emily.'

Emily shrugged. 'So, you'll always remember you have a big sister who can kick your behind.'

Aria let out a giggle.

'Listen,' Emily, said. 'Don't blame mother. They raised her that way. She thinks all girls need to, well, be elegant. Just give her what she wants, and when you come back from that diving trip,' she said winking, 'I'm sure we can explain I urged you.'

Emily was a good sport.

'You would do anything for me, wouldn't you, Emily? Even lie to mother and cover for me.'

'That's what sisters are for. We're like two branches off the same tree, and we keep the tree balanced.'

Aria drew Emily into a hug. 'Thank you.'

Emily smiled and walked to the door, 'Now hurry,' Emily said, pointing to a brown box on the dressing table. 'It came for you.'

Aria studied the box. 'What is it?'

'You've inherited your first heirloom. Things grandmother wanted you to have. I was sent a similar box three years ago when I was fifteen. The bank releases them to us as instructed in grandmother's will. Age fifteen, eighteen, twenty-one and thirty.'

Aria shrugged as she examined the box. She shoved her fingers inside, and her hand grazed a pouch. She pulled it out and unravelled it. Brown and with a solid leather cover, with the words *East India Company* embossed on it, she flipped open the lid. The diary must've been her great-great-great-grandfather's from the date on it: 1846. She knew the British East India Company formed during the British Empire to trade in the Indian Ocean region. The little history she recalled told her the Company seized large parts of the Indian subcontinent. It also colonised territories out there. She also remembered the Company ruled India at some point.

Aria studied the name written in dark cursive inside the diary, Thomas Brownstone Asterley. Lord Asterley had once headed the East India Company, and Asterley was a name that had survived generations at Asterley Castle. This had to be his private diary—and one that never made it to the family or official archives.

Her eyes fell on several notes written in a hurry, hidden between the sheets of the aged document.

The diamond was split, and we must make haste.

Someone had written the lines in a hurry.

'Aria!'

Her mother's voice brought her back to the present. She flipped through several more pages. 'Coming!'

She read more;

We found it after the meteorite hit.

Several lines below, a diary entry dated November 17, 1847 read.

We found the evidence and caves in an Indian village, in the former territories of Sultan Mahamad. By all counts, isn't this how the Koh-i-Noor was first mined?

Aria knew little of her great-great-great-grandfather, Lord Asterley, but possessing the diary now made her want to investigate the Whip politician who'd played a role in ensuring the rule of the English in India.

The little she knew was that he'd been a controversial man —at least according to recorded history. Her eyes fell on his half-written page.

This diary was at least a hundred and fifty years old. She took in every detail. The handwritten contents came from an ancestor she hardly knew, yet with each page she read, she discovered more about the man who once commanded the East India Company.

What was his fascination with diamonds and gems? Most of the diary focused on that topic. But more than anything, his charm was in the mysterious way that he wrote. Sometimes the sentences made sense, and at times he referred to things that could only be interpreted as mythology.

She sensed a fluttering in her chest as the details mesmerised her. Aria indulged just for a minute longer.

. . .

'Today, we will go deeper. If we mine exactly where the meteorite hit. Perhaps we can find out why the villagers have been acting in bewildering ways. The locals call it vengeance from the gods. I know that there's something here that's linked to the origins of the Maharajah's diamond.'

'Aria?'

Aria shut the diary and dropped it in the box before shoving it under her bed. She gave her reflection one more glance in the mirror and headed for the door.

'I forget to mention that I bought you some makeup. Here, try this lipstick and mascara,' Clarisse called, returning to the room. 'You're now fifteen, so it's about time.'

'I don't know how to apply makeup,' Aria said.

'If you'd only asked, I could've gotten someone here to help you.'

'That's fine,' Aria said, smiling and applying lipstick for the first time. 'Well?'

Her mother studied her from head to toe. 'You have certainly tried. You're a beautiful girl, Aria. Nature has been kind to you. You truly need little on your flawless face. You remind me of my mother.'

Aria shot her a warm smile.

'Tonight, I'd like to introduce you to some important people. Tonight, you and your sister will make me immensely proud.'

Aria nodded as her mother left, then she turned back to the diary. She'd already grown accustomed to its good company.

15

'Father,' Aria said.

She realised how carefully her father was estimating her.

His eyes squinted with amusement. 'Happy birthday, Aria. You're a big girl now. I'm not sure this is the birthday party you wanted. You possibly expected a beach party, perhaps somewhere in the Mediterranean.' A glaze seemed to come over his smiling eyes. 'Your mother tries hard, I'll give her that.'

Aria shrugged, the rueful acceptance of a terrible fact. 'Father, can I ask you something about my great-great-great-grandfather? You're quite a historian, so I know you may know about him and when he travelled to India.'

'Both your families travelled to India. Which one would you like to hear about?' her father replied.

'I didn't know your family had also been to India?'

'Indeed. Why the sudden interest?'

'Just want to know more about my heritage,' she said.

He pulled his mouth at the corners. 'The Raiths have

always been travellers. Take me, for instance. I moved from America when I fell in love with your mother.'

'Was that after you met at Princeton University in the United States?' she said.

'Yes.'

Aria had always found their story romantic. There was a sweetness to it. Her father was probably far from the man her mother would want her to end up with. After all, he'd broken all her rules. Yet she'd married him. He was an American for one. He wasn't aristocratic, but instead, he was a man her mother had eloped with and with the vast steel fortune he came from, the match made sense. No one used his title, and he liked to be known just as Garen Raith.

Her father had struggled to earn his place as a career diplomat in the Foreign Service, but he'd worked his way up the civil servant ladder of the British Foreign Service for years. He'd gained his second degree at Oxford after he'd married Aria's mother—a move that had given him the right connections and propelled him into a career to be envied. Now an ambassador, in many ways Aria couldn't be prouder.

He loved to gain knowledge about everything, yet history and political affairs remained his forte. He'd become a British citizen out of necessity but also to please her mother.

Perhaps he'd felt he had to earn the title the Wartner family had bestowed on him—Earl of Asterley, and later, the Duke of Asterley. Was he finally trying to live up to her mother's expectations? A mother who'd come from an extensive line of earls and lords.

Aria took a mental note of her ancestry for a moment. Her father was an American boy who'd fallen in love and married well, not discounting the American steel empire background he came from. He decided never to move back to the United States.

Her father remained uncomfortably still as Aria drew closer. 'Father, you have several photos of our family, and you've kept them for generations. You constantly remind me that your mother never wanted you to forget your heritage when you moved here.'

He raised an eyebrow. 'Look at you. You've taken a keen interest in your family all of a sudden?'

Could she say that a specific large emerald fascinated her? An emerald that had spent a great deal of time in India and had possibly been the in possession of her ancestor, Lord Asterley of the East India Company?

She moved to a picture on the grand old piano. 'Your own great-great-great-grandpa is the only one here who has a photo that's taken outside the United States in your family.'

She eyed the sepia picture of an ageing man in a smart suit leaning on a tall counter. 'He must've been an explorer or an archaeologist. Adventure was in the hearts of both my great-great-great-grandfathers. Maybe he was a travelling merchant. I don't know. Tell me more.'

'Except for the fact that I inherited his eyes, the family wrote him off a long time ago,' he said. 'He was curious about many things. As a boy, I heard he was forced to work in mines. So not the romantic, explorer story you were hoping for.'

Aria's eyebrows squished. Both sides of her family had been in India—one a miner, and one fascinated by a diamond, the Koh-i-Noor, while working as part of the East India Company. She was undoubtedly cut out for a line of adventure, just like the men in her family. It was the other rare jewels of India that interested her, though. Certainly not diamonds.

Her father set a hand over his heart. 'Something he found in the gold rush in America raised his curiosity further. He began to study the mining history of other parts of the world. Then he ran away from home. That's how he ended up in

India. He joined a group of diamond miners, and so began his fascination with precious stones. I believe he nearly died in the Kollur Mine.'

'Did he ever find any diamonds?'

'No. He died never once setting eyes on any precious stones in India.'

Aria bit her lip.

With shoulders back, her father lifted his granite jaw, then searched her eyes. 'Now, he did find something interesting.'

'What?'

As if changing his mind, he turned his back to her. 'Enough of this, Aria. They branded him as a mad man. For years, we Raiths set ourselves the task of reviving the Raith name to erase the sins of our father's fathers.'

'I don't believe they had sins,' Aria said. 'They were curious about the Earth and its minerals. Like me. I want to know more. What do you really think, Father? He wasn't mad, was he?'

Garen stopped what he was doing. 'I think both were geniuses, like you and Emily.'

Her father, though guarded, had given her much to think about. India sounded fascinating, and the wealth of resources enchanting. So much so that both sides of her family had been drawn to it. She could go there one day, but first she had to tell her parents she'd signed up for a diving trip upcountry that they wouldn't be in favour of.

Parkinson would have a few ideas.

She made her way down the maze garden, past the lake. A small path led up the door of the back house. She then hiked up the hill towards the cottage. Parkinson was getting on in his years now. He always sat in the same chair by the lab table and still always had a stone, plant, or chemical in hand. Like her father, he liked to read. Aria couldn't understand her family, but she understood Parkinson.

He always had something intelligent to say. He would make sense of what she'd found out about her great-great-great-grandfathers.

'Parkinson?'

He looked up and smiled. 'And to what do I owe this visit? My, don't you look well?'

Parkinson had never lost his American twang. Even in the ten years he'd worked with them. Aria wondered if he would live with them forever. Her parents wouldn't mind it. He took such good care of the grounds at Asterley and was a great mentor for Aria and her sister.

'You never cease to amaze me, Parkinson. When will we finish the study on rubies that we began last week? I hear there are rubies abound in India. Tell me, Parkinson, have you ever been? You seem...travelled.'

His eyes lit up with amusement. 'Why the sudden interest in where I've been?'

'I don't know. I've been reading up on the East India Company and particularly its interest in gems and colonial goods.'

'The loot of war, some may call it—the loot of years of colonisation. Even the word has an unsettling ring to it.'

'You left your life in America, just like my father did. Parkinson, I've always wanted to know,' she said. 'What is that small cylinder you wear around your neck?'

'You want to know what this is?' he said, pointing to his neck.

'As a little girl, I would watch you. You never let it leave your neck. I thought it was photographs or notes from your family. You never talk about them, Parkinson. Well, at least that's what I thought it was, but I was so small.'

He stopped what he was doing and faced her. 'You'd be surprised what meteorites can tell us about our very own world —especially when they release precious items into the earth.'

Three Months Later

The morning had started with a downpour. By mid-afternoon, the sustained whine of the police car had brought the news. The faraway sirens stretched across to them.

Three hours later, Aria balled up in the corner of her bedroom. She had pulled the blinds and closed the windows. The sound of the spluttering rain against them would have been a welcome comfort, but could anything really bring Emily back?

She lifted her chin when she heard a faint knock on her door, and her father poked his head through the door crack.

'Have they found her?' Aria said, her eyes welling with burning tears.

Her father shook his head, his face grim. 'The police have been everywhere on Altaneus's property. The explosion came so suddenly. I'm afraid she's gone. Nobody saw what happened to her. There's no use.'

Tears stung Aria's eyes. 'I spoke to Emily this morning. She and I are supposed to go on a camping trip tomorrow.'

'The police say they've been everywhere on the grounds and nothing. Aria, I'm so sorry, but Emily is gone, sweetheart. They have CCTV footage that followed her to the labs. Her car was still parked in the car park when the explosion happened. There's no sign of her ever leaving Altaneus's labs in India, and every place has been turned over.'

It felt as though her heart literally broke as her pulse began to race; the thudding of its speed was unbearable. She wanted to scream. 'You need to send someone there. Use your government contacts!' Aria implored.

'There's nothing I can do,' he said, steadying her by her shoulders.

'It's all your fault, Garen,' her mother said, entering the room.

Aria turned to see her mother and dove into her arms for comfort.

Clarisse raised her eyes to Garen. 'You did this. You always protected these girls, but you let Emily slip out of your hands when you let her go to Botswana and India with Altaneus. I told you she was just too young.'

Her father's lips pouted. 'Perhaps if you'd paid more attention to them and not spent so much time worrying about the heritage you'd pass onto them, Clarisse, Emily might still be with us. I, for one, wasn't about to stop these girls from being who they wanted to be.'

'That's how we have lost Emily!'

Her mother's voice rang loudly in Aria's ears.

Three Years Later

Aria had never known it to rain so much as it did that day. Mist had hung over the Asterley Castle chapel for the good part of the morning. She stared at the picture of her mother for what seemed like an eternity. 'First Emily. Now you?'

Aria remembered little of the morning's activities that day when she stepped into the private service.

'We're here to commemorate and remember Countess Clarisse Raith,' the vicar began moments later.

Aria barely heard the words as she took her place at her mother's funeral service. The arguments with her father had never stopped since the day Emily had left. That had been three years ago. There was nothing for her here anymore.

'I'm so sorry for your loss,' Lady Madeline Asterley, her mother's sister, said with tears in her eyes. 'What will you do now? What will you do without your sister and mother?'

If it had been meant as sympathy, the words had bitten at her like the cut of daggers. Aria had lost much.

She cradled the meteorite from the cylinder that Parkinson had left with her the day he too had disappeared right after Emily's death. He had wanted her to have it. Parkinson was the only person who had understood her well.

There was no going back as Aria clung to the void her mother had left, one that would never be filled, especially by a father who put his career before her.

With the two people who'd glued the family together gone, where could she turn but to her first love?

The oceans and the world of geology were calling to her—and just maybe the gems on sea and ocean beds would now fill her desperation.

She had one thing left and raised her head to her aunt. 'I'll be fine. I think it's time find out who I really am and where I belong.'

When Aria graduated from Oxford three years later, the seas and oceans called to her stronger than ever.

16

Vienna
Present Day
16:17 hrs

One thing Aria knew now was her father was trying to prevent the Koh-i-Noor from leaving British possession, but did it really belong to England? Aria knew history well. They'd brought the stone to England as a gift for Queen Victoria, presented by the young Maharajah Duleep Singh, but was there an agreement or another prearrangement that had been agreed and signed? Was her diary alluding to this prearrangement? Is this why everyone wanted the journal and why Emily wanted it destroyed?

The international court hearing to be held in The Hague would soon be upon them. Another ten days and the courts would decide the fate of the Koh-i-Noor—even in its absence.

She glanced at the papers on the desk and tried to make sense of the various pieces in front of her. What they had gathered connected various parts of history, but it all culminated and led back to her family and her father.

Similarly, it also led back to her mother's ancestry. Her father had a past that connected them to Britain's colonial history. It wasn't all cohesive and straightforward.

Aria sensed a pair of watchful eyes on her.

'Don't take this all to heart, Aria. It's history that you didn't write,' Jave said.

'But this is bad. I can't understand why my father wants to keep the Koh-i-Noor so badly if it truly has blood written all over it. Granted we know that the Koh-i-Noor passed many hands and many borders way before it got to the last Maharajah Duleep Singh, but why now? I now understand why my father didn't want to tell me much. It's because I know enough about diamonds to avoid them, and I feel adamant about private property and borders. He didn't want to tell me anything about it.'

She took a pause. 'This stuff has gone on for centuries, and I'm stuck right in the middle of it, Jave. Then there's this government group you call the Department of Economic Intelligence.'

'Don't think about it,' Jave said. He watched her, and a streak of uneasiness crossed his face. The East India Company existed at a time where your country could seize resources at their disposal and advance their economic gain across the British Empire.'

Aria let out a short sigh. 'It's simply wrong.'

'You're an oceanographer, and you know jewels. You understand the value of what's at stake. A diamond of such size had never been found or discovered, so when they found it, it created economic tension. It always has.'

'Who was involved? How did this tension start?' Aria said.

'Before it got to England, a prearrangement took place.'

'Says here the diamond was acquired by two brothers from

London both working for the East India Company, they then enlisted a man from the Boston Tea Company to move their assets to the Americas. Is that the unpaid debt my father was talking about? Then a fight broke out.'

Jave drew near. 'Then, a fight?'

'Yes. There was another diamond, according to Lord Asterley's diary. This photo here is an illustration of what they think the diamond looked like before it was split and they took a piece each. The Koh-i-Noor was part of a much larger diamond, split by a meteorite event possibly several centuries before anyone ever owned it.'

'Here,' Jave said. 'The documents secured by Valex's family.'

'We know one ended up in Queen Victoria's crown.' She raised her head to face him. 'And a second one, no one's ever heard of, is at large. It's claimed here as one of the biggest jewels ever found in the world, but this is only half the story.'

Jave scrutinised the documents. 'We need to fill in the blanks before the hearing in the International Court.'

The Tower of London had displayed the Crown Jewels for decades. Little did Aria know the hidden history that came with such a fascinating gem, and now her sister's life depended on it this very history.

The Count entered the room and took her hand in his. 'I know I can't do much, but I certainly can offer some help. This is a mystery to all of us. The jewels date back to the British version of history, but you need to go a little further, maybe even go to where some of these documents were first crafted. Three historic letters can discredit the jewel as belonging to Britain because it had been promised by an earlier agreement made by Lord Asterley to the colonies in the New World. Also, everything around the Indian authorities who signed it over remains controversial. That's what is at stake here. Should this become known, it would be an international scandal for Britain. You also now have a diamond out there somewhere that is larger than the Koh-i-Noor. Which tells me that meteorite started India's diamond history and mines that no one alive now has ever laid eyes on. That's where the Koh-i-Noor came from.'

Jave's warm palm on her back gave her strength. 'The British Library may be able to tell us more. I bet you something in their archives can give us answers.'

Central London

London was under smutty darkness when they landed from Vienna. As they rented an Audi from Heathrow and headed towards Central London, city lamps pushed at the gloom, casting an orange shadowless glow along the carriageway.

'We need to get to Richmond first,' Jave said, programming the GPS. 'I found a name here on the billionaire's list Count Valex shared. Sondra Dryden's name stands out. It's the only one that cross-references with all the information relating to your father and his diplomatic missions, and Sondra has been buying documents for years.'

Aria studied the file. 'She's an archivist at Kew Archives. Doesn't sound like she's a billionaire. But she's had access to some money.'

'She must have used false credentials to bid in that auction at Christie's,' Jave said.

'She put down three-hundred thousand pounds for the

letter and other documents from Valex. Why would she do that?'

'Guess we need to find out. I have managed to hack into the auction house's security system,' Jave said. 'Her home is in Richmond. We can make it there in about forty minutes.'

Close to an hour later, Jave curved the car into Richmond in West London. He parked the car outside the address he'd just found on his hacking software. The large house was lit by a single light in the front window.

Jave parked, and they stepped out of the car. 'Let's see if anyone is home. It's after eight, so here goes. Stay close.'

'You care what happens to me, don't you?' Aria said.

He zipped around, a look of surprise crossing his face.

She'd caught him off guard.

A shy smile crept to his lips as he prepped his gun and rang the doorbell.

A head popped through the door crack. 'Yes?'

'Sondra Dryden?' Jave said.

She squished her brows as Jave continued, 'You were an archivist for the Foreign Office.'

Hesitating for three seconds, her beady eyes narrowed. 'What do you want?' Sondra said.

'Just to talk,' Jave replied.

'About what?'

'The documents you bought at an auction at Christie's. Can we talk?' Aria said.

Sondra didn't move an inch. 'You still haven't told me who you are?'

Aria felt her throat go dry. 'A friend. Aria Asterley Raith. I think we want the same thing. We want to make sure the Koh-i-Noor is returned to its rightful owners, but equally, your documents aren't complete without the ones we have. Maybe we can help each other.'

Sondra narrowed her eyes one more time but then pulled the door open. 'I sympathise. I can help a little. Did you say Asterley Raith? You must be Garen Raith's daughter. I knew him from afar when I came in at entry-level to the Foreign Office. I suggest you ask your father for access to FSO government files if you want to go any deeper into the Koh-i-Noor's history with Britain. It's the files of those who worked in the East India Company that you are looking for.'

'The East India Company? It seems to pop up in every conversation on the Koh-i-Noor.' Jave said.

Sondra moved farther into the house. 'I suspect you want to know why anyone would steal or even take an unprecedented interest in a diamond like the Koh-i-Noor. Come with me,' she said.

Aria nodded. 'Think we need to know exactly what we're up against. Your reason for purchasing Lord Asterley's letter at Christies interest us.'

'I see.'

The woman took them to the front room of the house. She brought out three glasses from a cupboard and a bottle of gin.

'Hard day?' Jave said.

'You've no idea,' Sondra said puffing. 'Now tell me about these documents of yours. If you have Lord Asterley's other two letters that make up the pre-Lahore Agreement then you are ahead of that court hearing. You can prove that the British never intended to bring the Koh-i-Noor to England at all.'

Jave drew in a sharp breath 'Why is this so important to you?'

'Because I'm an archivist, and I don't think history should be tampered with.'

'Fair enough,' Jave said.

'Let me show you something.' These letters say something about Britain's past that not many people know, and I have been searching for them for more than fifteen years. Until you appeared at my door just now, I assumed they'd dropped out of history for good. Wait here.'

Several seconds later, Sondra went upstairs and returned with three large boxes. 'You sure you want to open up all these secrets. Especially you, Aria. You may not like what you see.' She suddenly stopped eyeing her. 'Be careful what you wish for. History's bite can hurt if you aren't ready for its secrets—especially when they come from your own family.'

Sondra disappeared once more through the double doors and returned with her hands full. She took a seat next to Aria at the kitchen table. 'Your father is the High Commissioner to India now, isn't he? That's prompt.' She shoved a newspaper in front of them. 'He's been in the newspapers. The High Commission ambush has been all over the news. The media are following the Koh-i-Noor trail like nothing else now.'

Aria studied the paper closer where a journalist had taken her picture with her father. 'Yes, that was taken a couple of days ago when we were at the reception before the ambush happened.'

Sondra wasn't done with the questions. She arched an eyebrow. 'You're also a jewel expert, aren't you?'

'Jewel hunter rather than an expert. The expert was my sister, Emily.'

'But that's why the High Commission was ambushed. With the Koh-i-Noor gone, you're who everyone wants. You recently found the ruby treasure of the Indian Ocean also linked to India. It's been twenty years since the "so-called" map was first auctioned at Christie's.'

Aria breathed a sigh of relief.

'How do you know so much about her and her father?' Jave said.

There was that protective streak again.

'I'm just an archivist at Kew Archives trying to bridge the truth together after the Foreign Service Office fired me. They initially recruited me from Altaneus Corporation to give them much as I could on the company's operations around diamonds.'

Jave moved to the windows and glanced outside briefly before turning back to them 'That explains why you bought the letter at auction. You disguised your entrance into that auction, didn't you? Using money from government funds, might I add.'

'They deserved it!' Sondra snapped.

'If we show you Aria's diary excerpt, which constitutes part of Lord Asterley's three letters, what can you tell us about the Lahore pre-agreement?' Jave said.

'I can give you a lead, but it's just a lead, and by no means will it be everything you're looking for. My suggestion to you is to get all three letters together and avoid the international courts. It will open up a whole assortment of problems no one will ever be able to put back.'

'That's fair?' Jave said.

'I'm knowledgeable about the various parts of British history, but I shudder when sections of it go missing. Some of our history has been crossed out and rewritten in other nations' history books instead, including India's own history and that of the United States. Very soon, a new chapter of that history will be written if the international hearing goes ahead. Yet again the diamond might cross borders, and it could even end up in the United States,' she said, eyeing Jave.

'Will the hearing still go ahead if the diamond isn't found?' Aria asked.

'Yes, because this hearing has been in the works for several years, and now, with it just a few days away, it's critical to both governments that it does go ahead,' Sondra replied.

'The fact that the diamond's gone missing is rather interesting. It means either side could be guilty of theft and obstruction of justice. I knew this day would come. Bloodshed has always followed this diamond, and now you can imagine a disagreement around its ownership that began centuries ago can finally be settled.'

'You've known this a long time, haven't you, Sondra?' Jave said with curious eyes on her.

'I joined the National Archives Office at Kew because the office files history people want to remember, but it seems many are willing to file history that people don't want to remember. Those people are more powerful than you think. The reason I joined the Foreign Services Office was that I wanted access to history of our dealings with other nations—public and non-public.'

Aria held back a thought she'd had since meeting Sondra, but on second thought it surfaced on her lips. 'Do you believe my father is hiding something to protect our government?'

Sondra pursed her lips before speaking. 'Honestly, I don't know. One thing I can say, even from the little I knew him, is your father is a career diplomat rather than a political appointee, which says to me he isn't after power, but what's right. I had so much respect for him, and so does an overwhelming majority of the Foreign Service.'

For a second, Aria thought she'd been too hard on her father. She smiled. 'You have one of the three letters. Can we see it?'

Sondra nodded and pulled out the letter from her boxes. 'Yes. Here we go. What you have is an agreement with plans for the Koh-i-Noor before it went to Queen Victoria. Without this letter, it's hard to tell all the facts, but from what I gather on these two letters from Lord Asterley,' she said studying the images on Aria's phone, 'is that three parties made an agreement that involved the East India Company in India, the US Boston Tea Company, and the maharajah's officials in 1840. This agreement involved the use of the diamond as payment for a service provided by the Boston Tea Company. What it doesn't say is what that service was, but it overrides what happened to the Koh-i-Noor.

'Lord Asterley, who I take it is your relative, and the then head of the East India Company, agreed to have the Koh-i-Noor go to an entirely different place to where it eventually went. He then swindled the Boston Tea Company.'

'My ancestor conned India, the Boston Tea Company, and Britain...' Aria said, a lump settling in her throat.

Sondra set a gentle hand on her shoulder. 'I think your father has been trying to correct that history for years.'

Aria took in the information. Could it explain why her father had been so secretive? That's why his life was in danger. Many stood to gain from history remaining as it was. He was trying to protect her mother's family's reputation.

Aria and Jave glanced at each other but said nothing.

Sondra took a sip of her gin. 'Lord Asterley's letters were split decades ago to hide history. My opinion is only a suggestion of how events could have transpired, but without the third letter, you can't know the full story. That's what your family is entangled in.'

'What about Emily? My sister. What has she got to do with all of this?' Aria said.

'My guess is your sister was a bargaining chip. I knew her at Altaneus Corporation. When I heard of the corporation's interest in developing diamond technology, I got curious. So I enlisted as a researcher for them. Emily Raith's only fault was she knew more about gems than most. She was the prodigy child who understood how to piece together jewel history and geology. Looking at you and what you do, it must run in the family.'

'You knew my sister?' Aria said her heart thumping.

'Yes.'

The revelation silenced Aria. All she could do was study Sondra's face.

Sondra opened her mouth to speak, but before a sound could leave her lips, her eyes grew large at something she saw out the window.

In a fraction of a second, the kitchen glass smashed, sending shards shooting across the room.

Jave drew his gun and shoved them out of harm's way. He threw them under the table and charged to the window his firearm at the ready.

Deafening gunfire followed, extinguishing every light. In the darkness, Aria crawled behind Jave, her hand on his arm. His eyes followed the direction in which the can had smashed, through the far kitchen window.

'They're gone,' he said.

'Jave!' Aria said. 'They got Sondra, and the documents and my flash drive are gone.'

Aria cradled Sondra's head.

She patted her forehead and found a couch cushion for her head. Together they helped Sondra to a chair as Jave checked the rest of the property. He returned to the kitchen.

'You okay? How's she?' Jave asked.

'I'm okay,' Sondra replied.

'I think they're gone,' Jave said.

Aria nodded, her hand shivering under Sondra's as she drifted in and out of consciousness. The stench of the gas can had stunned their senses for several minutes, allowing the intruders to make off with the documents and data.

What had the intruders used? Everything that Sondra had said about the technology breakthrough had to be true, including its link to the ancient Koh-i-Noor and how it came to England.

Sondra stirred.

'Jave, she's gonna be okay. Sondra? Can you hear me?' Aria said.

Sondra opened her eye slowly and tried to sit, coughing the fumes away that had stung her gut. She sat up straight and stared at them both. 'What happened?'

Aria set a hand on her shoulder. 'Someone has broken in and taken the letters. Yours and mine.'

If Sondra had heard right, she didn't show it, but she rose slowly as if she could just take off from where she'd left off. The shock was wearing off.

Sondra had been struck and swallowed hard before speaking. 'You've got to get them back. Those letters can't get to the international courts.'

She seemed to want to tell them more. Aria wasn't sure they should leave Sondra alone. She too was now a target. She was fully conscious now and pointed to the newspaper they'd been reading earlier. Aria reached for it and handed it to Sondra who ran her finger across the image of the diamond the paper had run.

Aria read the caption.

'The diamond, made of about 793 carats, was owned by the Kakatiya dynasty.'

The article went on to express the bloody history of the Koh-i-Noor. She read further as if digesting the brutal history for the first time, a history that went back more than 5000 years. The Koh-i-Noor was first mentioned in a Sanskrit manuscript, and the current name, Koh-i-Noor, in Persian, meant 'Mountain of Light.'

Aria knew that after that, the diamond wasn't mentioned much for over four thousand years before it reappeared in 1304 in the possession of the Rajas of Malwa.

She scanned the article further.

In 1304, it had worked its way into the hands of the Emperor of Delhi, Allaudin Khilji. Then in 1339, it was sent to Samarkand, where it stayed for almost 300 years.

There was more. One detail was new to her. A curse was found in a Hindi text. She read the curse word for word then turned to Sondra.

'I'm not superstitious. Is this curse really true?' Aria said.

Sondra rubbed her chin. 'The curse is real all right. History can tell you that. Look at what has happened to every male sovereign who has worn it.'

'Why would the East India Company decide to gift the diamond to their sovereign with such a bad omen surrounding it?'

'Maybe it was just about money. Most things are you know,' Jave added.

Jave was right. The diamond's real history had been cryptic to them all, and there was more to be unearthed, but much more was known. According to the article, Persia's conquering of Indian sultans and the surrender of the diamond to them was unavoidable.

Jave studied Aria and drew her to him. 'Are you okay?'

Heat rose to Aria's cheeks at his touch. It was the first time he'd touched her this way, and she didn't fight it. 'Yeah, just puzzled. It just doesn't make sense. If the British government, in the form of the East India Company, was ready to gift the diamond over as a gift to Queen Victoria, why would they keep this information? Why not destroy the letters? Why did Lord Asterley send them after the diamond?'

Jave withdrew for a second and rechecked the windows. 'Maybe they wanted to, but it never happened, and that's why we find ourselves here.'

Sondra was fully alert now and rose from the floor, rubbing her head. 'They tried to hide the information I believe. What I discovered at the Foreign Service Archives is that the Company learnt not only of the Koh-i-Noor diamond's curse, and the particular ownership issue, but also where it came from. That's where these letters grow cold in their information. Lord Asterley penned these three letters alluding to something so secret it's not even fully disclosed.'

'How did information about the letters get out?' Aria asked.

'Lord Asterley sent them after the Koh-i-Noor on its way to Queen Victoria with the Maharajah, but they never made it to the Queen. My research shows that the ship carrying the letters was shipwrecked and taken over by pirates. I believe that's how the letters were split. Centuries later, Lord Asterley's diary went to your family, one letter was found by Maharajah Duleep's family, and the third was bought by the Valex estate. That's how I knew to hunt for it and buy it at whatever the cost at the Christie's auction.'

'This is important,' Aria said.

Jave made a move towards them. 'We need to move before they come back. Sondra, can we get you somewhere safe for now?'

'I'll be fine. They've taken what they came for,' Sondra said. 'That's all they wanted.'

Sondra coughed and went to the sink for a drink of water.

'You have many parts here. The East India Company knew a time would come when the Koh-i-Noor would be contested,'

Jave said putting away his gun. 'Aria, we should go. You aren't out of danger yet.'

'He's right,' Sondra said. 'There are two sides who in a few days will battle it out for the ownership of the Koh-i-Noor diamond. The stone changed hands several times between various factions in South Asia for seven hundred years,' Sondra continued. 'This is just another contest showing that no one will ever truly own that stone.'

Jave strode to the window one more time before closing the shutters. 'Let's go.'

'These letters have been lost for years,' Aria began, 'and I'm beginning to believe my family has been instrumental in hiding much more. It's just driving me mad. All I can think about is getting Emily back—if she's alive—and I know she wouldn't want the diamond ending up in the wrong hands.'

Jave turned to Sondra. 'What is Altaneus's part in this?'

'I'm not sure. I was trying to find out, but I think Emily found out what Iver Fenderson was up to and that's why'—she shot Aria a hard look—'they got rid of her. Now,' Sondra continued, shaking her head, 'I was a data filer. Someone far from key company information. They didn't really give me any access to what they were working on at Altaneus.'

Sondra's voice was beginning to crack. The shock had been more impactful than they'd thought. 'I've amassed a great amount of knowledge on the Koh-i-Noor. Aria, you'll have to find the rest from here on.'

'How long were you at Altaneus?' Aria asked.

'Seven years in India, then two in Boston. I saw your sister on a couple of occasions. I knew she was in trouble the minute she joined the research team working on the desalination project.'

'Desalination?' Jave said.

'I don't know more. I wish I did,' Sondra said.

Aria dug her hands deep in her pockets; her head was throbbing with the agony of searching for answers that eluded her. 'Emily wants me to destroy the diary. Why?'

Sondra shrugged. 'She's alive? Not sure. My expertise is documents and data. If you want to know more, I suggest you go to the British Library. Alternatively,' Sondra said, 'you might want to go to the National Archives as well, where I work. I must admit my research hasn't focused on the British Raj, more on the diamond itself. I won't stop you from digging around here as well, but you will find that the role of the British in India is one of the most fascinating subjects in modern history. I would also question Iver Fenderson's involvement in all of this. He headed Altaneus. You might find something on the solar panel desalination projects.'

'His name pops up in every single file the Foreign Service Office has on the Koh-i-Noor,' Jave said suddenly.

Sondra observed him. 'Don't rule out anything. There were many other places that the British conquered such as North America,' she said looking at Jave. 'You also have Australia. When it came to India, especially in the 1700s, you'll find that the nation was just as developed as British society, and no one would admit we subjugated that nation to Crown rule, and the Koh-i-Noor sits at the whole heart of this debate. It's no wonder that now with a new prime minister in the United Kingdom, the international court case will be quite heated.'

'What does stealing the Koh-i-Noor achieve?' Aria said, her eyes narrowing into the newspaper article on her father and her.

Sondra took the paper from her hands. 'It slows down the process of the international courts.'

Aria mused, talking to herself more than anything else. 'How's it that we—the British—managed to enter a country with vast resources that was well developed as a society, just like that?'

Sondra's tone rang with conviction. 'The country wasn't united as you know it now. It had vast resources, armies, and kingdoms, but it lacked the one thing that the British had, unity.'

Sondra was right. India was a Commonwealth country and had its roots of democracy moulded after the democracy of her own country.

Early the next day, they drove up to the National Archives building and made their way into the entrance of the official archive of the UK government. It kept some of the most iconic documentation, dating back a thousand years and more —everything from Doomsday records to the present.

Once inside the building, they asked for the Foreign and Colonial Office correspondence file section. They followed various corridors until they found the section they needed, then began scouring the shelves of stacked archives folders in order of history.

Aria stopped when her hand fell on a file dating from 1612. Her eyes scanned a letter signed by Lord Asterley himself. 'Look, Jave, a letter from the British to Admiral Kulluk from the day the Company won trading concessions from the Mughal Empire.'

Jave moved to her side.

She continued. 'It says here they traded in cotton, silk, indigo, and spices from southern India. I wonder when diamonds come into the picture.'

There was something else in the neighbouring archives that caught Aria's attention. Five bookshelf documents related to *The New England Company, Indian Ships in the United States for Export to the Middle East, Indian Ships in the United States for Sale to Britain,* and *The History of the East India Company*.

Aria's attention was suddenly drawn to a man she recognised studying quietly at the table. He had a volume open on the Company's takeover of parts of the Indian subcontinent. He set the volume down and shot them a quizzical glare.

Aria strode past Jave, advancing to his table. 'You pick an interesting part of history,' she said.

The man raised his head and studied her for all of two seconds.

He then pulled a gun to her arm, gripping it tightly. 'As do you,' he said. 'Let's go quietly. I understand you have an interest in the Koh-i-Noor diamond. Maybe I can help.'

Her voice wavered. 'Jeff Avent? What are you doing?'

Aria drew her head back. 'Jeff Avent? What are you doing? Who are you, really?'

'You'll come now if you know what's good for you. I'm with MI5 special projects, but it's not important who I am, right now.'

Jave stepped between the gun and Aria. 'Take it easy, agent.'

Avent ignored him as he plastered his eyes on Aria. 'You leave quite a trail behind you, Miss Raith.'

Aria let her guard down. 'What's this all about? I may be a jewel hunter, but I don't have this jewel. Even my father knows that. I don't even like diamonds.'

He glanced at her hand, spotting Maxwell's ring on her finger. 'Yet you wear one courageously.

'I...the true value of diamonds doesn't reside in money alone,' Aria said.

'You've clearly done a lot of thinking about this,' Avent said.

'Sometimes I think that's all I think about.'

Jave intervened. 'Put the gun down.'

'You're outnumbered here, Lincoln—and out of jurisdiction.' He turned back to Aria. 'Now back to the Koh-i-Noor. You've been following me. Why?'

Aria drew in a sharp breath studying the gun. 'I want to know what my father's up to. I saw you in India.'

'You're asking the wrong questions,' Avent said. 'You must ask yourself what the significance of giving the diamond to Queen Victoria meant. That's the question that needs to be asked. Your father is trying to make sure Britain stays on the right side of history. Also, who stood to lose more with the transaction? My men are outside. Let's go.'

The gun remained firmly aimed at her. Jave was motionless.

'Let's take a walk,' Avent said, this time more forcefully.

Jave's jaw tightened. 'Where she goes, I go.'

Avent shrugged. 'Suit yourself.'

Three armed men moved into the secluded reading room. One took Jave's gun, and a second restrained him.

Jave didn't resist.

Twenty-five minutes later, they found themselves in a closed-off interrogation room at Thames House MI5 headquarters.

'Right, we'll keep this simple,' Avent said taking a seat. 'I've looked over the flash drive, the auction letters, and the other documents.'

Jave sat across from Avent, his right eye squinting briefly. 'That was you? You ambushed Sondra's?'

'Yes,' Avent said.

'Why?'

Avent loosened his shoulders. 'I need your help.'

That surprised Aria. 'Why should we help you?' she said.

'Because helping me helps you, or should I say your father.'

Aria was not convinced. Avent was her father's lawyer with quite a hidden life, yet now he was working with MI5. She leaned forward. 'What do you want? Really?'

Avent settled back in his chair. 'There's an economic transaction happening in these letters. What does it mean? It could change everything in The International Court of Justice next week.'

Aria moved forward. 'We don't know.'

Avent nodded, then watched them silently for several seconds. 'What do you know of Altaneus Corporation?'

Aria spoke first, cradling the meteorite rock around her neck as it dangled on the same chain as her sister's necklace. 'I know that my sister was the bargaining chip in all of this, and the government did nothing to help her. What's your interest in all this, Avent? You were my father's attorney for years. Are you now with MI5?'

'Let's just say I help him in international cases between the US and the UK.'

'I saw you at the High Commission in India. What's going on here?' Jave said.

'Emily Raith disappeared about the same time Altaneus Corporation closed down. It was all over the news. At the time of Altaneus shutting down, they were two diamond mines owned by Altaneus that were also closed after that fatal accident took place,' Avent said.

'That was the accident after which Emily went missing. We were sent a report that documented how she died,' Aria said.

Avent raised an eyebrow. 'And now you're starting to question the validity of that report, aren't you? What do you think happened?'

Aria shrunk back. 'Don't know, but I want to believe she's alive.'

Avent tilted his head. 'Miss Raith, your search for answers may not bring her back. Your father tried. Why do you think you can succeed? What have you found?'

'Not much more than what's public knowledge,' she said. If archivists like Sondra know about Lord Asterley's letters, more people will too.'

'Your sister was involved in a lot more than you know. She perfected the formula and the rollout for production of clean rain in the desalination project that Altaneus funded. Clean rain is the future and can be used by people like Iver Fenderson as a biological weapon in the light of climate change. You see, his research is important, but so is the Koh-i-Noor. Your sister cracked the possibilities of a weapon in the form of saltwater desalination. That alone can be powered into a weapon, simply by Altaneus's keeping a monopoly on that research.'

'Go on?' Aria said.

'Fenderson has been campaigning for years for the return of the diamond to India. His scientific interest in diamonds made him swear that he'd retrieve the Koh-i-Noor working with India when the project was completed.'

'Why?' This time it was Jave who spoke up.

'Because his family is connected to that of Maharajah Duleep Singh.'

Aria ran a hand through her hair. 'Is that true?'

'Yes. Also no one who witnessed the Altaneus mine

collapsing has lived to tell us what happened, and if they have, Fenderson has since silenced them. Altaneus Corporation was on the verge of discovering superior technology involving diamonds—hence how Emily comes into the picture. The Koh-i-Noor is supposed to be the first diamond to go into that experiment. For Fenderson it's personal. It's his men you've run into up to now, like in the Maldives. They think you have the diamond, and so does half the world.'

'But I don't,' Aria protested. 'How do we know this Iver doesn't have it?'

Shoulder's straight, Avent faced her squarely. 'We don't, but he's desperate to know who does, and he has you marked.'

Jave shot up from his seat. 'Are you saying Altaneus Corporation is still in operation?'

'Yes. They are the ones on the hunt for you, just like they hunted your sister. I've been following this for a while,' Avent said.

Emily could feel her stomach churn. 'He won't stop until he has me.'

'No, he won't,' Avent agreed. 'Emily completed the solar panel desalination breakthrough before she died. There's another person I'm on the hunt for. A James Parkinson. Do you know him?'

Aria raised an eyebrow and set her sweaty palms on her kneecaps. 'I've known him most of my life. My mother hired him when I was five to manage Asterley Castle's gardens. I haven't seen him in thirteen years since Emily died.'

Avent rose and dropped the documents taken from Sondra's house, and her flash drive, on the table. Aria gathered up all their papers. 'Here you go. I haven't told MI5 about this. The truth is your father sent me when he couldn't reach you.'

Aria studied the contents on the table. 'Can you tell me if Emily is alive?'

Avent headed for the door. 'Not even I know what fully went down at Altaneus. I suggest you go now and be careful. I'll keep British authorities away from you as much as possible.'

'I...' Aria began.

Jave held her back.

They stood staring behind Avent as he left. When they glanced down at the table, he'd left a new flash drive and Jave's gun.

17

Water Club House London
18:00 hrs

London's evening sun, behind the city skyscrapers, dazzled off the windowpanes in the exclusive members' only club. Garen slid his fingers over a folder. The words 'EYES ONLY' stared back at him. His mind refused to disconnect from the words that the file confirmed. The Foreign Service Office had charged Emily Raith with treason before she died.

Garen felt eyes on his back as he stepped into the room, then took a seat opposite the windows of the upmarket clubhouse. He didn't want to keep anything from Aria anymore. She was the only child that he still had, and he needed to tell her the truth about her heritage. What had happened before she was born and why had he let Emily go to a dangerous corporation like Altaneus at such a young age.

He sat by the window, holding the folder, his hands tight around it as if for protection. What was he going to do now? He glanced up when he heard expensive shoes clicking by his chair. Michael Robey's gaze locked into Garen's, cold fury melting from his eyes. If this meeting with the Foreign Secretary didn't pan out today, right now, he would have to turn to more laborious methods.

The door to the kitchen flew open, and a woman wearing a green suit appeared with a tray containing his order. Robey moved out of the way until she'd set the plate down and left.

Robey sank into a seat across from him and took a sip from his Remy Martin whiskey he'd brought in with him. He set the glass down. 'What's so important that it would require a meeting in such a public place?' Robey said.

Garen thought about his next words. Before he could speak, Robey raised a finger. 'I understand you're sincerely in need of some kind of miracle, but before I do you a favour, I also need a favour from you, from the Indian President and our talks on the Koh-i-Noor.' Robey arched an eyebrow. 'I need something to be kept under wraps.'

'I'm tired of this. What do you need, Secretary Robey?' Garen said. 'What do you need me to be quiet about this time?'

'Let me first hear your ask,' Robey said, taking another sip.

Garen's tongue felt too thick to form words. 'Here's how this will work. I also need you to release information on my oldest child, Emily Raith, from the archives in the Foreign Service Office, and I need you to clear her name.'

Robey raised an eyebrow but said nothing.

Garen cleared his throat. 'You listening to me?'

'I can't. There's nothing I can do about it,' Robey said.

'You have to do much better than that,' Garen said. 'I know you can get this done. What's your price this time? I need you to release everything that was classified on my daughter, Emily, when she died—especially around any dealings with the solar power anti-salination project the government commissioned Iver Fenderson to work on and then later disowned him after the explosion.'

Robey's gaze penetrated deeply into Garen. 'Come on, Garen, we've known each other for a long time. Don't tell me that little secret of yours is back to haunt you? No, not here in broad late daylight.'

He was thinking about the incident. A time in history he wanted to forget. *Damn it.* He had served his country. He had served his country, but his family had also served the nation in its history. Was it his fault that his family had traded secrets between the US and Britain decades before he was born? Decades before his daughters were born. He had come a long way, and it wasn't time to give up now. He could easily blow this man's cover, even as the Foreign Secretary.

The dirt on him was knee-deep. He'd orchestrated the hiding of the Asterley letters from the public eye. He had also been involved in a government conspiracy to hide East India Company secrets. He was knee-deep in a muddle. Garen owed it to Aria, to the Raith family.

Garen rammed a fist on the table. 'Damn it! Do we have a deal?'

'You tell me. I need you to testify in the Koh-i-Noor hearing.'

'We agreed I would stay out of it,' Garen said.

'It's the only deal on the table. Why do you think I sent you to India? Don't you think I knew about Clarisse and her family? She was supposed to be mine. You married the women I was supposed to have.'

Garen suppressed the instinctive desire to snort at Robey. 'Don't you ever speak about my late wife like that again.'

Robey sneered with a huff. 'Then decide for the last time if you want Emily Raith to be connected to treason. It's the only report this office will file in our archives unless you testify at the hearing and keep England out of its shady past with India. We have to protect the Crown.' He raised his glass. 'For Crown and country. Your choice.'

Garen held back a threatening remark. If he testified at The International Court of Justice, Clarisse's family would be forever tainted. He couldn't. If James Parkinson could surface, this whole thing would go away before they stepped into The International Court of Justice. If Garen released any information on Robey, the man would be knee-deep in trouble, but then again, the evidence could lead back to his family. That's the chance he'd have to take when the time came.

Robey took a sharp breath. 'This is what I can do. I'll expunge the files on your daughter and clear her name of treason with that one condition. Testify and keep Britain on the right side of history. Tell them Lord Asterley was a mad man. It's out of my hands if you do not respect Britain. I can no longer protect you or your family. London's darkest and deepest secrets in India will be on your head, but it won't bring your daughter or wife back.'

'Do you believe Avent?' Aria asked.

'We don't have time to figure it out. Let's go,' Jave said.

They took the London Underground back to Richmond to collect their car. After a brief check on Sondra, they headed for Central London. Jave came to a rolling stop at a traffic light, and a Land Rover Defender appeared along his right, its windows tinted.

'We have company,' Jave said.

'What?'

The window pulled down, and a man reached inside his coat for a pistol.

With the traffic light halting at red, Jave slammed his foot on the accelerator and tore the car away to the right turn, speeding down the avenue.

Weaving in and out of traffic, the Defender whined, hot on his tail, and it nearly rammed his Audi at a junction. Jave wound through an opening through traffic and flattened the gas pedal, taking them straight into Richmond Park. The Rover, not once losing him, sprayed the gravel as it stayed at his tail, closing the distance until Jave tore around a corner behind a field and into a wooded area.

He glanced into the rear-view mirror, observing the tinted windows of his pursuers until he came to a dead-end in the woods.

Jave slammed down on the brakes as a deer crossed in front of the wall ahead of him.

They were trapped.

The Defender reduced speed and came to a stop, metres behind him.

'What now?' Aria said.

'We make a run for it. I'll get out first. They'll mark me. Then I want you to climb over the wall and make a run for it. I'll contact you,' he said. 'Wait until I'm concealing you, then run behind me to that tree, where you'll climb over. They won't see you.'

Blood pumped through her veins at a feverish pace, but she nodded as the Defender revved its engines remaining stationary.

Jave opened the door and set his boot on the ground, and Aria slipped unnoticed behind him and crouched behind the branch before hauling her body over the wall. On the other side of the wall, her feet hit the ground, and she bolted towards the main road via a tunnel.

Aria heard a gunshot, then swerved. Darkness forbade her from seeing much.

Footsteps pounding behind her grew loud, and she swirled, this time finding herself face to face with a tall man with a gloved hand. A red laser eye of death blinked on her chest.

Her heart clenched in fear, and she shivered a little at his dark expression.

'I'll make you a deal,' he said. 'Let's stop this nonsense of me chasing you across capitals. Give me the flash drive and your sister will live.'

Her head drew back quickly. 'You have Emily? Who are you?'

'I go by the name Daniel Pepper, and let's just say I know who does,' he said.

Aria held on tightly to the flash drive Avent had left with them.

The gun tracked her.

Shots rang out behind him, and Pepper dropped to his knees, holding his arm.

Jave surfaced from the darkness and grabbed her hand. 'I only got his arm, so we need to move...Now!'

Jave led her to a road with oncoming traffic. He shot his pistol in the air, and a Toyota shrieked its brakes in front of them. A startled man froze at the wheel as Jave pulled her into the passenger seat and threw both him and her onto the seat. 'Drive,' he commanded the driver.

The man surged ahead until they came to the nearest Tube station.

Jave reached into the glove compartment and pulled out the man's car registration details before they stepped out. 'Tell anyone about us, and I'll come back for you.'

The man nodded frantically and hit the pedal as the car sped off.'

'Come,' he told Aria. 'I'll take us somewhere safe. We need to get out of here. The longer we keep this information, the worse it will get.'

'We can't let that happen before we find Emily,' she said as they raced down the Underground escalators at Richmond Station.

'If we lose the flash drive, we lose any bargaining power to find Emily. That man, Pepper, said he knew who had her. Jave, she's alive somewhere.'

He stopped running, then turned to face her as they stepped onto the Tube. 'Aria, I think he was pulling your leg to get the drive and documents.'

Central London
21:13 hrs

'Timothy can help,' Aria said.

'Him again,' Jave muttered.

'I believed that man.'

Jave squished his eyebrows. 'I don't trust either man.'

'You're overreacting. Timothy can be trusted. He flew us out of Jordan when my father's plane couldn't.'

'I'll get us out of here, Aria. First, though, let's see what's on Avent's flash drive.'

Shock silenced her. Why was Jave overreacting? She could trust Timothy. Jave seemed subdued, even with the knowledge that Emily could be alive. Was it possible, though? Thirteen years?

Where would she be?

What did she look like if she was at all alive?

Was the answer in the history of these letters?

The letters had been written during the British occupation of India. When exactly? They had to find out. All this news about the East India Company taking spoils from India was starting to get on her nerves. She just wanted to find Emily.

Aria rubbed her forehead as if she could erase the tiredness she felt. She hadn't slept properly in days. She hadn't even had a proper meal, and now they were about to go to God knew where.

The hum of the Tube nearing Central London stung her nerves, but Jave knew more than he was saying. On the plane from India, he'd briefly mentioned the Department of Economic Intelligence. Just who were they in this whole picture as well?

Their car was empty, and Jave kept watching the door with each stop. Shortly before South Kensington, she set a hand on his lap. 'Thanks, Jave.'

His face softened. 'For what?'

'Saving my life. More than once. Perhaps keeping me sane.'

He smiled and put his warm hand over hers. She hadn't expected that reaction, yet Aria welcomed his silent affection.

'Tell me more about the Department of Economic Intelligence? I overheard Avent speak with my father about them. Tell me, what is their interest in this? Why this diamond?' Who exactly are they? How's it that you know so much about them?'

Jave's eyes watched her, not judging her as they had done so many times when they'd first met. 'The DEI's interested in matters that involve economic events that may spiral into international security matters. If the Koh-i-Noor is disputed across borders, it affects economic relations as well as national security matters. The DEI started as a branch of the United States government that does not exist, but their interest is to seek out any economic threat to the country and their allies. I guess they must believe the myth that if the diamond's ownership is questioned, it will lead to economic mayhem because it will bring into question every single thing the British acquired over the years. That alone destabilises everything. Ungoverned it would be disastrous for them.'

He paused as if thinking before continuing. It's about the diamond's history, but it's also the future of all diamonds that's at stake now that Altaneus has perfected their research. They use solar panels and other materials to create artificial rain, and they need the diamonds to facilitate this quantum power. If this research was in the hands of any government that alone would make a country invincible in the future. Imagine the ability to constrain rain production whenever and however you want. Fenderson would get all of this at the cost of disarming Britain of the Koh-i-Noor diamond, reopening his operations in India and elsewhere.'

Aria mused. Jave was right. 'When Parkinson came to work for us, I remember him saying gems just don't shine, and jewellery has more significant purposes.'

Jave nodded, smiling. 'Remember the files that Sondra gave us. I looked through them all and especially honed in on the East India Company, and then the Dutch East India Company. I was also in Amsterdam, hunting through their files. The place was tightly sealed to the bone when I got there.'

'You were in The Netherlands?'

'Yeah. Finding anything on Altaneus Corporation. Your father asked me to look out for you a few months ago when they announced the day of the court case.'

'Emily? When?'

'I'll let him answer that,' Jave answered. I believe he owes you that much.'

'What did you find in The Netherlands then?'

'I sneaked into Altaneus's warehouse—the only one that's

still recognisable. It pretends to be a technology factory. I didn't find much,' he admitted.

Jave's lips pressed into a hard line before he continued. 'Must be difficult, for you. Not knowing what happened to your sister.'

'It is. Does anyone know about this?' Aria said. 'I mean about The Netherlands?'

'No.'

Aria's skin prickled at the attention Jave was giving her. 'I can't read my father. Never been able to. Does my father have any suspicion that Emily may still be alive?'

'Don't know,' Jave said. 'Maybe he just wanted matters cleared up after she'd gone missing. He didn't tell me much. Whatever information is out there on Emily, he needs it to be destroyed or found. That's why he sent me to Amsterdam.'

'Jave, you're an agent for hire. Is that what you really do?'

The Tube stopped at Sloane Square, and he rose abruptly. 'We get off here.'

Outside Sloane Square station, they walked for five minutes through the heart of Chelsea and came to a private apartment house behind a set of railings. Jave scanned his palm to open the gate and then each door until they were in a highly secure modern apartment on the third floor of the building.

'You live here?' Aria asked, studying the grand, luxurious place. Mostly grey in colour and void of any sentimentalities, it was sleek and decked to the brim with the latest technology, including a spying camera viewing each window, door, and entrance.

Jave smiled but didn't respond. 'Can I get you anything?'

'Now, I see business is good. I'll have some water please.'

Jave brought her a glass of cold water and settled on the state-of-the-art sofa. It was the first time she'd relaxed in days.

'I know my life is in danger, but, Jave, thank you for keeping me alive.'

Aria took Avent's flash drive from her pocket. 'Should we look at this?'

Jave found a laptop and settled on the sofa next to her. 'All right.'

He slid the drive into the laptop, then checked the files. Sure enough, the data included information about the British Raj and the East India Company—everything from its formation to every part of its business endeavours. How could something so historical be so significant and so crucial to what happened to Emily?

She wished she'd paid enough attention to India's past in history class. She'd been more interested in geology and science. Avent's files showed Altaneus had inaugurated its biggest research arm somewhere near to where the diamond had been mined.

'Could that be India?' Aria said.

Jave shrugged.

Aria's heart beat fast at the next information she read. A document within Avent's records with the seal of the Foreign Service Office opened up. The name was clearly marked.

Emily Asterley Raith.

It was the first time that she'd seen Emily's name connected directly to East India Company historical files or the Foreign Service. Was she right? Had her father had known more than he had let on when she had died?

Parts of the document were unreadable, blacked out by encryption.

Her sister had been part of whatever this was. Emily had been researching Altaneus Corporation—she hadn't been working for them directly. She'd been spying for the government at seventeen. They'd fabricated her employment at Altaneus to spy for them. The government had sent her there because she knew the desalination research inside out, and Altaneus needed her.

They'd used Emily.

Something had gone very wrong. Either way, the government hadn't come in to help her during the explosion, but instead, they had left her there to die.

Her father must've known. Emily would never have stood up to whatever was wrong or stood for what the company was trying to do.

Aria's shoulders fell back, and she felt a heaviness in her core. Her muscles grew weak as tightness grew in her chest.

Her father had left Emily there, too, just like the government.

What had her father been part of thirteen years ago?

Jave took both her hands into his. 'Aria don't read anything into this. We don't know.'

'But the files here say that she was spying. They sent a child to do their jobs, and my father stood by and watched. He must've kept this from my mother too.'

Aria couldn't believe that her sister was a scientist who'd created a technology to produce water and rain using solar panels and diamonds, and this was the very technology that the DEI and the British government wanted from Altaneus.

Jave neared her and held her in his arms. She glared at him for a few seconds, feeling his warmth next to her as she felt a well of tears coming on. 'Aria, don't judge him yet. We need to know the whole story. I'm with you all the way on this.'

Her mind still in shock, and she watched him with teary eyes now.

He would protect her; she knew that well. Why did he care? Aria couldn't understand why this affected him so much. He wasn't doing this for himself but to...

'I just want to find her, hopefully alive and...'

'Don't overthink it,' Jave said, now tenderly kissing her teary eyelids. 'Wherever this takes you, I'll be right behind you,' he said gently.

He meant what he said. He really would. She had misjudged him in India. She nodded. 'Okay.'

Jave took in a deep breath. 'The DEI will be all over the fact that your sister is still alive if they haven't found her before we have. Emily has a great deal of information valuable to so many people—and some of them are all wrong. They must have figured she sent you some communication and are after you—and her if she is still alive. We need to stay one step ahead of them. The information we have is crucial to keeping her alive. The minute the evidence leaves our hands, it's all over.'

'I know,' Aria said. 'We also have to find the Koh-i-Noor now. It would clear up so much.'

'Your sister was one smart girl. The very fact that she was working on something so crucial at such a young age... I must admit the Raith family has some super talent,' Jave said, now smiling and trying to cheer her up.

'That was thirteen years ago. I can't believe that she was so young and doing something so significant like this. I know Altaneus offered her the job within hours of meeting her. My father has never been able to control either one of his daughters.'

Jave let her lay her head on his chest. It seemed natural. Taking in a deep breath, he felt his heart under her ear. 'Aria, we are now in this together. Perhaps if we get to Fenderson's old Altaneus headquarters? What if they've hidden evidence on Emily? I, for one, would like to find out. Want to come with me?'

Aria nodded.

'Is there anything we haven't looked at?' Jave said, closing the laptop with his free hand.

She lifted her head and smiled. 'Treasure hunters are constantly looking for old gems. Some diamonds are like vintage clothing. We know they exist, but few people wear them. Jave, I can't figure out who stands to gain from keeping the Koh-i-Noor.

'I think you can, Miss Treasure Hunter. When was the last time Emily communicated with you?'

'Not since I left the Maldives,' Aria said. 'Do you think we can learn if the desalination technology has been fully developed? What's to say that whatever Emily was working on was ever stopped? And who are the buyers for that technology?'

'We'll get to that, but I think I want to talk to you about something else,' Jave said taking her ring finger with Maxwell's diamond in his hand, then removing it slowly with his lips. He took it in his teeth and gently set it on the table. 'If you were going to marry him, you would've by now.'

Aria watched him as if absorbing shock.

She was breathtaking.

There was so much confusion in her head.

All he wanted to do was to alleviate it. He watched her intensely. Her beauty was intoxicating, a balm on his wounded soul. Wounded by secrets in his own family, he'd spent much of his life away from home, wanting to get away from the dark memories of his past. He saw things very differently from the day he'd met Aria. He'd started to care.

He no longer saw her as a job. He only knew one thing now. He wanted to be with her. She was built to drive men wild, and she didn't even know it. He'd been bold taking that ring off, but he saw the relief on her face when he had. Thirty-three years old, when was he to settle down? Jave hadn't been lucky with relationships, and as a rule, he stayed away from beautiful women, and yes, this wasn't the time to get involved with Aria.

His fingers traced the delicate softness of her lower lip, and she squirmed slightly. 'I...' she began.

He smiled, and she returned his affection with a shy smile of her own.

'If you really loved him'—he started, then stopped, and his breath whispered over her lips before he teased them with a kiss before lifting his chin to speak—'then you wouldn't be kissing me like this.'

They both had been under a lot of strain the last several days, but she had returned his embrace. 'What's bothering you?' he said when she rose from the couch and moved in a shy sweep to the balcony.

He stepped onto the balcony behind her.

'I don't know,' she said. 'I—'

'You haven't called him once since I met you. At least, I haven't seen you do it. You've only called that Timothy guy, and the way you speak to him, I can't imagine you have something with him, unless...'

She swallowed hard. 'No, there's nothing with Timothy.'

Jave didn't respond.

'You know you can trust me,' she said in a sultry voice.

'I'm sorry,' he said, moving back into the room. 'I don't

want to put your life in danger anymore. I'm sorry I did that just now.'

Aria let out a small laugh and followed him. 'You're not putting my life in danger.'

I don't want to complicate your life any further. I want this to happen for the right reasons.

'Still, I want you to be safe,' he added.

'Why?'

Jave couldn't formulate the words. He didn't know these feelings. They weren't normal for a man like him. 'We have just been through so much.'

'I need to know that I can trust you, Jave. You see, I can't trust my father. I've never been able to trust my family. Emily was the only person I could trust, and she was taken away from me,' she said.

'Tell me about her,' Jave said.

'I find myself in the biggest mess of my life. Emily would have known how to sort me out. She was the best sister anybody could want. She was kind, generous, considerate, and brilliant. I can see now why the government used her. I only ever wanted to build a museum in the Maldives,—and maybe more places—so the world could see what nature offers. Emily got her love for science and explaining the unexplained from James Parkinson. He just took off one day, left without a word to anyone, but left me this jewel I wear round my neck. It's a meteorite rock, he once told me.'

Jave could see that Aria was working hard, trying to uncover her past. 'You're very special, Aria.'

'Why?' she said, coming closer and placing her hands around his neck.

'Because I...'

Jave couldn't believe what he felt as he pulled her close once again. Her body was telling him something different.

Stark and vivid eyes shone at him. Her dark hair swung about her shoulders, but she didn't resist him. Her eyes encouraged him as she drew her arms around his neck, tighter.

This was the woman he wanted to be with and what he'd been running away from all his adult life.

He ached for her touch, and she drew near to meet him in a moment of unrestrained passion.

07:03 hrs

Sunlight strained its way past the heavy drapes of the bedroom and bathed the room in light, banishing the shadows of doubt about last night that Aria would have otherwise had. Jave's masculine sense, next to her, teased her.

Her pulse raced, palms dampening at the sight of him. The night had been one of mutual passion. She'd not felt any need to resist Jave. He stirred a little, and she realised how much she loved the sound of his low, husky voice when he spoke.

Maxwell had never made her feel like this, and so she'd resisted him, and now she knew why. A new sense of identity engulfed her. She had an intoxicating respect for this man with whom she'd spent the last several days.

She was falling in love—something Maxwell had not been able to do to her. Being with Maxwell had been about pulling teeth and trying to manufacture a relationship that didn't exist, but with Jave it all seemed natural.

The man could handle himself with a gun or in a fight. He could protect her. There was a rawness about that approach.

Jave slept peacefully, half covered by the sheets, and she allowed herself to appreciate his athletic beauty. She knew he was all man, inside and out.

Quietly, Aria slipped out of bed with a sheet around her.

She passed the table where Jave had left the flash drive and copies of the documents they'd tried to make sense of these last few days. Everything that they'd discovered about her family, her sister... At the top of the papers, she noticed the name that she'd not paid attention to before.

Stoker John was written at the top of the document. Then next to it was another name—Lincoln.

Lincoln was Jave's surname.

Lincoln.

In 1856, someone by that very name had signed this document. This among other document that had imprisoned her father's career and her family's reputation. Not to mention her great-great-great-grandfather, all because of the blasted Koh-i-Noor diamond.

She decided to make use of the time and paced to the office next to the living room. Neat boxes lined one wall of a long shelf. She moved to the sleek desk and pulled open the drawer, and her eyes fell on an Altaneus company identity pass.

Jave Lincoln's and Emily Raith's.

She heard the shower start and realised she'd not heard Jave waking up. Several minutes later, he came into the room with a towel around his waist and leaned in for a kiss.

She drew away from him for an instant.

A quizzical glare crossed his face. 'You all right?' he said.

She nodded briefly. Then her hand slid and pulled his gun from the side table. She aimed it at him.

His eyes widened in a moment of confusion.

'You've been lying to me,' she said, her eyes heating with anger. 'You worked for Altaneus with Emily. You were there when she disappeared! Also, Mr Lincoln, you are a descendant of the Lincolns who had ties to the Boston Tea Company, aren't you? Jave, why didn't you tell me you knew Emily? What the heck is going on?'

She could tell that Jave was self-conscious about his near nakedness. He was in a very vulnerable position facing his gun and her rage.

Her finger quivered on the trigger, her anger raking over her like hot coals. 'What does your family have to do with this diamond? There's something I've seen in these documents that wasn't in Sondra's files and those from the National Archives. Pages have been torn out. Pages that reference the Lincolns—and that would mean you. What are you hiding? You have been involved in all of this, haven't you?'

He put his hand out, trying to steady her shaking hand, the gun still aiming at his middle.

She wasn't done. 'Tell me,' she said, leaning forward and placing both hands around the handle of the gun, aiming it directly at his face. 'Isn't your surname Lincoln?'

'Listen. Let me explain,' Jave began.

'Start talking. You're hiding something from me. I know there's a link between your family and the diamond as well. It's not just my family. For all I know, Emily is dead by now. For days, I've been running around believing you. You knew Emily, and you didn't tell me, and even worse, you were there at Altaneus with her, Jave. How did you get this?' she said pulling out Emily's ID card.

'Listen, Aria. I was going to tell you. I knew your sister.'

'When? Right after you'd been with...'

This time, Aria dropped the gun to the floor, and a shot left the firearm in a thunderous blast that cracked the side of his shelf, knocking one leg off.'

Jave's eyes moved to the shelf. 'Aria, please.'

'Why should I, Jave? I spent last night with you. Why didn't you tell me you knew my sister? You lie. Just like every man I know!'

'Aria, I have your best interests at heart. I'm not hiding anything.'

Tears now flooded down her cheeks. 'When I find my sister, I don't want to see you.'

She started walking, and the sheet fell off her body, leaving her nude as she stormed to the bathroom and slammed the door behind her.

Within fifteen minutes, she'd dressed and gathered her things, then she made for the front door. 'Open this blasted thing. It's not a normal door.'

He complied, releasing the electronically surveyed door. 'Where are you going, Aria. Please wait...'

'What do you care? I'll find those after me and offer my services or find the diamond. It can't be any worse than having your so-called protection.'

She stormed to the lifts.

Jave stared behind her, unsure what had hit him.

Edinburgh
08:09 hrs

The Edinburgh sky, dark in the aftermath of the strong gales that had hit Scotland the night before, began to clear.

Iver glanced out the window. He smiled at the thought of what he was about to do.

His left arm, charred in the Altaneus fire, ached, and he massaged it gently.

He knew he looked a lot younger than his age. Nobody could tell anyhow.

Iver had tasted enough of life to know that he wanted more. Working on the rain project had kept him young. Even now his thirst for getting the diamond and restoring his family's dignity still burned within him. He couldn't let go of everything done.

They had waited long enough and needed to go to the next step. The International Court would bend things his way. Not long now. Just four more days.

It would all be over soon if Robey did as he was told. The bloody Foreign Minister was wanting a cut in his rain project, too.

He took in a sharp breath. Only a fool would mistake the Koh-i-Noor diamond as belonging to England. Not after Duleep Singh had been forced to bring it to Queen Victoria. It had humiliated not only his family but everything that it meant to his heritage.

He picked up an old copy of the portrait of Dorian Grey, a character much like himself.

Dorian Grey had been his inspiration after he'd lost his arm. He pulled his hand from his glove and stared through steel and aluminium. An unsightly scar. Flesh burned off in the fire of his warehouse. He placed his hand back in the glove, God forbid anyone ask...

Fenderson needed drugs, and that girl, Emily Raith, knew how to make them.

He had no idea how she'd done it. The Raith girl would do anything he wished. He was tired of waiting. The Raith girl, that sister of hers, had to know where the diamond was. Was it that simple? A sister for a sister?

She had to produce enough of what he required for the rain project to succeed. Her research showed that diamonds created communication that made the networks extremely secure. Diamonds were quantum power enablers unknown to most of the scientific world—starting with the Koh-i-Noor. No one would look to ever own it again.

The idea wasn't known, but it was the Raith girl who'd known how to set up the procedure. The Koh-i-Noor had to be the first diamond to undergo the trial. It would be redemption. No one could even seek to own the diamond ever again. The Koh-i-Noor debate would end with the desalination project. Everything had been set. Finally, diamonds would show their true worth, giving the world what it needed most. Rain.

In the climate change environment that they were in, he would hold a monopoly for years to come. His family had traded in diamonds, silk, and indigo; he would sell the simplest, yet most valuable of commodities—water.

How had she done it? Iver had no idea, but when Emily Raith had started the fire at Altaneus, destroying his investment and burning his hand in the process, just what had come over her?

She was a damn good scientist and one he intended to keep an eye on. She would complete the project tonight to continue phase two of the experiment. Convert properties of the diamonds into storage they needed for the networks and produce neutral silicon vacancies in diamonds.

'Cicero! It's time,' he said.

18

Edinburgh, DEI Office
10:21 hrs

Silence engulfed the void office. Three soundproof walls surrounded the lone table in the centre of the small room in the Edinburgh centre. He glanced around. For an organisation hiring the best, the DEI's Edinburgh office had only managed a pop-up office, albeit in Bruntsfield, the leafy neighbourhood and one of the most prosperous in the city.

Iver hastened to the table, two attendants hurrying behind him. He turned to one attendant behind him and stretched out his hand. The man set a cold glass of water on the table and handed him three pills.

He took a swig of the water and swallowed. The medicine was not going to last.

This was going to be a long day.

'Fenderson.'

He turned his head.

'This can go away quickly.'

It was the moron, Hudson.

'Just turn away from this case. You can't bring a case against your own government. That will be treason.'

'You snake! You're working both sides of the table,' Fenderson said. 'Soon the DEI will have to choose. Just make sure I get what is rightfully mine and stop following me for my money. If it weren't for my money, the Department of Economic Intelligence wouldn't even exist, and you wouldn't be hiding in the centre of Edinburgh parading as an insurance company. The unveiling of the Koh-i-Noor was supposed to be tonight. Damn it, man! Haven't your agents found it yet? Why is there no evidence, even on your secure CCTV cameras?

'Ten minutes of footage are missing.'

'That's your carelessness. Remember, without the girl the diamond is worthless,' Fenderson said.

'Where is she? I thought you'd buried all of that.'

'Not until Altaneus is back up and running,' Iver Fenderson said.

'We've known about you for a long time, Fenderson.'

'You know nothing. Just a bunch of agents looking for things they don't understand, nor can afford. You need people like me.'

Hudson smirked. 'Then let's make a deal.'

House of Garrard
Central London

The House of Garrard wasn't as her mother had described it. Clarisse Raith had frequented the establishment all too often.

Aria hesitated at the memory of her mother and her connection to the house that had the honour of serving every subsequent British monarch. She hadn't known what to do when she'd left Jave's place. How could he have done that to her? But then the unexpected had happened. As Aria had walked through Chelsea aimlessly, her phone had rung, and she recalled the conversation that had brought her now to the House of Garrard.

He'd said he would meet her here.

The call had been brief when Aria had picked up.

'Aria?'

'Yes?'

'Little Aria?'

'Who is this?' she'd said.

'If I can fix a broken doll, twenty-three years ago when at Asterley Castle, then I can find my way back to that little girl. Lord Asterley's daughter.'

'James Parkinson?'

Her heart had almost stopped at the realisation.

'No time to discuss this on the phone, but meet me at the House of Garrard.'

And here she was in front of House of Garrard, which sold royalty and the rich the most exclusive jewellery. Her mother had been in perfect company. But she'd avoided such shops most of her life. Aria placed a hand over her heart and glared at the sign above the jewellery shop. Was she ready to see him? She pushed the door open and made her way through the exquisite entrance. A lady in a smart suit approached her. 'Can I help you?'

'Yes,' Aria said. 'I'm looking for a man by the name of James Parkinson.'

'You mean our head jeweller. Come with me. This way. Is he expecting you?'

'Yes, I believe he is,' Aria replied.

'He hasn't been here long, but he has already made a remarkable difference to the place.'

A flush of adrenaline tingled through her body when she laid her eyes on Parkinson. The man had barely changed. Except for a little ageing around the eyes and the forehead, he was still the same James Parkinson who'd fixed her doll all those years ago.

'Little Aria Raith,' Parkinson said in a faint voice. 'Thanks,' he said to the lady who had brought her into the back room. 'I think that will be all.'

'You're now the top jeweller here?' Aria said.

'Well, somebody's got to make a living—mine just happens to be in jewels.'

'How did you get my number?'

'Years of hiding have taught me how to find those who want to stay hidden,' he said.

Parkinson drew her into a big hug, and the tightness in her chest dropped. 'Please sit down. It's been a long time.'

'James. I've missed you. Thirteen years. Where have you been?' she said, taking a seat.

'Mostly parading around the world under different names and aliases.'

She felt her heart in her throat.

'Perhaps we can get into that had another time. It's time the Koh-i-Noor finds its home,' Parkinson said, closing the door. I've resurfaced because we need to help Emily. She's in deep trouble.'

'You know where she is? Is she alive? I had my doubts, but you saying that makes me think that she really is alive. Where is she?'

'I don't know, but the fact that the rain project is going ahead, and I found evidence in India of a new undercover Altaneus project disguised thanks to old Indian folklore, says she completed the project or was forced to. I told you a little bit about her and my work at Altaneus Corporation. And our time in Africa,' he said.

'Africa?'

'Yes, Emily and I worked there, in Altaneus's diamond mine as well as in India.'

With every new piece of information she found out about Emily's work at Altaneus, Aria began to think more and more that she knew her sister truly little.

'I was the one they trusted to guide their mining in Altaneus in Botswana in the interest of the USA, Britain, and Jave Lincoln was the one who made sure I stayed in line.'

'Jave Lincoln?' she said, raising an eyebrow.

'Yes, I believe you've already met him.'

'Jave Lincoln came from a private diamond Empire in Illinois and knows a bit about diamonds too,' Parkinson said.

That was news to Aria, but it shouldn't have been now. Was Jave really an expert in diamonds? That was an exciting idea. Aria raised her chin. 'Jave has been hiding just as much from me as my father.'

She bit her lip.

'Don't blame him, blame the diamond industry today,' Parkinson said. 'You need to know the truth.'

'So, please do just that, and don't leave out any details,' she said.

'Diamonds are the world's most major natural resource,' he began. 'Their value is estimated at 13 billion, and of those that are roughly produced, about 8.5 billion of them are found in Africa. There is about sixty-five per cent of the entire diamond industry down there.'

'Tell me more,' Aria said. 'Do they have any other value?'

'Yes. Beyond going into your jewellery and everything else that sparkles,' he replied. 'There's more to be said about diamonds. Many have been used and searched for their rarity. They're beautiful in appearance, but only about three per cent of diamonds are of gem quality. Seventy per cent of diamonds are used for industrial applications including cutting, drilling, grinding, and much more. We now know and have the technology and scientific development that uses diamonds. Especially in computers and artificial intelligence.'

'What about drugs or anti-salination qualities?' Aria said.

'There're many things about diamonds that the world doesn't know,' Parkinson said as he polished a diamond on the table. 'The largest one ever found—for its rarity and beauty alone—demonstrated that diamonds are unique.' Parkinson stopped grinding and stared at her. 'As the hardest natural material known to man, they're the most effective at conducting materials, and they also expand extraordinarily little when subjected to high temperatures.'

'Why would someone connect them to rain production?' Aria asked.

'Unlike most material, they're resistant. The diamond you're looking for one is like no other, but there's an even bigger one than the one in Queen Victoria's crown that came from the same mine.'

She squinted an eye. 'Bigger?'

'Your sister knew this. Your sister, Aria, was one of the most advanced experts in diamond theory and their compositions. I think that's what made her disappear.'

She touched her throat, a sudden coldness hitting her core. Aria couldn't believe what she'd just heard. She neared Parkinson, his eyes full of sorrow, sympathy. 'James, you of all people know I need to find her. I need all the help I can get to find her.'

'I only saw your sister once at Altaneus mines in Botswana. I saw her the day I met Jave Lincoln, when we were there six years ago. Many countries produce diamonds—Australia, Botswana, Canada, the Democratic Republic of the Congo, Namibia, Russia, and South Africa. I believe your sister could be anywhere where such diamonds are mined. The time I did see her, she was down in Botswana where I believe Jake Lincoln was hired to protect her and to find her. Your father sent Jave almost the minute she got on the plane to Botswana to work for Altaneus.'

'He's known Jave that long? Thirteen years.'

'Jave once saved your father's life when they were on a joint UK and US military mission in Iraq. They were captured, and if it hadn't been for Jave—as young as he was then, only twenty I believe—they would never have escaped enemy lines. Their friendship goes back to then.'

It all made sense now why her father trusted Jave with her and Emily's lives.

Parkinson continued, 'Several scientists were recruited, and your sister was the youngest of them—but also perhaps the most skilled. She was recruited either perhaps involuntary on *Operation Mountain*.'

'The government sent her as a spy on this mission. Did she know she was being used?'

'She volunteered because she didn't believe diamonds should be used in this way, to create a new form of energy monopoly that could one day dominate the world and be used as a drought weapon. I was in the garden at Asterley working on the lawn when the MI6 agents arrived one day and told her about it, asking to recruit her. Your sister and Jave were part of the original twelve people who were on this mission. She led the diamond operation. It must run in the family. You know, the knowledge about gems, especially this very particular one.'

'My sister? Really, she was all that? But the government let her down. They abandoned her when Iver Fenderson found out about her true purpose there, right?'

'I don't know, but it wouldn't surprise me. We were both working in the mine's technology facility, but then one day she just disappeared. She was doing research downstairs. Then the fire happened.'

Had Aria judged Jave too harshly?

Parkinson took her hand. 'After about two months of her work there, I believe that's when the problems began in the tech facility of the mine. Now, many factions not only want to be on the right side of the Koh-i-Noor conversation, but they also want a piece of that drought weapon. Imagine governments' interest in diamonds when used in the desalination of water and become a weapon. That's what Emily was working on. Altaneus funded a lot of the research. The Scottish billionaire has a huge stake in the operation.'

19

Garen stared ahead at the traffic, drumming his fingers on the driving wheel. His strength turned to bone-weary exhaustion. It had been a while since he'd visited Whitehall and been down into the city. London reminded him of his ex-wife.

He'd first seen Clarisse at Trafalgar Square at the National Gallery cradling a notebook in front of a van Gogh. She'd been sketching. A true artist in appearance and everything she touched. From the beginning, he'd been taken with her sensual lower lip that she twisted when in thought.

Garen waited for the lights to turn green. He'd found his car in a private park where he'd left it. Checking his rear-view mirror to see if he'd been followed, all he could see were the lines visible on his face. The trip had taken its toll on him, not necessarily the flight from India and the visit to the Foreign Service Office earlier, but one glance in the mirror had told him this issue with the diamonds had to stop.

He had taken this trip many times before, but this time, it would be different. He needed to get to his home.

To Asterley Castle in West Sussex.

It was time he unearthed the dark secrets he kept there.

He wove the car through London traffic before hitting the suburb and then swerved onto the A25 out of London.

He remembered what Clarisse had told him before she passed away. It was the last time he'd seen her. She'd said he needed to get this business away—as far away as possible—from their daughters. The girls were never to know the truth about their great-great-great-grandfather. She was right. She had to be correct, and he felt that once he lost the files, ultimately he may still have a chance with the only daughter that he still had left, and maybe he could save the family's reputation at the same time.

His Jaguar wound up towards the family home, a couple of hours later.

Asterley Castle was mostly tranquil this time of year, due to fewer tourists. The first thing he noticed was the quietness in the lawns in the distance.

When he was away from the private wings of the castle, he typically asked the housekeeper to keep it in case any of them came home.

He liked to come back to a place that was tidy and ready to be lived in. There was no sign of the housekeeper nor the gardener as he walked through the door quietly. Something was not right.

As he made his way up the stairs through the building, suddenly he realised that someone had been here.

The place had been raided. He stepped into the kitchen where he noticed cabinets and bins had been overturned. He then made his way into the den towards his favourite chair. A knife had run right through the sofas, leaving the foam underneath jetting out of the wrecked leather. He moved around the house until he had checked every principal room.

He suddenly turned around, hearing a noise behind him.

'Timothy, what are you doing here?'

'I came to help. I was in town when I saw them leave. Thugs came with three defenders and scared the housekeeper.'

Garen had known Timothy since he and Aria were at school together. He arched an eyebrow. 'Why did you come here?'

'Come on now, Garen. I remember a time when I used to come and no questions were asked—back when I started dating your daughter. Now it seems she is firmly in Jave Lincoln's arms.'

'I wouldn't exactly call it dating,' Garen said. 'You were just teenagers playing around, mostly bickering in the garden.'

'What happened here?' Timothy said.

'I don't know, but I intend to find out.'

They went through several more rooms. Garen wasn't sure why Timothy was here and why now, but he'd always been a regular at this house when the girls were growing up. His family only lived up the road. So, he had come home to visit and decided to stop by and check on things.

Timothy had a way about him and how he moved around the house. He had an intense curiosity about things. He always did.

By the time they went into the girls' rooms, a sudden shrill from Garen's phone interrupted them.

Garen didn't recognise the name. He set the receiver to his ear and listened. 'High Commissioner Raith?'

It was a digital voice. 'If you are listening to this now, then you know that the files have been expunged. Let's hope you keep your end of the bargain or Asterley Castle will have more than just tourists visiting again. We need to find as much as we can. Anything to do with the research that Emily was involved with.'

'Who are you? Why do you keep calling me? And how do

you know so much about my daughter? I swear if you are the bloodied Department of Economic Intelligence I will...'

'It doesn't matter who we are.'

He set down the phone in his pocket and turned to Timothy straight on. Those had to be Robey's men. The Foreign Secretary had not taken his threats lightly.

'Who was that?' Timothy said.

'Nothing. Nothing to worry about right now.'

18:12 hrs

It took every ounce of courage for Aria to call Jave. When she did, he picked up after one ring.

'You okay?' he said.

'Yes. Jave I'm sorry—'

'You have every right to be pissed off at me, Aria. I'm sorry too. Can we meet?'

'Actually, I was wondering if you'd come with me to check out that Altaneus unit in Scotland we talked about. I will be on a flight in one hour. Could we meet there?'

She gave him the address, and Jave agreed to meet her there in a few hours.

When Jave landed in Edinburgh, Aria had already rented a Honda to take them to Altaneus Corporation's old storage unit warehouse. She'd found the details in Sondra's file. James Parkinson's had called in an old favour from a colleague who still worked in the abandoned, yet highly secured facility.

'Miss Raith, I'm only letting you in here because of the help James Parkinson gave me with authenticating my wife's family jewel collection. You've less than seven minutes before the alarm goes off in there. I'll leave now before they notice I am gone.'

The quiet man who helped them seemed nervous. They stepped into the warehouse unit and glanced around. Rows of sealed black boxes lined all the walls. They were labelled with the words Altaneus Corporation Desalination.

They split up, each rummaging through several dark boxes. Early moonlight flooded in through the small window behind them. Jave had been noticeably quiet. He stared around the dusty warehouse. Every few seconds his phone would beep, but he kept ignoring it.

The next time Jave's phone beeped, he picked up the call, but on second thought, he clipped it off. His face settled into hard lines of determination.

'It could be important,' Aria said.

'Don't think we have time to talk to the authorities. They now know of our involvement,' he said.

It was impossible to change the man's mind. She stared at him, her mouth slacking a little. 'We still have another four minutes.'

He motioned to a Defender across the street from the little window that came to a halt. He turned and picked up a file of a pile of files and shoved them in his travel backpack. 'I think I have what we need now. Let's go.'

20

Nothing mentioned the Koh-i-Noor or any suspicion of who would take it. The odds were running out. The flight back to London was uneventful as they studied the files they had gathered.

Jave pulled out his tray table on the British Airways flight and set the files down on it. 'If we don't have the diamond, and Iver doesn't either, then who would take it?'

'Jave, does it still matter? We tried. Going to that warehouse was our last hope of finding out.'

He studied her as if seeing her for the first time. 'If we don't find the diamond, then you, Emily, and your father, will be running forever. I don't want that to happen.'

Jave cared, but she still found it hard to grasp that he shared a past with her sister he'd chosen not to reveal. Tightness in her jaw and chin caused mild discomfort.

He closed the files and took her hand. 'Aria. It's important to me that you only see that my relationship with your sister was just friendship. I went to protect her and stayed far from her or her work. I swear. I wasn't there when she disappeared, and it has haunted me since. That's why I'm so protective of you. You do something to me, and I—'

'It's okay, Jave. Parkinson told me how you met my father.'

'Your father trained me after we left the Middle East. I learnt a lot from him, and in many ways, he fathered me more than my own father. I told him I would help him in whatever mess he was in when he told me about Altaneus.'

She tilted her head. 'Why?'

'Because I respect him, and I trust him like no other. Your father was a highly valued MI6 agent before he joined the Foreign Service. He taught me how to survive. The day that the diamond's shady past had been presented to the Pakistani authorities, our names got tangled up with the Koh-i-Noor. It would be detrimental to all of us.'

21:12 hrs
Claridges Hotel, London

After everything she'd put him through, Iver decided he was going to make Emily Raith suffer.

Really suffer.

His family was slowly dwindling. Everything that they'd worked for going all the way back to the Scottish Lords. Just where was that diamond?

They had a clear argument, and the case would be won. They would win the Koh-i-Noor diamond in court.

Finally, his day of justice had come. Who had stolen the diamond, and why didn't he have any kind of information, yet?

Hudson watched him as he took a sip of water from the table in the grand dining room at Claridges Hotel in London, then he shoved a piece of white paper in front of him.

'What's this?' Iver said.

'Our agreement, and the deal that is on the table. I'll make sure that once the Koh-i-Noor has been granted back to India, you be fully compensated for any harm or inconvenience. Should it be found, we would like to acquire it and be part of Altaneus's prospects for the future. The DEI will make sure it gives you every backing in The International Court of Justice. We know people, and we know the jury.'

Iver huffed. 'I don't agree. The diamond belongs to me fully. I'm not prepared to make a deal, Agent.'

'Sir Iver Fenderson. It's the only deal that's on the table.'

Iver's eyes heated with anger, and he set the paper away from him. 'No.' Sure, his glare could have burned a hole in Hudson, he pinned him with his eyes. 'I'm not prepared to make a deal.'

'So,' Hudson said rising, 'it looks at the race is on. Whoever finds that woman, Emily Raith, and the diamond will be crowned the winner of this challenge. May the best man win.'

07:02 hrs

The shrill sound of her mobile phone woke Aria with one ring. She staggered out of bed in the hotel she'd chosen to stay at in London and picked it up.

'Aria Raith?'

'Who's this?'

'Meet me at Beacon's Café on the corner of Thurloe Place in an hour if you want information on your sister.'

The man hung up.

Aria set a hand on her throbbing chest. Jave had insisted

she stay with him, but she'd declined, wanting to sort her feelings out.

Should she go?

The café was still dark in the morning hour when Aria made her way into the space. The smell of roasted coffee beans combined with the sweet aroma of pastries in the French-style café in the air made Aria sense her hunger. She had no idea who she was looking for, nor if they were even here. Her eyes scanned the quiet café, and she took a seat by the door.

Just in case.

A man, chewing a piece of gum, stopped in front of her table. He was tall, in his late forties, and had a glint in his eyes. His harsh features were carved with manly pride. 'Golly,' he chuckled, moving to her table, 'if you want to play nice, I can get you the rest of your breakfast.'

She took in a deep breath, and there was a moment of silence.

'Who are you, and what is it that you want?' she said.

'Amos Hudson. I'm from the Department of Economic Intelligence, which might mean nothing to you. You are a hard woman to find, Aria Raith. The real question is what is it that I can do for you,' Hudson said. 'If you want to see your sister alive, I suggest you start to cooperate.'

Aria's mouth fell open. So now the DEI, as Jave had explained, was in her face. 'I don't understand.'

'We have a lot at stake, and you're right in the middle of it,' Hudson said. 'Your father was involved in quite a lot of things—and has been for quite some time. He has the information we don't want him handing over to the Indian source and the Pakistani government.'

'What exactly do you mean? Why would the Indian authorities need anything from the British government?'

'Well, for one, your father is still in trouble. The best thing you can do for him is to cooperate with me by giving me the Koh-i-Noor,' Hudson said.

'I don't have anything that you need.' After a few moments, her voice broke into a full laugh. 'You don't scare me, whoever you are. I suggest people stop thinking I have this diamond.'

He wasn't amused and trapped her arm in an excruciating grip. 'I'll make you cooperate. You want to see Emily, get me the Koh-i-Noor. That's what you do, isn't it? Find gems and treasure?'

His eyes were full of fury, and Aria decided she'd hush her next words.

She'd been trapped.

He continued, 'This will be a two-way street.' He moved close to her, chewing noisily at his gum. 'Do you understand exactly what I mean by a two-way street?'

Aria shuddered. She deliberated on what path to choose, run or scream, but she decided against it when an icy expression entered his light green eyes. Hudson was a sizeable man.

'You're going to get the diamond, and when you do, I need you to make sure I'm right behind you,' he said.

Kalahari Desert
Southern Africa
07:27 hrs

Aria had taken the overnight flight to Botswana with Jave within hours of meeting Hudson. If she was to find the Koh-i-

Noor, as with any gem hunting case she took for clients, she wanted to know as much about the treasure as possible. This time the treasure's connection to similar diamonds and Parkinson's information about the mines in Southern Africa was all she had to go on.

When she stepped off the plane, they found their booked taxi waiting to take them to Koenraad Rog Diamond Mining —a mine that sat on Altaneus's old mining plot. After Altaneus had shut for business in Botswana, the government had joined forces with Koenraad Mining and formed a joint venture, having confiscated Altaneus's earlier operations.

Jave opened the door for Aria as she settled into the passenger seat. 'I suggest we say nothing about the letters or anything else that we've uncovered.' He shot her a smirk. 'Your cover is you're my fiancée. They'll believe that, and we are on an engagement ring gem hunt together.'

Aria realised that she had no choice. She followed Jave quietly as they made it into the building to one side of the mine that housed the headquarters.

Light reflected off its fantastic windows as a tall African man greeted them at the entrance. Aria walked into his office with both curiosity and excitement, eyes wandering wildly around the room with interest as she tried to decipher the type of work that had gone on when her sister worked here.

'I'm glad you've have chosen us for your diamond purchase. We service a lot of prestigious customers like yourselves,' the man said as he offered them refreshments.

'We're here to buy the best diamond you can get us, but first, we've heard of the fine history of this mine and its contribution to the diamond industry,' Jave said and then continued, 'This is my fiancée, and we are stopping by very quickly on the way to a pre-wedding trip. We would like to be educated on the history of diamonds, and then perhaps we can find the right one for her.'

'Indeed, not only can we give you a history lesson on the diamonds here, but we can also make sure we find the finest diamond for your beautiful fiancée.'

Aria gave Jave a play-along smile.

'I'll give you a short tour,' he said, rising from his seat. 'That's the best way to see what we do here and entice you as to what diamond you want.'

He took them to the far end of the mines on a hill that overlooked the drilling pit.

Jave and Aria could see several people working in the mines. She couldn't help but imagine that this was where her sister had worked all those years ago. The sun beat down on the pit, and despite what she'd read on the plane, the mine was much larger than she had predicted.

The man took them around proudly. Vast in the Naledi river valley of the Kalahari, in the middle of the mine, a group of concentric circles were cut deep into the ground. The ditch was circled by a network of roads and structures used in mining operation.

Once they had toured the outside from afar, he took them back to his office. 'Yes, we will have a history lesson today, and perhaps I can start with diamonds in general. First, let's begin with the ten largest diamonds that have ever been found.'

He took them to a door in the far corner and led them into a quiet room.

'Excuse me, sir, while you're looking for a diamond for my fiancée, I would also like information, if you have it, on how diamonds have been used by not only corporations but perhaps governments. Is there any one large diamond that stands out?'

Aria shot Jave a knowing look. He was clearly after the DEI's hidden interests.

'No doubt what you're looking for may be amongst this list that we compiled. We created this list about thirty years ago, when the CIA began to understand the importance of diamonds and how they could be used for, let's put it this way, espionage. If the diamond isn't amongst this list, we'll try to source more information for you. That's because we've been tracing all the diamonds from this list and would know anybody who's even come within ten feet of them.'

'Wow? Espionage? Really?' Aria said.

'Yes. In fact, unless we look at data that NASA has taken while scouting diamond locations on Earth and outer space. If you take a mining crew somewhere near the sun, you'll find a lot more diamonds, but anyway, that's twenty-two trillion miles away. Let's start with something closer to Earth and with the most significant ones.' He started up a programme on his laptop. 'Some of the most significant diamonds ever found haven't made it onto the most wanted list. One of them is known as the Sergio 3000 and weighs one hundred and sixty-seven-carat diamonds. It's one of the largest rough diamonds ever mined. There's also a black one, a carbonado diamond from Brazil, that beat all its rivals in weight and is quite rare. I don't think that those we found recently can match anything close to the ones on this list.'

'Why is the CIA so interested in diamonds?' Aria said, interrupting him. 'What sort of espionage is involved when it comes to diamonds?'

'As an industry, diamonds, in the beginning, had the potential to be used for transactional purposes to fund the nuclear arms race. The more we dove into it, the more we saw that people wanted diamonds for other reasons, and the bigger they were, the better. The diamond industry has a value of about $72 billion a year. You can see that's exactly why it's essential and valuable to the United States government and economic well-being of many prominent nations.'

'What about the Koh-i-Noor diamond?' Jave said.

'There are many thousands of diamonds that could be up for grabs. When I think of the Akwatia Mine diamond, which is 303,106 carats, amongst others. The most momentous time was when it was discovered by a mining superintendent in South Africa in 1905. He's named after the mine. It was taken to be cut and an estimated value of two billion dollars.'

'And the Koh-i-Noor diamond?' Jave insisted.

'If it is 793 carats, it's not as big as the other ones. What's important about it is where it came from. The part that was sent to the United Kingdom was set in front of the Queen Victoria's crown, and it forms part of the Queen's jewels that many visitors view at the Tower of London.'

'Hang on a second,' Jave said. 'The part?'

'Yes. The part. I've made it my personal interest to study diamonds, and I believe the Koh-i-Noor was once part of a much larger diamond that was split naturally by a meteorite.'

Jave shot Aria a quick glance but remained silent. 'What happened to the other parts?'

'When the CIA started snooping, when this used to be Altaneus, many did not believe me, but I know they knew more than they let on about the Koh-i-Noor. What you want is in the Tower of London.'

'The Tower? But the diamond was on loan in Paris and is now gone.'

'That is the actual Koh-i-Noor. I'm talking about its sister diamond from which it broke away from. I believe, and I could be wrong, that the East India Company acquired it, and someone used it in a transaction with the Boston Tea Company, but the diamond was never made public. Still, I think the British kept it, and it has been hidden in the Tower of London ever since.'

This time it was Aria who could not hold her shock.

The man coughed. 'It's a theory. I understand now it's been stolen from the Louvre Museum in Paris. Somebody got to the Koh-i-Noor before anybody else could, and it proves my theory. People want diamonds for all sorts of reasons—including espionage.'

'And to start an international debate,' Aria said.

They left the mine an hour later.

Jave raked his hand through his hair. 'If you're going to see your sister again, we're going to have to go to the Tower of London and steal a diamond that was mined at the same time as the Koh-i-Noor.'

She shot her head around. 'Really?'

'We'll be looking for a diamond that's never been on display. In fact, it will be so secret that the government doesn't even know about it. It will be identical to the Koh-i-Noor diamond. Secret agents, several decades ago from the East India Company, brought it to the United Kingdom—as the man said. Before they could present it to the Queen, they wanted to do some tests on it, because they had been rumours about where these diamonds have been found in the Kollur mines in India. Rather than expose the government on paper that British government had two diamonds; it was hidden in the private collection and never archived.'

Her eyes enlarged. 'So, it's true! How do you know?'

'Your father told me, and with Emily already set up as a spy for the British government, my job was to help rectify this information. When Emily and I were at Altaneus, we came across the information leaked from the Foreign Service Office and Commonwealth archives. Many factions want this to remain secret. That's why I couldn't tell you everything. The more you knew, the more your life would be in danger.'

She exhaled a pent-up breath in a long sigh. 'It's going to be an international crisis.'

'If they found it,' Jave admitted. 'In the absence of the Koh-i-Noor, our only hope in finding your sister is to grab the only diamond that's invisible to the world. We grab it in exchange for your sister. We're gonna have to steal it.'

'You're kidding me? We don't know the first thing about stealing a bloody diamond. How can we pull off something like this?'

'We're going to use all our resources, Aria. It's time we paid the Tower of London a visit.'

21

Anderlecht, Brussels
10:18 hrs

'You're telling me that this person is a security systems expert. Won't they be suspicious that we're asking all this information?' Aria asked Jave.

Her eyes followed the length of the skyscraper as they stood in the Plaza. They had flown into Brussels only an hour prior. Jave had made several calls until the details of a contact and a man in Anderlecht had been made known to him. The man in Brussels owned a security company.

'Aria, it's time you put away your moral ground so that we can find Emily,' he said.

Aria swallowed hard, unable to respond. Jave was right. It was the only way to get Emily back. If they presented the diamond, the whereabouts of Emily might become clear, but were they crazy? How would they do it? Aria only retrieved jewellery and treasure that was hard to get, but it certainly wasn't behind metres of concrete, steel, and a fort of security systems.

The diamond had to be highly protected. Jewel House in the Tower of London was a massive vault. The changing of the guard happened every two hours. The sentry at the Jewel House, plus the Yeoman Warders and other wardens, had the sole duty of protecting the Crown Jewels. These were highly trained officers.

The Crown Jewels themselves included an extensive, incredible collection of 23,578 gems. Also, Aria had admitted to herself that the jewels were the most potent symbols of the British Monarchy. However, she could not help but wonder if it was the stories behind the treasures, most enshrouded in centuries-old mystique, which continued to interest the public and other groups. Jewellery and gem history always included tales of curses, wars, and treachery, and they were right in the middle of one.

Aria and Jave took the lifts to the 55th.

'How do you know these security experts?'

'In my line of work, you meet all kinds of experts. Sometimes the wisdom is not asking how they became who they are and what they do. Just pay the money and run. There's an honour code in this underworld; *'you don't tell me, and I don't tell you'*. Everyone stays safer that way. It's a known fact.'

Aria realised she was learning more about Jave by the minute. The man's past and life was a wall of mystery. 'Well, Jave, you know a lot about it.'

The security expert would be able to tell them more. By now what they really needed to do was gather a plan.

'We'll need Timothy's help,' Aria said.

'As much as I would like to disagree with you,' Jave said, 'you'll be happy to know that I've already alerted Timothy. He's on his way to meet us.'

That had been a change of heart in Jave. Aria couldn't believe that he'd made that move without her asking, but if they were going to break into the most guarded place in the world, they were going to need the best out there.

They needed someone who knew enough about the Tower's technology, security, and could move in and out swiftly —and someone who had the muscle as well. It was too much for both to break into a high-tech security building. She still could not believe what they were doing, but she told herself they would return the diamond. They only needed it to bargain for Emily's life.

Timothy was waiting in an office they were directed into a few moments later. He gave her a quick peck on the cheek, and she sensed mutual respect, yet a discomfort between the two men.

'I got your message early last night,' a short, stocky man said as he slipped into a seat in the office. His greetings were brief as he extended a handshake out to each.

They took seats across from him in his well-lit office.

'What is it that I can do for you?' he began.

'We need to know how one secures a large diamond,' Jave said. 'What security needs are necessary?'

The man shot each a glance before answering. 'What kind of diamond?'

'Any?' Jave said.

'Many security companies can give you this information,' the man said.

'Yet, you pride yourself as the best,' Jave answered, raising an eyebrow. 'You possess the expertise.'

Timothy leaned forward, having been briefed by Jave on their new project. He would want to find Emily as he'd known her so well when they were growing up.

Jave continued, 'Right, so here's the deal,' he said. 'We'll need your security expert to at least penetrate through or shut off some motion detection devices. I believe we will be up against systems that monitor human movement and are linked to police systems. You hack intelligence as much as we do.'

The man smirked. 'My fee is one million sterling.'

Jave nodded.

He continued. 'That includes a fully-fledged security expert, possessing the technology and knowledge around diamond security, and who is an exceptional jewel thief.'

11:36 hrs

Aria pulled out her mobile phone, then studied an article about desalination procedures and creating pure water.

The file also referenced India and a meteorite that had hit several centuries ago, including evidence from NASA. Most of the damage had been in India. The meteorite activity caused an energy reaction within the soil and diamonds were created. The locals gathered many of these diamonds, but over the centuries, the exact location of the hit had eluded many, including a rumour that the East India Company had tried to locate these 'miracle' diamond mines as the files put it. Several photos from space guessed at the location.

She made her way out to the Plaza where the men were waiting. Timothy and Jave sat at a café, each huddled over a laptop. It was clear they were going to avoid any casual conversation with each other.

'They are two diamonds,' Timothy finally said. 'Who would have known? I, for one, say we say little to the jewel thief and keep them at arm's length. Emily's life is important. Trust you to foot such a high bill, Lincoln. You must be serious.'

Jave winced. Aria knew he didn't like Timothy, but Timothy had a point. Jave slid his hand around her waist, and she went into his shoulder. 'We'll find Emily. I promise.'

This caused quite a stir from Timothy.

Aria's weary body sank deeper into the chair.

'If we don't find the diamond and court is in session, Emily might as well be dead.'

'We bargain for your sister's life with the diamond. I doubt anyone but you will be able to tell the difference between the two diamonds,' Timothy said.

'We will get to the bottom of this,' Jave said.

Aria shoulders drooped. 'I know, but this makes me realise the importance of my sister's work.'

'The jewel thief will be here any minute. I agree with Timothy,' Jave said. 'She's on a need to know basis.'

Aria sat up with a spring. 'She?'

'Yes, *she*,' Jave said.

22

Vauxhall, London
11:27 hrs

Standing at close to six feet tall, the dark-skinned man had an out of place feel about him. He had a round face, a turned-up nose, and full lips. Light brown eyes shone large at Garen as he studied his computer.

Garen leaned in front of the MI6 officer. A day ago, he'd ask Count Valex to join him. If Austria surrendered what they knew about the rain project, Garen would have an easier time in Vauxhall. MI6 was going to be a hard one to convince. He'd used any credentials he had left to go back to his old office. He would need guarantees before he complied with any bargain Robey had.

'What is it that I can do for you, Mr Raith?'

'A lot.'

'You're a long way from the British High Commission.'

'Wilbert, we go back a long way. You owe me one. I have now come to ask for that favour that I need from you.'

'Don't...'

Garen wasn't done. 'MI6 has a lot of information on my family. I knew this when I joined the Foreign Service, and I know you have a way of keeping things secret that you want kept secret, but I need you to dig into what that information is. MI6 has a lot of connections around the world. There is a network of people, some of whom I call friends.'

'I'm afraid we can't release the files on your daughter or release any information on the mission your daughter was on. Everything within these walls remains on a need to know basis.'

'Come on, Wilbert, you don't believe that,' Garen said.

Wilbert gave a disdainful snort. 'She knew the rules. She knew what she was getting into.'

'She was barely eighteen!' Garen said, slamming his hand on the table. 'She didn't know what she was signing. All you guys wanted was her expertise.'

'The intelligence that we have on her will remain classified,' Wilbert reiterated.

'Why can't you give me this one break? Point me in the right direction, at least. There's a list that details scientific developments the MI6 considers a threat to our nation,' Garen said.

Garen shot Valex a concerned look. Both men were no strangers to the workings of the spy organisation.

'Your daughter committed a crime.'

'That's a lie,' Garen said. 'My daughter did not commit a crime of any sort. If anything, she was doing you a favour. She held the keys to something that you all wanted badly. She could save this world, and I know you better than that.'

'Whatever your daughter was working on was of a classified nature. So, unless she's here to defend her position, the charge for treason remains on her record.'

Valex, who'd accompanied Garen, leaned forward. 'Perhaps we can work together.'

Garen knew he could not trust the man. If Emily were alive, this would be so different. He turned over to Valex to see if he had anything to add. The Count's eyes shimmered with the intensity of his anger.

'I'm sorry that I can't do anything any further. That's all I can tell you. It's out of MI6's hands now. For all we know, she was speaking to interested parties about her work at Altaneus, selling it. If she were alive, today, she'd be on the wanted list. What that girl knew was more valuable that most classified files in MI6. There's nothing I can do.'

'You are so full of it! You know damn well I came here because I don't know what happened to her, but something tells me you do. Where are the reports of the explosion at Altaneus? Why is it that no one has ever been able to produce anything that happened there? You guys all silenced any witnesses from that day—just as much as the Department of Economic Intelligence. What is it that you're doing with them? What is it that MI6 is conspiring with the DEI about? You owe me. My other daughter has now been targeted by a criminal organisation and needs help.'

'I know Miss Emily Raith may have had information,' Valex said. 'She had the last piece of tech and research that Altaneus needed. Her research was seen by a few governments as a superior weapon.'

Wilbert glared at both. 'You've wasted your time. I've already shared enough.'

He stood up. 'Please do have some of the coffee here, it is the best in the country.'

With that, he showed them the door.

'I'm not leaving without seeing what happened that day at Altaneus.'

Brussels
12:15 hrs

'Leila Marshall is the most sought-after security expert in the world,' Timothy said, reading the details on his phone that they'd been given only a couple of hours earlier.

'And my price is not low. I'll expect thirty per cent of the value of whatever jewels you need stealing.'

They glared up when a tall caramel-skinned woman took a seat at their café table. 'I'm the chief security officer at this company. At least that's what my passport will say. I don't care if you are looking at something expensive or not, the cut stays the same, coz whatever it is, it's already mine.'

Aria bit her lip watching Leila's sure way with words, and it seemed, security locks as well.

'It's already taken care of as long as you get us in and out of the Tower of London as planned,' Jave said.

'There's no need to doubt, Leila,' Timothy said. 'She's a very well-connected person. Her reputation precedes her. Leila is the only person who can break into any safe anywhere in the world. No matter the technology. She has access, and she will be able to give value for money.'

'Is that so?' Aria said.

Leila smirked. 'All you need to worry about, my sweet princess, is identifying the right diamond to snatch.'

'Looks like all is in order then,' Timothy said.

Aria didn't know what to think of Leila. She was pretty and had a way with tough men—something Aria admired.

Jave saw Aria's discomfort and set a hand on hers. 'Hey, Leila is one person who can help us live through this. No one will know it's missing, and we will have enough time to return it after we find Emily. Besides, this might delay the court hearing as well.'

London
17:00 hrs

When Aria, Jave, and Timothy left Heathrow after a short flight from Brussels, Leila drove them to a suburb of East London. Fog bathed the woods as the car pulled up to the small city cottage on a quiet road.

The roof was leaking when they entered the house, the scent of pine wafted in the air, and the acrid taste of regret blistered the back of her throat.

Leila dropped her bags on the floorboards, then studied each face. 'We'll stay here tonight, so we can go over the plans. I warn you; this is your last chance to back out. Either way, I get to keep the money.'

Aria had no choice but to trust Leila. Her instincts told her something else, though. The tendons in her neck tautened. Were they really going to do this?

Aria pulled Jave to one side. 'I haven't heard from my father, and frankly, I am worried. He should've contacted us by now. It's not like him to stay quiet this long, even when I didn't speak to him for months, he always found a way to send some sort of communication to me.'

Jave glanced up and watched as Leila and Timothy settled into conversation at the kitchen table. 'Your father knows what he's doing. I wouldn't worry.'

Aria moved to the window. Evening shadows shifted into different shades of night grey. Jave followed her gaze to the road. His deep sigh whispered across her skin as he moved close 'Hey. It'll be all right.'

He moved to the kitchen table where Leila and Timothy studied hacked CCTV footage.

Arai squinted at the screen.

Jewel House had never looked so frightening.

18:03 hrs

Garen's eyes shot open, and he studied his surroundings. Sprawled on a bed, he tugged at a handcuff on his wrist tied to the bedpost. A pounding pain throbbed in his behind his left eye.

Pain throbbed from his shin, and light pierced through the cracks of the shutters, then he turned as a figure framed in front of him sat on a sofa. A strong stench of medication came from the other room. He could hear muffled noises, and every few seconds he heard a beep.

'Garen?' a man's voice said from across the room. 'Good, you're awake now.'

Garen's legs trembled and pain flared in his chest. He could not remember a damn thing. His face flushed, and he studied the dark figure in front of him with rage.

'...Garen, you idiot! What do you think you we're doing! You shouldn't have come to Vauxhall like that. I had to shut you up.'

Garen tried to respond, but his voice had no impact, his mind and body full of God knew what drugs.

'You'll stay here until the hearing. Those are the orders,' Wilbert muttered softly.

'No!' Garen yelled. 'Y-you bastard!'

'What? No, you bloody, high-brow diplomat! You had to snoop around what happened thirteen years ago. Why didn't you just leave it? You could have ruined everything,' Wilbert snarled.

'No!' Garen blared, trying to kick at Wilbert with his free leg.

He felt his heart pump, and his fists clenched tightly. No matter how much he fought, he still couldn't reach Wilbert.

They'd put him here, so he couldn't jeopardise the court case.

Wilbert rose from the dirty sofa he was sitting on. 'Do as you're told. It will go a lot easier on your daughters. Both of them.'

23

Tower of London
23:47 hrs

The Tower of London staff had settled for the night, and a supreme calm claimed the air. They took the path leading to the top of the long staircase and could see Tower Bridge from the top of the stairs.

They would wait for Leila's signal. Clad in black attire, their suits had been prepped for them by Leila. Each had a distinct part to play.

Jave glanced at the blueprints on his smartwatch as Timothy helped Aria up the first wall.

Leila had devised a plan that involved going under the historic tunnels that linked the abandoned Tower Subway and the Tower of London, with a couple of blast points to shoot them from the Tower to the river.

Once they had the jewel, it was a fail-proof plan of escape.

Had Leila known? Tower Subway was the second oldest tunnel running under the Thames, and until Leila had mentioned it, it was an often-forgotten reminder of Victorian engineering. The tunnel stretched between Tower Hill on the north side of the river, through to Vine Lane on the south side of the Thames, west of Tower Bridge. That was the escape route, a seven-foot-diameter passageway, with a wrought iron tunnelling shield bearing through a layer of clay below the riverbed, forgotten by the public this time of night.

Aria gasped when she looked down the staircase, reminding herself she hated heights.

Jave was focused like the other two.

They'd made their way in through the water and historic sewers. The Thames had to be commended—it was a dark and murky place. A witness to history served by tunnels to the water that could lead one anywhere they wanted to go in London.

Jave observed ahead of him and mouthed, 'Let's go past the security guard post.'

Aria glanced up at him in utter shock. His expression was just as unreadable as his voice.

They made it to the first post. Soon they were past the security guard and were now at the innermost ward—an area immediately south of the White Tower. It wove out to what was once the edge of the Thames. They would need to make haste to the Waterloo Block.

In the foreground of the Tower of London, darkness forbade them to find the exact spot, until Timothy produced night goggles. They passed the armoury building and headed straight until they were outside Jewel House. They had to go in at precisely the time that clock struck midnight.'

'Okay,' Timothy said. 'We need to get behind the vault at Jewel House.'

Aria swallowed hard; she was trying the impossible. Despite everything she'd learnt in the last several days, she never imagined she would be robbing the Tower of London.

Leila manoeuvred herself like a stealth cat, leading them with a security box tied to her waist that deactivated each alarm with each step they took. How she'd hacked into the security system, only God knew, but so far it was working.

Once inside Jewel House, at the end of a corridor, two laser alarms beeped. The Crown Jewels were protected by bombproof glass and a million cameras it seemed, but they were not after the Crown Jewels.

At least twenty Yeomen Warders, mostly ex-military personnel provided on-site security and lived in the Tower itself. Two were currently about seven feet away, then when satisfied with the surrounding, they returned to their quarters.

With Leila's disarming of the security systems, they slipped into the vault room. Leila clipped open the large bolts that unlocked the back room where more treasures were held.

They found the room where the Koh-i-Noor had been stored before the Paris Exhibition—its velvet cushion empty and solitaire was an encouraging sight. A noise behind them alerted them. The thin thread holding her nerves together frayed, as a beefeater appeared through the door. His wide shoulders barely fit through the door.

Leila held the beefeater with a tight grip around the neck and secured him. He could barely breathe, and his air passages were blocked by the fury of her grasp. 'Now I'm going to release you,' she said 'but you have to cooperate. Don't make me break your neck,' Leila warned.

Frail as cotton in her martial art hold, the man's body went limp, his hands clasping at Leila's arm around his throat. He gave a sign of surrender. 'Just have a few questions,' Jave said.

The beefeater nodded slowly, his neck in a highly compromised position, a look of desperation crossing his eyes.

Jave wasn't done, and he unarmed the man of his weapon

and radio. 'Where's the safe?' Leila said. 'It's not on any of my blueprints.

'I don't know,' he muttered.

Leila pulled out her gun and held it to his forehead.

'Hey,' Jave said. 'Killing this guy gets us nothing. I don't think he knows anything about the safe. We'll have to find some other way.'

Leila landed a fist in the man's stomach, and he spat blood. She released him, and he fell back, hands to his middle.

It came as a whisper, through the window.

Garen's eyes shot open.

'Hey, who's over there?'

Drugs still clouding his vision, Garen couldn't see exactly who it was.

'History repeats itself,' said a voice.

'Who's this?' Garen said.

'If you want to get out of here, I can help you,' the voice insisted.

'Who are you?'

'Doesn't matter who I am. What matters is that you have a choice.'

The voice was coming from an intercom. Garen searched through foggy senses for the device, finally spotting it overhead.

'I don't really care what yours or their reasons are, but I certainly can tell you this. I can help you.'

'Whoever you are,' Garen managed, hobbling to the window, 'I don't need your sympathy or worse your sudden development of a conscience.

'I don't think I can take your offer,' Garen finished as he approached the window.

'Your daughter's life depends on your consideration.'

This time, Leila knocked the beefeater unconscious.

'The diamond must be in the White Tower in the chapel where no one would expect it to be,' Aria said.

'Why?'

'Because before the Crown Jewels were moved here, they used to be stored in Westminster Abbey in the Chamber of the Pyx. History shows jewels were often kept in a chapel. I suspect nobody would expect them to be there. That's where we need to go—to the White Tower. The chapel is on the second floor.'

Timothy made a move to the outer wall and glanced outside. They were locked in the beefeaters' quarters. It would be a few more moments before they could cross the plaza to the White Tower using Leila's night technology.

The Romanesque chapel on the second floor of the White Tower, found in the oldest part of William the Conqueror's fortress, was silent when they made it up to the level in question.

'Now what?' Leila said. 'By my count, I can only hold the alarms down for a maximum of ten more minutes before all hell breaks loose and all of London is after us.'

'Sounds like you do this for a living,' Timothy said.

Jave ignored him and stared at Aria. 'I know you're scared, but I trust your instincts as a jewel hunter. Where would they store the jewel? I know this is something that you've probably never done before. Nobody's going to find you out. You're with us.'

Timothy stepped forward. 'Jave is right. We can do this and in all of nine minutes be at out in the Thames via the Tower Subway.'

Aria glared at both men. She was keenly aware that Leila had her eyes on her too.

'All right,' she said. 'In the altar. If the East India Company stored away pirates' hordes, and if I am right, that altar floor hasn't been opened in at least a century and a half.'

Leila stomped to the altar.

'Careful,' Aria said. 'The chapel has many things that are nine hundred years old. We're not here to destroy property.'

'Then, princess, you have seven minutes to secure that diamond in your hand.'

'State records used to be stored in this chapel and were removed in 1858. A convenient time to stash a diamond. I believe once large presses were installed to help store documents. This meant they removed the original altar and a spiral staircase was installed, but when the records were taken away, the military wanted to use this space as a storeroom. Prince Albert, Queen Victoria's husband, refused, wanting this place to be returned to religious use. I think the spiral staircase was removed and a new tiled floor was installed,' Aria said, stepping around the altar floor. We need to slide the altar across to access that floor. I believe that is where you'll find the diamond.'

Leila got to work, with Jave and Timothy helping slide the altar. Aria joined in, never imagining how jewel hunting was so second nature to her—she'd even begun to think like the hoarders she sought day and night.

Once the altar was several inches to the right, they lifted tile after tile until it revealed a solid metal casket.

Leila broke into the chest. 'Payday.'

Leila's hand emerged with a rock partly concealed by her fingers, but even in the dim light, nothing prepared Aria for the sight. The size of two large eggs, uncut and in a raw state, her sharp mind told her it was the real thing and over 4000 carats.

Gasping, Leila handed it to Aria to authenticate. 'I must admit, I didn't think we'd find anything. Check it, then we go. Is this the real thing?'

Aria quickly pulled out her instruments and studied the rock. 'Yes, this is the real thing. Much bigger than the Koh-i-Noor.'

The alarms went off. A deafening shrilling that nearly made them forget the task at hand.

'We need to split,' Leila said. 'Time is up, so we revert to plan B.'

Scrambling to the lower floor, they charged along the innermost wall until they stood over a sewer leading to the Tower Subway. One by one, they threw themselves under until Timothy, last to go in, pulled the grid over the gutter.

By now sirens were sounding and blaring across the Tower grounds. Their boots thundered as they each scuttled through the tunnel to the abandoned iron tube, now fully submerged in the Thames.

'We swim for it,' Jave said. 'We'll meet at the Shangri-La Hotel at London Bridge. Be there tomorrow morning at nine in the lobby and follow the plan.'

Aria had done this several times before in the Maldives, but not in murky water. Swimming in the Thames wasn't going to be that much different, or was it?

Aria gasped. The water was faster and stronger. They had

to swim across, through the tunnel to the other side. They each pulled on a diving mask.

'Okay,' Timothy said, and in one deep breath, he secured his mask and submerged under the darkness.

Leila followed.

'I'll see you soon. Now go,' Jave said as she secured her mask and stumbled forward.

Darkness engulfed her as dimness overshadowed any sense or form in the water. Aria preserved, fighting a current with a force that she'd never fought before. After minutes of utter darkness, the tunnel spat her out a few metres from shore on the South Bank.

She pulled herself through the mud, breathless, and tore off her mask, gasping for air.

24

00:31 hrs

Aria moved away from the docks, alone. Though she was a strong swimmer, the river current had been powerful. Why had the guys not met her as planned before they took off to the hotel separately?

She moved her legs, pulling herself through mud and smut along the foreshore. Her ear strained at the dull thump of footsteps behind her.

She turned. 'Timothy?'

Timothy approached, his suit dripping mud.

'Where's Jave?' she said.

'With any luck at the bottom of the Thames.'

A flush of heat rose to her face and neck, mentally replaying Timothy's words. 'What have you done, Timothy?'

'He came between us, so he has gotten what was coming to him.'

Aria wiped mud from her chin, and in the dim midnight

light, she could just about make out Timothy's sneer. 'This isn't the time to joke. We just bloody robbed the Tower of London!'

She lunged for him and laid a strong strike across his jaw.

He pulled his pistol to her face. 'Enough. You should've listened to him when he told you not to trust me, but you were so blinded by our past. It could be completely amazing,' he said, aiming closer.

She blinked rapidly and froze on the spot. 'You wouldn't...'

'You could make me a happy guy. We can keep the diamond. Speaking of which? Hand it over.'

She shook her head, the gun still aimed at her. 'No.'

Her eyes strained as she felt the cold steel on her skin and shivered. 'No, Timothy.'

He gritted his teeth. 'Give me the diamond.'

She made a move forward, then hesitated, Timothy would smother her, or even shoot her. Perhaps leave her to die. How could he? He reached for the diamond in her breast pocket, then withdrew the gun and slotted it back into its holster. 'Your American won't be joining us.'

Aria's knees locked, nausea threatening to take over. 'What have you done?'

'If the Thames hasn't swallowed him, the police have him by now. You should be proud. He'll be a headliner tomorrow.'

Adrenaline welled in her, and she lunged for his neck. All her fitness paid off in one blow. Her hands chopped his neck like blades, then she finished him off with two quick left kicks.

Unable to digest where the fury had come from, she watched him. When he regain his senses, his eyes communicated he had no qualms about hitting a woman. His knuckles crashed home, knocking her senseless.

Aria pulled her face from the cold mud. A chilling breeze seeped into her bones, and she set off after Timothy who'd started for the stairs up the river bank. She reached for his shoulder, span him, and kneed him in the groin.

He recoiled.

He drew in for a punch, and she retreated. As a treasure hunter, she and Maxwell always had been ready for whatever criminals they would run into. And Jave had made sure she could handle the rest.

Timothy charged her. She scanned the foreshore then raced towards the bobbing speed boat that Leila had arranged for them. Timothy jumped in when she started the engine, and the boat waded out as they struggled for its control. Timothy had taken the diamond and placed it in the thigh pocket of his trousers. She could just reach the rock and saw her chance. Her snatch was sharp and fierce.

Timothy saw her intent. 'Not on your life, beautiful,' he said, retrieving it.

He aimed for and secured the rock. This time her kick was lethal as she booted the gem out of his hand, tossing into the river. Without warning, a police boat, its siren blaring, sped towards them.

On instinct, Aria threw herself into the water. Timothy roared the boat's engines. She didn't care if they got him as she dove for the diamond.

Aria thrashed at the current.

Nothing mattered anymore. When she made it to shore, her body refused to move further, her muscles quivering. She shut her eyes and awoke when sunlight hit her face. The Thames was no Indian Ocean, its current vicious and tidal.

Had Timothy done something to Jave? Was he that much of a thug?

If Timothy had trapped him, the police might find them. It was now a waiting game. She staggered from the South Bank.

Rush-hour was early in the city she struggled up the pavement heaving. She blended in the crowds that stomped the South Bank walkaway. An early jogger jolted past her, nearly knocking her to the pavement.

How long had she been out there, cold?

Her limbs heavy, cold rippled through her muscled as she made her way towards the Shangri-La Hotel, rubbing off as much mud as she could.

She meandered towards Borough Market crossing the street to the Post Office box with three package lockers they'd arranged. Aria punched in the code and pulled the first open. She found the change of clothes they'd arranged. The others hadn't picked up their things. Aria threw a coat over her shoulders and wiped her face with some cosmetic wipes. She then pulled out a money purse and a mobile phone. She headed towards the Shard and then through to the lobby, smearing away as much of the Thames experience from her body.

Three minutes later, she was in her room and collapsed on her bed.

Jave hadn't checked in.

Timothy had done something.

She had two choices: one, go to the authorities and tell them the truth, or two, do nothing.

It all depended on the morning's news.

She showered and grabbed a quick room service breakfast before heading to the lobby.

The wait was agony as she watched the door sitting concealed in the corner of the lobby. With every minute she prayed Jave would walk through to the hotel lobby. She glanced at an elderly couple across from her. Nearly toppling over, her pulse quickened as she read the headline on the newspaper the man was reading. The Guardian reported it all.

There was no turning back.

The heist was in the morning's headlines.

25

08:23 hrs

Timothy's eyes were firmly on Fenderson as he made his way into the private meeting room at Claridges Hotel.

'You had one job,' Fenderson said, tossing the paper on the table in front of him. His face grim, Timothy took a step back when he eyed Iver's men at the door.

Iver raised an eyebrow. 'Where is it?'

His voice firm, Timothy spoke for the first time since entering the room. 'I can still get you the diamond.'

'Your time is up. I sent you to the Maldives with one job only, Captain Seeds. Restrain that girl. Turns out she's a better swimmer than you are.'

Timothy had come this close. This wasn't the moment to let go of what he had worked hard on. Rightly or wrongly, Fenderson owed him money, and he wasn't leaving without it.

House of Garrard
Central London
09:13 hrs

'The police will know who I am. If I don't hurry, they'll certainly find me. I didn't know where else to go,' Aria said when she appeared at Parkinson's door, her pulse speeding.

Parkinson drew her quietly into his office and closed the door.

'You can stay here as long as you want. Or, I can help you disappear, I've done it many times myself,' Parkinson said. 'You found the diamond, didn't you?'

She showed it to him.

Deep lines puckered his forehead. 'Incredible. I hoped, but never once believed it was real. How did you? ... I'd better not ask. What are you going to do now?'

She set her hands on her knees. 'I don't know where to go.'

Aria's phone rang.

'Count Valex. Thanks for calling me back. Have you found my father? Jave?'

'No. Are you okay?' Valex said. 'Your father hasn't been picking up my calls for more than twenty-four hours.'

'Is there nothing you can do with your intelligence connections? Anything?'

Aria sensed hesitation in his voice, followed by a long pause. 'I'm sorry to inform you, Aria. Jave Lincoln's body was found in the Thames. He's gone. It was on the secure wires this morning. They have pinned the Tower robbery on him. Incidentally, the authorities haven't been able to identify what was stolen.'

She gave Parkinson a blank stare as Valex continued. 'I'm afraid someone has to come and identify the body. Jave has a blank on international databases. It's as if he doesn't exist. How well did you know him?'

Aria dropped the phone unable to take any more unwelcome news. A cramping moved to her stomach, and she clutched her arms. The only ally she had had was the very man who had betrayed her.

Leila was gone too, vanished, just like her credentials had promised.

And now, she was the only one who could identify the body of the man she feared she had loved and yet not really known.

Garen was badly hurt.

His last attempt at an escape had left him with a bleeding lip and a fractured knee.

MI6 officers had done their work on his ageing body. He wasn't thirty anymore. Twenty-four hours under house arrest in an abandoned safe-house facility was more than his bruised body could take.

He checked the wound on his leg and the cuff on his hand. He would live; this wasn't the worst that he'd seen. A simple hack to the security system could open the secured door of the room he was in, and a distraction would do the rest. He now had to find the right moment.

The moment came eight minutes later.

An overweight MI6 officer made his way towards him. 'Right. Toilet break.'

Garen waited until his cuff had been released and a quick slam into the man's neck was all it took. The man landed on the carpet with a thud, and Garen secured his gun, mobile phone, and earpiece. He hobbled to the now open door and drew it slightly. After looking both ways, he scuttled out of the safe house and into the woods, the fresh air stinging his nostrils.

In the distance, he caught sight of a river.

Just where the heck was he?

They had brought him here drugged. He shuffled past three MI6 guards unnoticed until he came to the river's bank.

He would testify at that hearing in twenty-four hours if it was the last thing he would do. Garen couldn't leave it to chance. He pulled out the mobile phone to see if he could get a signal and any GPS information on his location.

The phone was nearly out of battery. Maybe a few more minutes was all it would take. If he could send an encrypted signal to Caroline, she would make all the necessary arrangements. She'd taken him out of worse binds. The fifteen years they'd worked together had to count for something. She knew everything about his getaways.

He studied the device. It had to be one of the world's most connected phones.

Come on!

It had to work. The number of satellite networks connected to this little thing was beyond reason. He'd seen it himself at the surveillance offices of GCHQ.

The phone sprang to life but died as soon as it had started.

If he testified at The International Court of Justice against the Koh-i-Noor the way he wanted, it would be treason on both his countries, and the governments wouldn't take it lightly, but Aria would be safe. Which meant, the DEI would be his new worst enemy.

A branch cracked behind him.

He zipped around.

The blow caught him in the jaw, and his eyes trundled as he crashed to the ground.

26

Three Kilometres outside London
10:52 hrs

Aria's boots brushed against long grasses and wildflowers that grew against the hunting cabin. She stomped up to the front entrance and shuffled in, closing the door. She set her back against the door and breathed hard.

Her cabin was an hour outside of London. The place hadn't been used since her mother died. Her father put it on the market months after the funeral, and when it had failed to sell, Aria had asked they keep it. At least, for a little while.

It was a place of solace, one she kept to herself. She'd never come here much as a child, and now, no one would link her to it.

Leaves flapped in the wind outside, and Aria found the key in the hanging lamp box. She stumbled in and locked the door behind her. She reached for a blanket from the lone bed to shield her glowing, feverish skin from the worsening draughts seeping through the cabin walls and coming down the chimney. She longed to make a fire, but her limbs wouldn't move, and her burning fever would not let her shuffle a muscle.

Yet, she shivered in the darkness, struggled to the bed, and slumped on it. The swim had taken its toll, but something else had brought on the fever. Reaching deep in her wet suit with difficulty, she drew out the diamond.

She hit her head against the pillow and stared at it. The sparkle it let off even in the dim morning light mesmerised her.

Aria's eyes couldn't leave the diamond. She couldn't recall how long she stared at the blasted thing. Why had this diamond, much larger than all other diamonds, not been known to the world?

She was spent now. Everything had gone wrong.

The plan had been to grab the diamond and barter for Emily's life, and now Leila and Timothy were gone, and all she had was a stone worth possibly more than $11 billion, or a heck of a lot more than the Koh-i-Noor, but this priceless diamond couldn't buy back the life of the man she'd lost.

Jave was gone.

He'd been the one person that had made her start trusting again and affected her in a way that not even Maxwell had.

How was she going to find Emily now? A sister who'd disappeared thirteen years ago and was now supposedly alive. She stared ahead through the window—the earth made bare by dawn's light shining through the curtains. How she longed for the comfort of a fire's warmth, but she couldn't start one without drawing attention.

Her eyes begged for sleep. For a minute, she thought she heard the thump of boots across the creaking floorboards outside, but then she decided it was her pounding head. The nausea was now rising to her throat. She could barely see in the dim light, as she snuggled in the blankets. She had to sleep this fever off.

Her eyes closed. They opened at what seemed like hours later to the sound of a ringing phone.

Aria reached for it and swiped the answer button to the right.

'You can't get rid of me that easily.'

Timothy!

'It will only be a quick trip to the media to pitch you as the Tower of London mastermind thief. Don't make me turn you in. Do the right thing now. If you want to be safe, I suggest you listen to me carefully. I want the diamond. It won't take me long to find you, you know.'

Timothy could do it. Not only was he ex-SAS, but he was also severely determined. He would keep his word. How could he do this to her?

It would only be a matter of hours before he would find out exactly where she was. Anger welled up in her, but fever forbade her from concentrating.

She gathered every ounce of energy to respond. 'I'll never trust you after what you've done to Jave and to me,' Aria said.

'It's only business, darling Aria. Some of us haven't had the privilege you had growing up. We need to make a real living, and it isn't my fault that the education I was afforded created desires in me I couldn't pay for. I'll give you twenty-four hours to provide me with the diamond. If you want to see your sister alive, I suggest you cooperate.'

It was almost impossible to think, but she wouldn't deter in her determination. She wouldn't give it to him. 'How could you, Timothy? We trusted you. I will not help you.'

'You have one day. You'll receive a message with instructions of where the exchange will happen.'

Aria hung up the phone.

She didn't know how long she sat in silence, wanting to crush the phone between her fingers. Her mind forbade her to even consider his proposal. In all of about ten minutes, she dialled a number. 'Count Valex?'

'Aria? Where are you?'

Her beaded brow perfused, and shivers shot through her feverish body. 'Count Valex. I don't know, but... I need... your—'

Her hand released the handset, and it slipped to the floor.

New York City
05:27 hrs

He found the rental at the end of the low-roof car park at JFK international airport. Jave hurried to the last-minute Ford Escape he'd managed to secure and slotted the key into the ignition before sinking into the driver's seat. He eased the car out of the southeast of Lower Manhattan, past a Jaguar whose wheels squealed as an impatient driver made a sharp turn in front of him.

He stepped on the gas expecting an hour's journey with the traffic he'd caught out of JFK.

He rechecked the details. Jave had never been to any Department of Economic Intelligence building. Granted, it wasn't that obvious to most people. What he was looking for would be tucked away from the centre of the city.

Forty minutes later, he found a parking space between a secluded road with two warehouses and a tall stone building. He studied the five-storey tower in front of him.

A homeless man reclined at the corner of the street, obscured by sheets of newspapers. The isolated properties were at the end of the car park in the industrial district next to Gowanus Canal, behind the Ninth Street Bridge.

He checked his watch. The first time he'd been brought here he'd been blindfolded. He'd been shoved unceremoniously into the building. Thirty-six hours later, they'd released him with the shadow mission to find the scientist working at Altaneus Corporation. His cover was that he'd be a jewel expert to work on the desalination solar panel project. Hudson had been noticeably clear about that, but Hudson now needed to end this.

Jave knew enough about gems, but by no means did he have a graduate degree in geology like Aria. Yet, he'd had to brush up on a few things. He'd sworn to find his way back here if only to teach the bastards who'd brought him here a lesson in manners.

The DEI would be all over The International Court of Justice's hearing preparations by now, if at all, to keep order and obtain a verdict that ensured their interest stayed on the right side of economics.

He heard a noise behind him and turned. Agent Amos Hudson's office would be on the third floor. He made his way to the back of the building and found a service entrance. This is where all the catering was brought in and out for the two hundred or so people who worked in the establishment. He'd done his homework the night before checking up on anything his intelligence services at Interpol could tell him about the Department of Economic Intelligence.

He moved to the side of the door when it opened. A short man carrying two empty crates of vegetable waste stepped out into the open car park. Jave moved around the bins.

He snuck in through the doorway, found his way towards the fire escape, and looked up at the flight of stairs. He started his ascent and found the office only three doors from the elevators. He checked both sides. The halls were empty. Jave placed his hand on his gun and opened the door. Slowly. Then stopped.

Shuffling noises behind him alerted him, and he turned.

Hudson advanced, then stood back, an astounded look crossing his face. The large man reached for his gun.

Jave set one foot in front of the other. 'Not so fast. I'm a better shot than you are.'

Hudson knew better and replaced his weapon.

Jave studied Hudson's eyes. 'Why didn't you tell me you were after the desalination technology from the beginning?'

'What? And show all our cards? What you need to know is that we failed. We found the desalination research almost by accident at Altaneus. Our interest was first with the economic imbalance that would occur if the Koh-i-Noor was an issue of international politics. We never banked on the technology until MI6 started sniffing around.' Hudson gave out a disdainful snort. 'You can speculate all you want; your mission was simple. Get the girl, Emily Raith, so she could work for us.'

Hudson stepped inside his office and motioned to Jave. 'You better come inside.'

Jave moved cautiously through the unfamiliar room.

'Like I said, all you need to know is that we failed,' Hudson continued. 'We found Parkinson's data and the desalination research by accident.'

Hudson peeked up at Jave before continuing. 'You can speculate all you want. We're running out of time.'

Jave wasn't bothered. He wanted to find the underlying cause of the matter.

'What I do know may pique your interest,' Hudson said. 'James Parkinson worked for the Department of Economic Intelligence on a contract until he took off with our files in

1977 and made his way to England. He soon found employment with the Raith family, and eventually, that's where he transferred a great deal of knowledge to those girls. They may have been five and seven at the time, but they learned fast.'

Hudson strolled to the window and glared outside for a few seconds before turning towards Jave. He tossed a file to the table. 'Emily Raith, as a seven-year-old, had a curiosity only seen in the most prodigious of children. She continued to develop that knowledge as she grew and was the only one who held the answers to the connection between the diamond and the scientific effects thereof regarding desalination.'

'That so?' Jave said, raising his eyebrow. 'You knew that from the start. Why put her in danger and now her sister? You could've protected them, even at an early age when Parkinson arrived.'

'We lost trace of Parkinson when he left Princeton. For several years we had no idea where he was. By the time we discovered he'd been working for the Raiths, he was long gone, and the deed was already done.'

'I don't believe you,' Jave said.

'You don't understand, Lincoln. You think the Department of Economic Intelligence is the bad guy. Like you guys at Interpol, we're not the bad ones. We're just trying to keep your country safe.'

'At what expense,' Jave said, feeling his heart starting to pound. 'People's lives? Breaking up families?'

'You can't pin that on us. Raith chose his allegiance to Britain when he married that countess. For us, he just happened to be in the right place at the right time. You can see that the country is in grave danger and that important technology is exposed, and we can't have that.' Hudson raised an eyebrow. 'Shouldn't you guys at Interpol be looking for the missing diamond? How could that slip from you? You guys have moles in every police force and government intelligence unit from here to Jakarta.'

'What outcome do you want in this case?' Jave said.

'Follow me, and you'll find out,' Hudson said.

They left the office and took the lift to the fifth floor. A meeting was already in session. The lawyer-type at the end of the room distributed a set of papers to the ten participants who sat around a long boardroom table. The standing man gave Jave one glance and continued talking, 'We've managed to secure presence in the hearing as an independent observer in The Hague. When the Koh-i-Noor case opens, we will be there.'

Jave took a seat with Hudson in the back of the room.

Hudson nodded for the man to continue.

The barrister cleared his throat. 'The Koh-i-Noor doesn't rightly belong to anyone—according to history. What we risk here is years of Altaneus's research getting into unwanted hands. With both Parkinson at large, the girl Emily out of the picture, and the diamond missing, I would say that the answer to all of this is silencing the Raith family for the last time.'

Aria's eyes shot open. The sun's rays penetrated the curtains as she pulled her body upright on the bed. She checked the time on her smartwatch. A quick recall of the previous day's events made her twitch more than she wanted. The diamond was precisely where she'd left it.

Timothy's message had come to the phone two hours ago. She has slept for more than twelve hours.

The details were clear.

4:00 pm was the arranged time. They were to meet at a

carnival in the village up the road. The meeting would be at the county fair a few miles up the main road in the village.

She rose from the bed, her fever now a faint memory, but a quick glance in the mirror revealed her paling skin. Aria washed and found some old clothes and walking boots back in the room.

After her quick shower and change, she grabbed her few belongings, her phone and smartwatch, and left the cabin locked by the back door. She lifted the garage door at the back of the cabin where a dusty Defender had been parked for more days that she could remember.

Aria arrived at the carnival and parked the old family Defender in a parking space several hundred feet away from the main carnival grounds. Canvas tents with country agricultural produce bustled with activity. The expansive locality was brightly lit, and sounds of chirping and clattering made Aria turned to the grassy fields in the distance. That would be the most natural getaway should she need it.

She advanced towards the main stretch between the several amusement rides and carnival games.

A balloon man disguised as a clown brushed past her, and she jumped involuntarily.

Timothy was late. The demanded exchange place was near the fire breathers. The agreement was simple: information about Emily for the diamond.

How could Timothy have done this? If it hadn't been for Jave, he wouldn't have known about the existence of the long-forgotten diamond. Had Timothy always been a criminal? What had happened to him? They'd been so close in high school. Granted they'd fought like cockerels, but even she couldn't see him betraying them as he had.

Aria caught sight of the newscast on the BBC in a café at the end of the main stretch of the carnival ground. Loud music prevented her from hearing the details, but one glance at the images showed her that the news reports were covering the theft at the Tower of London.

They'd made international news now. She turned her eyes away from the story. That's when she felt the gun in her back.

Timothy and two men in dark clothing surrounded her like hawks. 'Let the only move you make, Miss Raith, be the one when you hand over the diamond,' Timothy threatened.

Aria took in a deep breath and reached down the side of her leg. Before she could move another muscle, a shot fired in the air. Terrified carnival visitors sprayed in all directions as a second shot fired.

Deep-fried food and grilling meat turned over on one stall. The crowds dispersed as balloons popped, and screams rose above the blaring music.

Her nose caught the waft of oily sweet batter as dusted doughnuts fell on the ground by her feet.

She took her moment.

Aria's feet hurried over grassy fields. She did not dare glance back. With her heart pumping fast, she crossed into the village near the carnival grounds.

She took cover in the first building in front of her—a business that stored industrial cleaning goods. Brushing through into the corridor doors, Aria burst into a room at the back of the first hallway.

She shut the door, needing to think.

Nestled between shelving units storing chemicals, glass

cleaners, floor wash, stainless steel cleaner and sanitisers, the smell of dust and stagnant water attacked her nose.

She waited.

Forty minutes later, an ache in her left leg alerted her to move. She pulled off her smartwatch and destroyed it. It could send a signal, and Timothy, with his connections, could pick it up. She heard the loud jingle of keys and the squeaking of a cartwheel by the door. Soon footsteps racing past the door made her hold her breath.

The door cracked open, and a gun poked through the door's edge.

She held her breath, her eyes, widened, her heart racing. When a face drew into frame, at first she refused to register the details.

She knew him.

Jave shot towards her suited in tactical gear. Too stunned to speak, Aria registered her deep breath of relief.

'Jave. What? ... How?'

She threw her arms around him.

'Not yet, sweetheart,' Jave said.

'What happened to you? Are you okay? I thought you'd left me,' Aria said.

He shot her an overconfident grin. 'Never. Timothy and gang won't be far, though. We need to move. Are you hurt?'

She shook her head, then planted a swift kiss on her lips. 'I had to keep his men away from you. When we got to the Tower Subway. They had been waiting for us and the diamond. He and Leila had other plans. Did you get the jewel?'

Aria hesitated, then nodded slowly.

Whatever she felt about his behaviour, he was the only

person she could trust. It was time she started trusting in someone.

She held onto his arm as he led her back the way he'd come, checking both sides of the corridor. 'What happened to you? I couldn't find you. You weren't at the meeting place.'

Jave withdrew from her arms and looked her in the eyes. 'I followed Timothy after he tried to drown me in the Thames. I knew he was threatening you. I'm sorry I left you, but I knew as a skilled diver you could make it. I knew the water wouldn't get you. Timothy wasn't strong enough to take you out. I saw you. I left when I knew you were okay. But only for a while. I'm back now.'

She smiled briefly and showed him the diamond. 'Now we really need to find Emily.'

27

Garen moaned, his head throbbing as the man dragged him in the woods.

No. They couldn't take him back to the safe house. He arched his back intending to fight his attacker, but his energy was spent and he let the man drag him, his legs hoisted at the man's waist.

Then gunfire...

A gunshot to the leg and the man dropped.

Garen crawled to a nearby tree trump and took shelter from any further shots.

He peered once in the direction of the fire. Behind the mist, Jave and Aria charged through fog and branches.

Too stunned to speak, he only managed a weak, 'Aria?'

'Father.'

'How did you find me?'

She shot Jave a look. 'He did. After all, you trained him. Caroline got your message and tracked your mobile phone. She then contacted Jave.'

Garen pulled himself together and turned around to see if they'd been followed. 'Come on, we need to get out of here.'

They moved to the edge of the woods where Aria and Jave had parked the Defender.

As Garen opened the passenger door, he stopped. 'I know you wanted to believe it, sweetheart, and for a moment I wanted it for you as well, and for myself. I wanted to believe that Emily was alive, but I think it was all manufactured by Fenderson to get the diamond and her research. All they were interested in was the Koh-i-Noor. They've used our most vulnerable selves to get to us.'

When they were in the car and heading towards London with Jave at the wheel, Garen spoke with difficulty, still suffering from bruises and drugged senses, but he wanted her to know. 'Aria, it's time you hear the truth for me. We lost Emily, and it was my fault. I should've stopped her from going to Altaneus Corporation and working for the government. Iver Fenderson created so many problems for us.'

'Let's not talk about it now. You're hurt.'

'No, I want to you to know. The minute we, the government, discovered Lord Asterley's letters and the East India Company documents, my family's fate was sealed too. I have to testify to make things right. I won't let your mother's family suffer any more.'

Garen leaned back in the seat, his wounds still stinging. 'Aria, your great-great-great-grandfather, Lord Asterley, knew Golconda was where the Koh-i-Noor had come from. The properties in the valleys where the Koh-i-Noor diamond came from were like any other. No one really understood them, though. They didn't have the know-how and technology then, yet Lord Asterley knew there was more to it, so he wrote about those valleys. The Boston Tea Company and the East India Company conspired. He wrote in his diaries on three occasions that one day, after it was given to Queen Victoria, should the Koh-i-Noor come back to haunt them, they would need to find a way to return it to India. He documented all this information in three letters that he placed in the East India Company archives, but then after that, they disappeared.'

'And we find ourselves here, more than a hundred and fifty years later at the crossroads of history?'

Garen took a deep breath. 'They were known as the Lahore Letters, and they were written as a backup plan should anyone need to return the Koh-i-Noor diamond to India to protect themselves and the nation, but over the years the letters went missing and passed through many hands. Eventually, the letters were split into three to protect the conspiracy—as you know.'

Aria watched him as if she was seeing him for the last time. 'Father, what are we going to do, now?'

'I need to tell the courts the truth. MI6 doesn't want me to, because it exposes them and Emily as a spy working for them. This would have stayed quiet, but then, in the sixties, James Parkinson was working for the DEI. He studied the meteorite activity in the rocks around Golconda and was certain that the properties could lead to superior technological research, but the DEI had his daughter, and he refused to give them more information, so he ran away, to us. He believed that there would be other added properties that he could find in the composition not only of the mines but also the diamonds. Both Clarisse's family in the UK and Jave Lincoln's family in the US at the time were sworn to secrecy to protect the Lahore Letters and the mining area, then I did the rest. I protected Emily and Parkinson's research.'

'I see,' Aria said.

'No one would ever have thought that my girls would have an inherent interest in geology. And that Parkinson and Emily would be the ones to unearth the true potential of not only the Koh-i-Noor but also the Kollur mines.'

'Do you have to testify? We could just not show up,' Aria said.

'I would then be running forever and that would pass on to you. The three letters are needed to prove that the Koh-i-Noor belongs to India. The truth is I will testify to divert any attention from the mines around Golconda and the meteorite activity Emily and Parkinson worked on, which will lead to mass production of desalination. This is exactly what Emily must have wanted to prevent. And now, the disappearance of the Koh-i-Noor diamond makes the whole problem go away.'

After dropping Aria and Garen off at their hotel, Jave cornered his rented BMW into Putney, in Southwest London. He took the Thames road, where a series of boathouses and morning rowers were in full activity preparing for the morning row along the Thames. He parked the car in a quiet street and got out.

A stack of unopened newspaper drops blocked his entrance. He reached from the Guardian paper, and his eyes fell on the headline story.

The Koh-i-Noor thieves strike for the Crown Jewels. The thieves broke into the Tower with sophisticated high-tech manoeuvres, but it is yet unclear what they walked off with. The Koh-i-Noor is still at large and will be contested in The International Court of Justice a day from now.

Two minutes later, he entered a boathouse and closed the door behind him. He'd made sure he hadn't been followed. His eyes strained in the dark space, but sure enough, he could make out the details of his private boathouse, still secure, and he hadn't been followed.

He checked his security cabinet and took a quick glance at the cameras on every corner of the building.

All good.

Jave fished through drawers and located the diving suit he'd used to make his escape and stay underwater for hours, only coming up to make sure no one had seen him that night at the Tower.

Aria was safe, and Timothy was taken care of—for now. He moved to the back of the building where a small storage unit was housed and keyed in the code to open the lock. It opened easily. He changed and suited up, placing his pistol within the suit.

Within the hour, he parked at 10 Downing Street and went through the security checks through a rear entrance—as he'd been instructed. Once in a grand office, he moved to the mahogany table and set the diamond on the table in front of the prime minister. 'I'm handing you this,' he said to the prime minister.

The middle-aged prime minister's eyes widened at the diamond. 'So, this is greater than the Koh-i-Noor. An unknown diamond to the world is now in my possession. What do you want in return, Lincoln, Interpol didn't make that clear? The Palace hasn't been informed. They understand the diamond's fate. Now, they believe the newspapers are just speculating, and that MI6 is onto the Koh-i-Noor.'

Jave eyed the prime minister, his gut telling him to beware. 'I'll let you deal with the Palace. That's not why I'm here, but what this does is keep everyone happy. You get a jewel to satisfy the Palace, and we deal with the media. Interpol can keep this all quiet and away from you and, now, we can clear

Garen Raith and arrest Robey and Timothy Seeds. He's not after the interests of your cabinet. I will find Iver Fenderson. I also want you to release a set of historical documents from the East India Company—I will let you know which ones. They won't be missed because history doesn't know they exist. I want you to hand them to Garen Raith, out of the public eye. Those documents pertain to his family, and he deserves them. You'll also release anything the government has on his daughters and expunge it. Am I clear?'

The prime minister thought for a moment, leaned forward, and asked in a broken whisper, 'Then, you go away?'

Jave nodded. 'Interpol disappears like smoke.'

Jave took the same back exit he'd used when he'd arrived. He now had to deal with a tougher business than Interpol's agenda.

How was he going to keep Aria's trust?

Rosewood Hotel, London

'And?' Aria said when Jave returned and poked his head around her hotel room door.

'The prime minister will clear your father's name. They don't have any information on Emily but will help where they can.'

Aria stepped aside as she let him into the hotel presidential suite she shared with her father. 'We've lost the diamond to keep the authorities off our backs and clear the Raith name, but I still don't have Emily.'

'We will find Emily, if she's alive, but we won't be criminals,' Jave said. 'Timothy was bluffing at the carnival. He had no idea where she was.'

She thought for a minute. 'I never wanted my father serving his country, ever since I was a child.'

'Why?' Jave said moving her to a sofa. 'Is he okay?'

'Yeah, he's sleeping. I had a doctor see him earlier. None of us in the family did really, even my mother. We all knew that one day he'd be torn between his two nations. Just never imagined it would be in this way. No matter what he does, he's stuck. He showed his allegiance to Britain by marrying my mother. In many ways, my mother's family wouldn't have it any other way. He was a Raith; she was an aristocrat. The only way for my father to prove his love for her was to serve the British.'

'Your father did what's right for his family.' Jave smiled. 'You need to cut him some slack. He's paid enough of his dues, and he's done everything he can to keep you safe. Whatever else you think of him, the one thing I do know is he cared deeply about his girls. Much like I do. Especially, this one,' he said with a hand to his cheek. 'Tell me this. Would your mother approve?'

'I...'

Before she could even mouth any words, Jave glanced at her for a sign of objection, then kissed her lips and crushed her to him.

The caress was a command, and the nearness of him gave her comfort.

She sighed and caressed the length of his back, then she pulled away briefly. 'Jave, we failed to find the Koh-i-Noor diamond. It has a lot of blood on it, and my family is the most recent victim. I should stop before I lose my entire family. That diamond has always been cursed.'

'Don't give up on them, Aria,' he said, his voice sounding tired.'

'But we can't win against the Koh-i-Noor diamond. Its

existence, and now political significance, has hit its latest target,' Aria said. 'Us.'

'We will. Together. From the little I knew of your sister when I was in Botswana, she was more than just brains,' he said, his voice trailing.

Her hand found his. 'I missed her so much when she left. She was incredibly young. She saw more in most things than anyone initially believed possible, like with the Altaneus project and its implications on the future. That's what she was always good at—proving theories.'

'I believe you are too,' he said. 'You're a good judge of character.'

'No, I'm not. I let Timothy hurt you. I'm sorry for bringing him between us.'

This time Aria rose, her hand still in his. The Koh-i-Noor has failed us too as it did Duleep Singh—and many a sultan before him. That stone was cursed for years. It crossed blood hand to blood hand and brought bad luck to kings and rulers—and maybe to the Raiths as well. The Koh-i-Noor curse has come to haunt us. All 186 carats of it, have become my worst enemy.'

'Don't say that,' Jave said with a gentle squeeze of her hand.

Aria turned when she heard a noise at the door.

'Come in.' Aria called.

A hotel attendant appeared, and he moved to the entryway. 'We have your suit ready.'

Aria thanked him and closed the door. 'Right,' she said, holding up the dress. 'This might bring us luck in tomorrow's court case. It's one way of having my mother with us. She loved a Givenchy dress.'

28

International Court of Justice
The Hague
10:00 hrs

The judge moved to the microphone. 'The opposing sides will each make an opening statement, then each side can pose questions to the other.'

Iver gave Garen a nod as the Indian officials representing the Indian government rose to give their statements. The first man moved to the microphone. 'India could claim much to be returned to its land, especially if you were to put a microscope on history and trace the profits made from India by the East India Company,' he continued. 'The Company had a monopoly of Indian trade over decades, and it intervened in Indian affairs.'

Garen took a deep breath as Jave encouraged him with a quiet nod.

Aria, seated next to him, knew it had to be done; this was the only way to keep international peace between two great nations.

'The British government took charge of all the East India Company's profits, but we're not going to get into that at all.'

The Indian solicitor-general took a deep breath. 'The history of the Koh-i-Noor is filled with violence, yet we seek to resolve this amicably. Wherever it has gone, the Koh-i-Noor diamond has brought destruction, division, greed, dread, envy, distrust, and war. It's a known fact that until diamond mines were discovered in Brazil in 1725, all diamonds came from India. Most ancient diamonds weren't mined but came down the river spewed from volcanoes. This means our forefathers received and extracted them like gravel on ancient riverbeds, like crystals. It was rare to see a large diamond, but it did happen, and the Koh-i-Noor is one such find, where, on occasion, one could pick up or find a diamond as large as a chicken's egg.'

He paused and looked around the room. 'One such place is called Golconda; these are diamond fields between Hyderabad and the Carnatic coast.'

He continued reading his statement, only looking up to glare at the faces in the room. 'Lord Dalhousie, the British governor-general, removed the diamond from ownership by force from 10-year-old Maharajah Duleep Singh in 1849 when the East India Company seized Punjab. Thus, the diamond belongs to India. For years it has been the single largest loot the British took from India never to be returned. It is now time to set that record straight. With the diamond not only mined in our country but unjustly seized from our rulers, it's time to own up to a disastrous past and return the diamond to India where it came from.'

Soft murmurs began in the room.

Garen rubbed his hands together.

The governor-general took a seat, and the British defence rose. He was a short man with a balding spot, and one of

Britain's top barristers. 'Members of the jury, you can't let history be punished when it is all in the past. Might I remind you that none of the people responsible for these acts can stand to defend themselves. At least as claimed by the opponent.'

'The East India Company brought prosperity, civilisation, and education to India for which the nation now currently enjoys. There's no evidence that the stone was robbed, nor involuntarily snatched. It was gifted by the successors of Maharajah Ranjit Singh to the East India Company. They say it was compensation for helping them in the Sikh wars. Contrary to what the prosecution has brought forward, no literature exists, nor any actual reference to their claim in any official documentation. Anything from mediaeval Delhi Sultanate and so on. Instead, what we find are textual references to large diamonds of all kinds—but not the Koh-i-Noor diamond. So, its ownership isn't recorded anywhere in history.'

He sat down.

The judge scanned the room.

'May we call the British High Commissioner to India, Garen Raith, to the stand.'

The judge nodded to the Indian barrister. 'If there are no more statements, then we shall begin the questioning. High Commissioner Garen Raith, you may come to the stand.'

Garen rose and took the stand. After he had sworn-in, he took a seat.

'High Commissioner Raith, you're the UK representative to India, and therefore versed in all matters on British-Indian relations,' the Indian barrister began.

Garen nodded and locked eyes with Jave for a brief second, then shot Aria a quick glance.

'High Commissioner Raith,' began the barrister. 'Can you

please read from exhibit A from these records by Lord Asterley, starting with this line.' He pointed to a section of the three Asterley letters.

Garen looked up to the jury. 'This hearing can't be valid for the diamond in question can't be authenticated.'

'You'll answer the question,' the judge said.'

Garen could usually hide his discomfort, but Aria knew he was struggling with that piece of information as he took a deep breath and read from the letter as instructed.

'I, Lord Asterley, as a result of this, state that upon witnessing the transfer of this precious stone to London, three unknown elements surround it that I will articulate in separate documents. The first concerns the mines where the diamond comes from. Here, the Company have discovered energies of nature we cannot explain—and we do not understand. It is still unknown to man what inhabits the soil. There are rumours of caves, but we found nothing. These energies—should they endanger our nation, or the Crown, and should we need evidence of where the diamond came from, so it can be returned without any contest—lead me to claim that the Koh-i-Noor came from the Golconda mines. The research conducted by Lord Dalhousie, on the history of the diamond, concludes that the composition soils should be questioned. Its formation is like no other...'

'Stop!' the Indian barrister said.

Garen swallowed hard.

'Now read this,' the barrister said, handing him a second document.

Garen continued. *'The second unknown is the fact that the diamond is claimed by three factions in India. How can we assume to claim it when they are two other lords with their hands at the ready, and I fear their claims could be equally justified? It should be noted that the Company has used the Koh-i-Noor as collateral for trade with the Boston Tea Company...'*

'Thank you very much. Now this,' the barrister continued.

Garen finally read the letter Clarisse had bequeathed to Aria. '*And the third is the fact that there might be more than one diamond. All cursed with blood and—*'

'That's enough. Thank you, High Commissioner Raith.' The barrister then turned to the audience and then the judge. 'You see, the British East India Company knew they were sending a diamond that didn't belong to them. This qualifies India as the world's first miner of diamonds. Regardless of where the diamond has gone, India rightfully owns it.'

The room grew quiet.

Aria headed for the door after the British barrister at recess. She took her father's hand as the barrister turned her way.

'What happens now?' Garen said as they took a few minutes in a quiet waiting room.

'We wait. It could go any way at this rate,' their barrister said.

'Put me on the stand,' Aria said.

Jave, Garen, and the barrister and his team shot curious gazes at her.

The room that morning had been filled with many interested parties. The media was plastered to the wings with representatives from both nations and had been in abundance in the room that morning

'Trust me. Put me on—as a gemmologist. I have found many lost treasures in the past, and I'm sure everyone is curious about what information I can bring on the Koh-i-Noor, especially after the media have speculated my involvement for days.'

. . .

They returned to the courtroom minutes later, and Aria took her place on the stand. Inhaling a deep breath, their barrister began. 'Your honour, we have a late development in the case, and I would like to ask Miss Raith to the stand.'

The judge nodded.

'As a gemmologist, and a treasure hunter of the highest grade,' their barrister began, 'can you tell us more about the Koh-i-Noor diamond and who would want to steal it? How would one go about it?'

'As a gemmologist, and history treasure hunter, I can confirm the diamond is of great value to anyone who would want to make history. Stealing the diamond makes it more valuable. I have seen this many times in my line of work. I'm no barrister, but I know the law around international treasure hunting. There's a law, about fifty years old in India, that disallows the government from bringing back antiquities taken out of the country before Indian independence—unless those antiquities and treasures were illegally exported. If a country starts claiming treasures of such nature, then the reverse would happen to that country or any other nation. So, to put it in plain terms, in this case, the British Museum, The Louvre and any other prominent museum in the world would be empty. Where does it stop?' She took a pause and scanned faces in the stunned room. In one statement, both sides of the argument had been robbed of their battles for the Koh-i-Noor.

She continued, 'I can't allude to the ownership, but I can confirm the diamond you're battling for, stolen days ago at the Louvre, is right here in my pocket.'

She pulled out the Koh-i-Noor and held it up for the courtroom. 'My job is to find hidden treasures, and I've found your diamond.'

'That was one crazy move, Mrs Raith,' their barrister said when the court had closed its doors.

'I'm sorry, but it had to be done. You were on the verge of landing and launching World War III in a United Nations courtroom. Not to mention the unease between the US and Britain, and possibly, several other Commonwealth countries. We need to keep these countries on the same side when it comes to this diamond and mining regulations. Diamonds are essential for the future,' Aria said.

'How did you get that diamond?' he asked. 'The entire world will be asking?'

'It's classified. It's a treasure hunters' code. We never reveal where or how we find our loot, nor who asked us to.'

She registered the shock still on Jave's face. He took a seat next to her. 'How? Where?'

'Does it matter? I just had a call from a Hazard Ramond from the Louvre in Paris. He's one grateful man. I can't reveal the client who asked me to retrieve it. The Koh-i-Noor will now stay within the court's custody until they work out what to do with it.'

Several moments later, Aria gave a press conference and attested that she'd been commissioned to find the diamond by an anonymous interested party. She wouldn't reveal her sources, except that the special relationship she held with her sister had also helped her immensely in finding the diamond. It remained unknown how the diamond had left the Louvre, but the most important thing was that it had been found. This had to be the best way. In less than two days, she'd found two significant diamonds, and the media hailed her as the world's chief treasure hunter, yet again.

Garen drew her into a full hug when the conference was over, and they prepared to leave the courthouse. When the three were alone, Jave smiled. 'Perhaps, you should have been the spy and not Emily. How... I knew your being in the Maldives and on the seas gave you excitement, but I underestimated you. The deal with the prime minster means you have been granted immunity—even from scrutiny from the press. I guess with the diamond back, that is the story they'll print.'

Aria shrugged. 'No, I think we are both good at it. My job is to find lost treasure, and frankly, that is what I did. After a very persuasive client asked me to.'

Garen left her with Jave to prepare their departure.

'So, this is it?' Aria's said, reaching for Jave's hand. She'd hoped Jave's eyes would tell her something that would make her stay in Europe and go to London with him.

He nodded. 'I have another job to attend to.'

He wasn't offering her much. Could he still have walls he was hiding behind? Surely not, but Jave would have to decide what he wanted most. For now, it wasn't her. She'd wished for too much.

She ran a hand through her hair. 'Are you off to protect some world president or celebrity?' she smiled. 'I envy him or her. I'm off. Back to my island in the Maldives and treasure hunting.'

'To Maxwell?' Jave said.

She regretted her thought but said it anyway. 'You haven't given me an alternative.'

Jave flew to London that evening. As much he'd tried, he couldn't get rid of the nagging feeling that he'd left Aria hanging. He couldn't explain his motives now—however much he wanted to. Jave took the BMW and drove halfway across London after landing at Heathrow.

'So, these came from Botswana, hey?' Parkinson said when Jave stole into his office at the House of Garrard in London.

Jave nodded.

'Parkinson motioned for him to sit down across from his desk. 'How did you get the diamonds you promised to bring?'

'Same way you connived yourself into this job—persuasion and skill. Afraid to say that my family goes back a few generations and has a bit of history in diamonds. I wasn't in South Africa by mistake, and I didn't take this case at Interpol by chance.' He took a little pouch of crushed diamonds out of his bag. 'You can use these here. These babies bought me the intelligence I needed that not even Interpol could get. I was able to find out a lot more. The person I hired to buy me intelligence refused to accept them.'

'She's a smart one, Lincoln,' Parkinson said.

Jave smiled. 'I actually don't know, but perhaps like she said, treasure hunters have a code of silence. These rightly belong to many people in Botswana and their families. Interpol can't use them. I need you to get these to them. Like you, I too have my secrets.'

'How did you get them, and how long have you had access to diamonds, Jave?'

'When you and Fenderson's men weren't looking, a man at Altaneus's Botswana mine gave them to me to get his family out of the country. His family and life were worth more to him than these. I couldn't tell Aria that when Altaneus folded. My family joined forces with the Botswana government and bought the Altaneus diamond mine. Altaneus Corporation fired people I cared about. They took a lot from those African people who worked in those mines over the years. Altaneus's interest was only to exploit the diamond mine and practise desalination. They didn't care who they hurt what families they broke up.'

'So, I guess we're even now,' Parkinson said. 'You got the scavengers off my back, found my daughter, and I've kept my part of the bargain. I convinced Aria to hunt the Koh-i-Noor for you—even though she had no idea you were her client. I cashed in an old favour, in exchange for a meteorite she prizes as invaluable. She feels we are even now.'

'For now, it's best Aria doesn't know that I'm Interpol. I'll tell her myself.'

'Or that you are a rich billionaire who owns a diamond mine with an African government. You keep more secrets than most.'

He shrugged. 'It was chance. I was born in a family that historically had a high interest in diamonds.'

'I guess it also helps that your family had historical ties to Boston Tea Company,' Parkinson said.

'What are you going to do now? Women can't be fooled, you know.'

He shrugged. 'I know I'm a crazy bastard for leaving her. I promised I would help you and your family. What you see here is one of the largest rocks mined in our business in Botswana crushed into hundreds of pieces. I know you can do something good with these diamonds. You can clear your debt to the Department of Economic Intelligence, and maybe get your daughter back. Make the most of your new life and use whatever you have left to get Agent Hudson off your back, and the rest ... well, that's up to you. I wonder if Aria knows how lucky she is to know you.'

Parkinson nodded and smiled. 'I don't know how to thank you.'

'Unless you know how to get the most beautiful gem that exists, and she can't be bribed with diamonds, then I don't know how you can help me. She doesn't trust men, and I gave her yet another reason not to.'

Parkinson set a hand on his shoulder as he rose. 'That girl is special to me. Garen was absent in her life. Don't be absent in hers too. It's the only advice I can give you. I think her heart is already yours, and Aria was always hard to please. You've gone further than most. Remember, diamonds are not the way to this girl's heart. You'll have to find something more valuable to give her. Perhaps start with the most valuable thing to you. Your heart.'

Jave's phone rang. 'Yes?'

It was Interpol headquarters. 'We have an urgent request for you.'

'From whom?' Jave asked.

'Don't know, but it sounds like Fenderson's opened hell in the Maldives.'

29

Maldives
03:16 hrs

Waking up in the dead of night was not new to Aria, but tonight felt different. She heard a noise by the door and struggled in darkness with a jet-lagged headache to check the window of her bungalow.

She zipped her head around when the deafening smash of a gas can shot through her window, landing by her feet. They had come in numbers.

She froze in silence and searched for a way to escape the house, the sound of more shattering glass cutting through her senses.

How many were there?

They'd been expecting her. How could she not have seen it? She flipped on the light.

Iver's face drew into frame, and he loaded a dart in a tranquiliser gun. 'You should've handed the rocks to me when you had the chance. I always knew you were the clever sister. That trick you pulled in The Hague has cost me.'

Aria shivered in her nightclothes. The dart fired, and he struck her once across the cheek.

Her nails raked his cheek, clawing for his eyes. Then darkness fell slowly, as the tranquiliser seeped in her bloodstream.

Aria opened heavy eyes, her head a pounding nightmare. She was still in her nightclothes, and the floor she was on felt cool. One eye strained for recognition around the room. The sound of soft purring engines and a hull slicing through water so familiar to her told her she was at sea.

Her eyes moved to her hand, now tied to a rail below a cabin window. There wasn't much in the engine room, just the resonance of crew above her murmuring to each other and the never-ending growling of the runner engine.

She pulled herself upright and looked through the circular window.

'There's no way out, even for you,' a rough voice called.

She zipped her head around as Fenderson stood at the open door, watching her. She'd not heard the door slide open, and only his voice had sounded his arrival. She narrowed her eyes, and for the first time, she noticed his left arm didn't move rhythmically with the rest of his body. It didn't take a medic to know that he housed a bionic arm under his sleeve; he controlled with a small device in his right hand. That's why his blow had felt so strong.

'What do you want?' she asked.

'That's not what I would expect from someone who I am about to reunite with a long-lost sister, but that reunification won't last long, because, Miss Raith, you've made me bloody mad for more than two weeks. You took something from me, so now I take something from you.'

If she could deactivate the bionic hand, it would be a start, but its grip of metal and strength was more than she could wrestle with.

'What are you talking about?' Aria managed through sharp breaths.

'You'll see.'

He slammed the door shut and locked it when he left.

She moved to the door and pounded hard, but there was no answer. A dungeon within a luxurious yacht. Suddenly, she heard noises above her. Muffling and soft footsteps followed. Someone was in the cabin above her. She reached above, stretching for the ceiling of the engine room. She glared up. 'Hello? Anyone there?'

Thumping footsteps stomped into the room above, and Aria strained her ears. Someone, like her, was a prisoner in the room above.

She heard men burst into the room. Muffled voices told her that it wasn't a cordial visit.

Iver Fenderson. Who was he talking to?

She plastered her ear against the wall.

'And I never will.'

A woman's voice.

Can it be?

She hadn't heard the voice in years, but she was sure it was her.

Emily?

It was a prayer, but it might as well have been a raw shout.

Her sister was on this boat.

Off the Coast of the Maldives

Sore muscles and cramping numbed Iver. The Raith girls had ruined his plans for the last time.

Iver glanced down at Emily's limp body. The girl who'd been so promising at Altaneus, now a bundle of defiance at his feet. She looked the same way she had when he'd pulled her from the burning laboratory. Thirteen years with the woman and all he had to show for it was a bionic hand, and he was nowhere near the Koh-i-Noor—thanks to that sister of hers.

He'd held her for several days on his yacht. Seeds had achieved one thing, at least. He'd made sure she'd stayed where he needed her and transported her from Scotland. She'd disappeared for forty-eight hours before his men had apprehended her. She'd left with her research she'd developed, but it was his money, his investment.

Damn it!

If Hudson hadn't intercepted an encrypted text she'd sent her sister fourteen days ago, he wouldn't have her now. Now that the Koh-i-Noor had eluded him, someone had to pay. The Raith sisters.

He moved like a hurt panther as he headed to the video conference unit and turned it on. 'Get me, Garen Raith,' he said, commanding the artificial intelligence unit to dial a number it had sourced.

The video connection found Garen Raith's secure phone.

'High Commissioner Raith. Don't think for one second I won't get the Koh-i-Noor after that move by your daughter. It will be the first sacrifice in my rain project. Now look at this.'

Iver turned the camera to face Emily, chained to a chair. 'This all ends today.'

. . .

Garen watched eager fingers twitch around his child. He responded in an emotion-choked voice. 'How dare you, Iver? You've had my daughter for—'

'For thirteen years. She was well treated and had access to anything she wanted—as long as she kept working on the project. It was her choice.'

'I don't believe you,' Garen said.

'She's a brilliant girl who manufactured her own disappearance for the sake and love of science to develop desalination technology with my money, then she developed a conscience. As luck would have it, only a few days ago, I found her crossing international channels, and she's been here ever since. You see, I needed a bargaining chip too.'

'You've held my daughter? All this time! You'll pay for this, Fenderson. I'll make sure you rot in prison.'

'Easy now, Raith. You're miles from here. I just want you to register that.'

'You son of a! ... You've taken precious time away from me. Now that you've made her develop desalination technology, let her go before every international organisation and intelligence service is out for your hide,' Garen said, not sure if he was demanding or begging.

'She could've been something, Garen.'

Garen's limbs felt too heavy to move. God knew where Fenderson was. His high-grade phone could usually trace a call.

'I will give you a little tour.'

Iver swivelled the camera and moved it to a different part of a room.

Was it a building?

No! It's a yacht!

'Here's your daughter, Raith, and I have one more surprise for you.'

Garen watched Emily's downcast face as her bloodshot eyes filled with fatigue. His heart ached for his child.

Emotion hit him as only a father could feel. Emily's look was weak at the camera. It was a face he had missed for thirteen years. This was his oldest child. His baby, now at the mercy of the one man who'd taken everything from him when his wife died.

'Before I dispose of her, she will finish the project!' Iver snapped.

'She won't,' Garen said.

He could feel his hand balling into a fist, but what good would it do? He was in London and had no idea where Iver was holding his daughter.

'She tried to escape five years ago with my technology, my intel, and my investment. She developed an expensive procedure.'

Iver removed the glove from his hand and revealed his mechanical limb. 'The machine was so successful that it ate off my hand!'

For the first time, Emily raised her weak head and then an eyebrow. 'A... a... a little souvenir. Just a reminder that you can't claim Raith women or Asterleys. They have been around for hundreds of years. Your family couldn't compete with the Raith bloodline.'

Her voice was tired, hoarse, but still full of courage.

'Fenderson, if you lay one finger on her I'll...'

'You'll what?'

Garen concentrated. Just where was Emily? His ears strained for any familiar noises as only a life of spying could have taught.

The yacht's horn sounded, and he heard a bridge lift that

he'd heard so many times when he'd spied on Aria in the Maldives Male harbour.

He knew precisely where Iver had taken Emily.

'Jave, he has my girls. He is threatening them both. They're out in the Maldives. We need to fly tonight,' Garen pleaded.

The agony of getting a long flight from London churned Garen's stomach. Jave and Garen spared no expense with a private jet to the Maldives, accompanied by several Interpol agents who'd also connected with the local police and authorities.

They landed at Male airport at dawn where a police yacht awaited them.

Garen's fingers shivered. Though he'd not seen his daughters much, the thought that he'd lose them again terrified him.

'Garen Raith?' a voice called at arrivals at the small airstrip. He looked up as a tall blond man approached him in the airport arrival hall, a feeling of dread settling in his gut.

'High Commissioner Raith. It's a pleasure to meet you. I'm a friend of Aria. Maxwell Amstell. Her fiancée. When I knew they'd taken Aria? I knew you'd come. Please let me help. I know these islands quite well, and we have Aria's boat.'

Garen's eyes widened. 'Did you see them?'

Maxwell shook his head.

Jave moved towards Garen as Maxwell continued. 'I checked her bungalow this morning. They left it trashed, and she was gone. I knew she'd returned from London. The only thing I know is that Aria was snatched this morning from her beach bungalow. There's also a yacht docked several hundred metres away from the harbour here. It's a yacht we don't see often. Aria and I hunt treasure in the seas here most of the time. We know most boats, and this one only docked last night. We need to hurry. I believe that's where Aria might be held. We need to get out there as soon as we can.'

'Excuse me,' Jave said interrupting. 'Sorry to cut this short, but the longer we chat, the less time we have. When was your sighting of the yacht?'

'Last night, around midnight.'

Jave motioned to the Interpol men and local police. 'We've less than a few hours to find them.'

'I think you'll need my help,' Maxwell said. I know the islands like no other.'

Jave raised an eyebrow. 'I think we're going to need jet skis and small boats. We need a stealthy approach. Know where we can get some?'

Maxwell smiled.

An hour later, they boarded jet skis courtesy of Maxwell's boating contacts. Seven jet skis took off behind the yacht. They appeared behind the majestic and fierce 537-foot yacht with tiered decks that swept upward, its sails towering above most buildings on the island. Garen imagined it could hold two helicopters by the look of its size. Hybrid diesel-electric engines were connected to powerful drives.

The jet skis slowed in the setting sun, waiting for a little darkness before stealthily making an approach.

Shots fired from the yacht at their position.

Jave glared through the binoculars. 'I go alone from here on,' he said to the local Interpol men.

'We can't let you,' Garen said.

'Fenderson is an international criminal. That's what I do. Catch criminals,' Jave said.

'There's a cove not too far from here. You can hide the jet skis in there until it's time,' Maxwell said.

Jave nodded, then dove into the waters towards the yacht.

What were they shooting at?

This was her territory.

Aria knew the Maldives intricacies, including this area of the ocean. She struggled to the little window as shots fired outside.

Her ears caught the sound of several engines, jet skis, circling the yacht. Maxwell must've alerted them. She'd only managed a quick hello when he'd picked her up at the airport, then later dropped her home. She peeked through the little window and saw him.

It had to be him.

Jave had come for her.

Shots exploded above the yacht, a cacophony through her cabin. Crew members shot to their stations as it became plain the boat was under attack. A massive blast rocked the boat and threw her against the back wall. The lights extinguished, and she tried to assess the situation through smoke and fire.

She waited.

Then a loud blast.

'Jave!'

His face, even in smoke, was a sight for her weakening eyes. 'You came?' she said.

'Later, sweetheart. We leave now.'

They made their way onto the deck as she lumbered after Jave. She saw several jet skis at the tail of the yacht, then held her breath. If she left with Jave, Emily wouldn't survive Fenderson's men.

She stopped. 'Jave, we can't go.'

'Why?'

'He's got Emily.'

His eyes intensified. 'I'll come back for her. Promise. I can't lose you.'

She took a step back shivering. 'It may be too late. Jave, I love you, but I can't go without Emily.'

With her ears attacked by the pounding of her pulse, Aria charged across the deck, her pulse beating loudly in her ears. Her time was limited. That bang meant that the yacht was being prepared for evacuation and she needed to get off.

With Emily.

She hurried to where she believed Emily was being held. The door had been left open by the blast, and she shuffled in. 'Emily?'

'Aria?'

The voice was faint, having experienced smoke poisoning.

'Not so fast!' Fenderson belted, his voice hoarse.

He wrenched Emily from Aria's arms.

Shots fired, and the gun slipped from Fenderson's hand as Jave charged into the room followed by Garen. Fenderson pulled out his hand from his glove. A bare skeleton of metal appeared and lunged for Jave. The metallic arm struck him across the face, and its swing missed Garen by an inch. He then reached for Aria.

'I'm not scared of you,' Aria said her eyes bearing to him. 'You can't get out of this. Let my sister go!'

'Not until I have compensation for the Koh-i-Noor!' Iver roared.

'You want me then! 'Emily shouted above the commotion.

All eyes fixed on her.

'That diamond took me and kept me prisoner in Altaneus, all because you wanted it to be the first to go through the rain project's inauguration.'

Fenderson's eyes burned with hate as Emily smirked and rose. Her cuffs had loosened in the blast. He went straight for her and kicked Jave out of the way.

'No!' Emily said.

Before Garen and Jave could fire, Fenderson's metallic skeleton wrapped itself around Aria's neck and drew her out of the room towards the deck. He glanced back at his pursuers before setting a hand over the rail. In one swift sweep, he went over the deck rail, taking Aria with him.

30

Jave charged to the edge of the yacht, a feeling of dread deep within him. He stole a look at the horizon observing the getaway boat as it raced off with Aria and Fenderson on board. By now, the Interpol boat had reached the tail of the yacht, and a stream of police officers and national guards boarded rounding up the crew.

'I'm going after them,' Jave said, turning to Garen. 'I can't lose her.'

'I'm coming with you,' Garen added.

'No, stay here with Emily,' Jave said.

'Let me come with you,' Maxwell said. 'I know these waters.'

Fenderson's boat was a dot on the horizon by now. Maxwell and Jave took the police speed boat and started the engine after them. Soon, Iver's boat pulled out of sight, miles ahead of them.

'They've disappeared,' Jave said.

'No,' Maxwell said. 'They are actually heading right into Aria's museum. It's a unique dive site that we haven't yet opened. Aria has collected an incredible amount of underwater treasures and art that she aims to have on display for exclusive dive groups, but without any diving gear, you can't get to it.'

'Why there?' Jave said.

Lines grew on Maxwell's tanned face. 'Fenderson is pissed. Aria found the Koh-i-Noor and returned it, and he holds her responsible for personally destroying his plans.'

Jave fed gas to the engines and moved the boat into high gear. 'Now he wants to destroy her museum—with her in it.'

His bionic arm working the engines of the ship, Fenderson circled the boat above Aria's museum site. 'We all have dreams, dear girl, and mine, you've ambushed.'

The bionic grip was fierce, agony on her skin.

Fenderson wasn't done. 'You should've brought the Koh-i-Noor to me—and the Tower diamond. Perhaps we could have come to an arrangement for your precious museum here,' Fenderson said.

Darkness was setting in, and Aria could see no sign of life on the horizon. Still in her nightwear, she breathed in quick, shallow gasps. That's why they'd chosen this spot. She'd wanted the underwater museum to be built in a secluded, protected area at a depth of fifteen metres. They had already built several large-scale installations and sculptures and even an underwater house in a protected case that would house the more precious pieces they would rotate to show her ocean jewel and gold finds. She had wanted to create a marine habitat that lent itself to social awareness and treasures lost long ago in oceans. Once this was successful, they would then replicate this museum in various places around the world.

Her eyes observed the depths of the waters, knowing if he

left her here, it would be her end. One only came to the dive centre by boat, and after that, one needed an oxygen mask.

Aria's eyes narrowed. 'What do you plan to do?'

'Let you have your dream,' Fenderson said.

His bionic arm jammed into her leg, releasing a stream of blood. Aria felt her eyes trundling. The pain was brutal, and every inch of her ached.

Fenderson approached, looming over her. He threw her against the edge of the boat, staring at her. 'You see, one day, the state of India will be given what it deserves, and the diamond will go back there. My desalination project will create an empire, dwarfing the East India Company's influence. When desalination of water—engineered by quantum power, and steered by diamonds—inaugurates, I'll have my dream, and the Koh-i-Noor will be the first to go under the knife as a symbol of reclaiming it. My project's first labs are already at work in India. Altaneus may have shut, but only on paper.'

Fenderson's eyes were menacing, flickering with anger as he approached her. He suddenly stopped and put his boot over her wounded leg. 'How did you get the Koh-i-Noor? You got it once, so you can get it again.'

Aria knew what was at stake. Her sister had been forced to create a technology in hiding for thirteen years. Aria inched back towards the back of the boat.

'It's over, Fenderson. Interpol will confiscate your labs. They are illegal,' she said to Iver.

'How do you figure that?' Iver said.

Fenderson dropped to a knee in front of her. Her leg was now beyond agony, an excruciating pain shooting up her ankle. Aria could feel the sting of the saltwater on her wound from where the boat had clipped her side. She reached over to her leg. 'So many corrupt dealings and blood have been shed over that diamond for so many centuries. I wanted to end it, so I returned it. The battle will continue over lost and exported, or even gifted antiquities, and no one will resolve them.'

Iver struck her across the face. 'Like I said, I have my dream and you yours.'

With that, he lifted her out of the boat and dropped her over the side.

Aria's hands gripped for the edge of the boat, terror gnawing at her. Iver's bionic arm did the rest as it slammed over her fingers, and she lost her grip.

The gloom of the water swirled around Aria as she slipped farther down into the ocean's depth without a mask. Aria took a long deep breath and closed her eyes, falling to her very own treasure-laden grave. She could not hold her breath long, and her leg forbade her from kicking fast enough to swim upward.

Her lungs burned for air as her energy left her, and she stopped struggling.

As her eyes were closing, a light circling among her installed sculptures shone a gleam in her direction.

Yet, still, she could not hold on. And then she felt a strong arm behind her, and oxygen entered her lungs as a mask landed over her mouth and nose.

Aria knew she had to stay alive. She took a big gulp of air. Her eyes now understood that the light in the distance came from a second boat. It shone against the depths of the Maldives triangle.

She could just barely make it, and she needed more air to even move. She took a gulp of the oxygen. Jave's eyes behind a mask came into frame as shots fired around them, zipping by in the fast current. Aria and Jave dove down.

She motioned for him to dive deeper, trusting her instincts as a diver.

Jave responded, trusting her skill and navigation. They descended as shots chased them, then when they'd lost their pursuers, they rose back to the surface.

Budding into the open ocean, Maxwell hauled them both into the boat. As Aria settled against the wood, she drew the mask off her face and breathed hard. Her leg was burning with pain.

'You all right?' Jave asked.

She managed a faint smile. 'Jave? You came?'

'Of course, I did. Just as I trust you might for me,' Jave said.

She felt her breath settle from her ordeal. 'How did you find me?' she said.

'You can't ever get away from me.' Jave said.

He kissed her as Maxwell turned to the rear of the boat, a shadow falling on his face.

'I know when I have lost, but let's discuss this another time. We've got company, and it's moving fast,' Maxwell said urgently.

With a parched tongue sticking to the top of her lips, Aria heard the roar of Iver's boat, metres from them.

'Quick,' Jave said. 'Now's our chance. We need to go.'

He charged for the controls and geared the boat at high speed towards land. Iver's boat showed no mercy as it thundered behind them. With their eyes fixed ahead, they were still several hundred metres from the beach. Jave slammed the gas and manoeuvred the boat towards an inlet beach.

Fenderson's boat rammed into his tail, and the boat skipped, lifting a few metres in the air from the beach.

'Jump!' he roared at them, and they jumped into the waters.

Fenderson slowed his boat and aimed its tip towards where Aria had fallen. Iron met steel as she used a pole that had fallen from their boat and rammed it into his bionic arm.

He stretched in pain and remote-controlled his arm with a device in his right hand. The arm's fingers spun into a blade of death, and he brought it close to her neck.

In the distance, Jave and Maxwell thrashed her way, but metal neared her skin, and Fenderson held her in place, drowning her with his knee to her chest.

Aria drew strength from the gurgles of the water. This man had taken her sister away from her, which had taken her mother away, and eventually, even her father. He had broken her family in more ways than she could count.

As metal blades made their way towards her eyes, a knee of astronomic strength in her lungs and saltwater drowning her, made her take one quick breath. She kneed him in the groin and claimed the remote control device. She pushed down on the lock and fastened Iver in his own metal.

Her body rose above the salt bath, and she struggled to shore where Jave and Maxwell restrained the big man.

She wasn't done.

Aria pressed down a second button, and the bionic arm twisted and knocked Iver out cold as Interpol boats streamed to their position.

31

Twelve Hours Later

Arms over her chest, Emily stared out at the expanse of the ocean as she sat with Maxwell on the beach watching Aria and Jave talk from a distance.

'She's happy, Maxwell,' Emily said.

'I know. I see the way she looks at him. She's never looked at me once like that.'

'Do you regret what we did?' Emily asked.

'No. I don't for once regret taking the Koh-i-Noor from the Louvre with you. When you escaped from Fenderson's grasp, we had to do it. You brought with you access to international alarm systems that made the job easy.'

'That bastard has been acquiring them for years. He's an international criminal on another level.'

'Looks like you, Aria, and I agree. Diamonds don't belong to anyone or anybody anyway.'

'Aria will be furious when she finds out you stole the Koh-i-Noor,' Maxwell said.

'I just had to do it,' Emily said. 'It was the only way to save humanity from the project that Fenderson was working on. Altaneus needs to shut once and for all. I'll donate my research to responsible corporations. I couldn't let him have the Koh-i-Noor, and stealing it was the best choice I had.'

Maxwell grinned. 'Still can't believe we pulled it off.'

'Well, we did have help. Wonder what James Parkinson will do now that he has his daughter back.'

Emily smiled and nudged him in the shoulder. 'Maybe start living, truly.'

'I don't understand why you let Fenderson trap you. Keep you under house arrest all those years.'

'I had too. Otherwise, he would've suspected something and killed my family. My Aria.'

'What now?'

'Well, maybe I stay here and help you and Aria with the museum.'

'You think she'll stay, now that she has Jave?'

Emily sighed. 'How did you take it? She's crazy about him and him her. That museum's her life's work, and somehow it looks like Jave is too.'

She mused, remembering their mother Clarisse and the legacy she'd inherited. Golconda was where her father and her mother had found a mine twenty-seven miles upstream. A mine closed long ago by natural causes and left to rot thanks to the whispers of the locals about a meteorite. The meteorite had made all things possible. It had manufactured the Koh-i-Noor and thousands of other diamonds like it. It was a landslide that buried the shaft during a lousy monsoon season.

Emily believed this is where the Koh-i-Noor has escaped from, after the meteorite hit and rolled down the riverbed, where it was mined in the valley.

Her parents had bought the mine months before Aria was born and sealed it for years until they could sort out the paperwork with India. They'd bought the land on which the mine stood, miles from where the diamond was mined, which was now saturated with tonnes of large diamonds where the only one had escaped—the Koh-i-Noor. The only one known to the world, and the second, her great-great-great-grandfather Asterley had written about.

It had happened when they'd first gone to India to explore with her parents as a child. She couldn't imagine what Fenderson would have done to her family if he knew the existence of that mine. Well, he'd received a permanent reminder of what it was like to mess with the Raith women. When he'd tried to restrain her during the Altaneus explosion, she'd fought back, resulting in his arm being caught between a beam that nearly landed on her. He should have known better than to attack her.

The result had been a threat to kill her father, and so she'd agreed to stay and work for him in exchange for her father's life. Since Iver wanted no one to know of his project, she'd had to be declared dead. But for now, India once again could produce diamonds much larger than the Koh-i-Noor. Just maybe that alone would settle the Koh-i-Noor debate.

The Next Day

'I have let you both down for many years,' Garen said, entering the room.

He took a deep breath. Dread consumed him, but it had to be done. He had lots of sorting to do with his daughters when they took seats in the breakfast room on Aria's yacht the next morning. He'd asked for a quiet audience with them before returning to India.

'When the Department of Economic Intelligence told me

Parkinson had come into our lives and I needed to spy on him, I refused. I saw how connected you two were to him. I knew he was perfect for you and for your education, but when your mother left us, I couldn't live with myself.'

Aria put her hand on her father's shoulder. 'It's okay, Father.'

'If I had revealed to you the true secrets of these mines you would've held onto such a weight of responsibility—one I didn't want you to have. Diamonds bring out the worst side of humans. Jave and I had to keep secrets about these mines. The Indian government allowed me to buy them as I paid for the entire operation. I would never be allowed to remove all the diamonds from India, but I could return some of the profits back to the nation. It is a sweet deal as it's extremely hard for foreign nationals to own immovable property in India.'

He slipped a paper towards them. 'You've both shown courage and integrity with the world's biggest treasure both at your disposal. I now hand you as an inheritance the deeds to the Raith mines in India, effective today,' Garen said.

Aria and Emily stared at each other in disbelief.

'But...' Aria began.

'Don't argue. I owe you both that much. Emily,' he said, 'you don't have to work for anyone but yourself as you do your research. Do the desalination project for yourself, and choose who works with you.' He then turned to Aria. 'Aria, you can finish your museum. You can show the world what a wonderful oceanographer you are.' Garen laid his eyes on her, loving every inch of the daughters he had raised. He wanted to share everything.

Both girls sat in silence before Aria spoke. 'Father, we have each other's back, and mother would be proud of you. You should be part of this too.'

Garen shook his head. 'No. I regret the time I stole from all of us.'

Emily set a hand on his cheek. 'Don't regret anything. I let you believe I was dead so we could have our family back together, and you made it happen.'

Tears welled in his eyes, and he kissed both his girls.

When Garen stood to leave, Jave sank into a seat next to Aria. 'Do I have any explaining to do with Maxwell?'

She put her arms around his neck. 'Hmm. No. I did all the explaining,' she said, landing a kiss on his lips. 'Incidentally,' she said, 'when were you and my dad going to tell me you owned half a diamond mine in Botswana? That was clever of you. I did wonder why the guys there were so receptive to us when we went there.'

Jave smiled. 'Busted.'

She pulled him closer. 'I too have a secret. Would you like to begin a partnership in diamond mining?'

'I thought you didn't like diamonds,' Jave said.

In one forward motion, she was in his arms. 'I could be persuaded.'

JOIN THE ADVENTURE

SHORT REVIEW

Thank you for joining this adventure!
As an author I highly appreciate the feedback I get from my readers. It helps others to make an informed decision before buying.

It only takes a few minutes. If you enjoyed **Blood Diamond in My Mother's House,** please consider leaving a short review where you bought the book by going here.
www.rosesandy.com

BE THE FIRST TO KNOW

Be the first to learn about new releases and other news from Rose Sandy, by joining **Real Time with Rose Sandy**, a podcast and fun e-update. See you there by going here :

rosesandy.com/signup

JOIN THE CONVERSATION

While you are at it, swing by the official Rose Sandy Facebook page (www.facebook.com/rosesandyauthor) to join a community of adventurers, history and technology enthusiasts.

Finally, if you enjoy pictures of travels, book inspirations, historical mysteries, science and technology thrills, check out my feed @rosesandyauthor on the Instagram app.

IN THE SHADOW FILES THRILLERS

IN THE CROSSFIRE BETWEEN TECHNOLOGY, SCIENCE, AND INTERNATIONAL ESPIONAGE

Book 1 -The Code Beneath Her Skin

Book 2 - Blood Diamond in My Mother's House

A series about intelligent women caught in the crossfire between technology, science, politics, international espionage, and the men who drag them there.

Guaranteed action adventure in each book, you'll fill the need for thrills, savor satisfying cliffhangers as you follow a secret organization, **The Shadow Files,** and two of its former agents around the globe.

Sworn enemies, one is on a mission to safeguard the globe from economic corruption, and one swears he'll protect the victims.

Each book can be read as a stand-alone story.

More here: https://rosesandy.com/the-shadow-files-series-2/

IN THE DECRYPTER SERIES

PULSE-RACING ADVENTURE

Book 1: The Decrypter: Secret of The Lost Manuscript

Book 2: The Decrypter and The Mind Hacker

Book 3: The Decrypter - Digital Eyes Only

Book 4: The Decrypter - The Storm's Eye

She's a museum curator, a doubter, and a skeptic. It all changed when the British government asked her to decrypt a code written in an unbreakable script on an ancient manuscript whose origin was as debatable as the origin of life. Then there was the issue of her long-lost parents.

Using her knack for history and technology, she bands with two faithful friends and is thrown into a dangerous journey of cyber espionage investigating the criminal, the unexplained, the scientific and the downright unthinkable.

More here: https://rosesandy.com/the-decrypter-series/

WHAT READERS ARE SAYING ABOUT THE DECRYPTER SERIES

"Takes you on a ride and refuses to let you off until you reach the very end."

"A brilliant read! I recommend this to anyone who enjoys mystery, suspense, thrillers, or action novels. The detail is astounding! The historic references, location descriptions, references to technology, cryptography....this author really knows her stuff."

"An action-packed adventure, technothriller across several continents like a Jason Bourne or James Bond movie, but with an actual storyline!"

"Brilliantly written. I loved the very descriptive side, which was a good way of visualizing and getting to terms with each new place, as the action takes place in several different countries."

"The description is so rich, so immensely detailed that it just draws you in completely to its world."

"There is great tension and chemistry between the two main characters, Calla and Nash, that has you begging for more."

BLOOD DIAMOND IN MY MOTHER's HOUSE

Created with Vellum

Printed in Great Britain
by Amazon

40904635R00182